*Dedicated to Edith Wharton*

*"The air of ideas is the only air worth breathing." ~ Edith Wharton*
*"The air of love is the only air worth breathing." ~ Coco Rousseau*

*Avec amour,*
*Coco Rousseau*

# Acknowledgments

Thank you Crimson Romance for enriching the world with stories of the heart. Without love, we would be mere flesh without soul. As Mahatma Gandhi says, "Where there is love there is life." Thank you, Tara Gelsomino, Julie Sturgeon, Beth Gunn, Jess Verdi, and the tireless staff of Crimson Romance who helped make this adaption of Edith Wharton's *The Age of Innocence* another shining star in the world of romance.

VOLUME 1

# The Age of Innocence

**Coco Rousseau**
*and* **Edith Wharton**

CRIMSON
ROMANCE

F+W Media, Inc.

Published by
Crimson Romance
an imprint of F+W Media, Inc.
10151 Carver Road, Suite 200
Blue Ash, OH 45242. U.S.A.
*www.crimsonromance.com*

ISBN 10: 1-4405-7490-1
ISBN 13: 978-1-4405-7490-0
eISBN 10: 1-4405-7491-X
eISBN 13: 978-1-4405-7491-7

# Part 1

# Chapter 1

On a January evening of the early seventies, Christine Nilsson was singing in Faust at the Academy of Music in New York. The pleasure of Newland Archer's company was expected. But he had not yet made his appearance for his attention had, as usual, been diverted elsewhere—or more accurately, he had been seduced. The lady, married within the ranks of New York Conservatives, would best remain unnamed at present for the sake of preserving subtlety among friends and others who might be predisposed to cast a disapproving frown. In Newland Archer's mind, tonight would be his final rendezvous with the lady, for the greater of society that of New York, the élite not to be catechized in the slightest, had called him to account. It was time for Newland Archer to settle down.

Over two winters, the lady had captured his attention in conversation. In the beginning, he did not fully understand her intentions; her words were simply stimulating. But in time, she invited him to experience pleasures that he had not yet known as a young man. Naturally, he was intimidated by her frankness, although his guard eventually crumbled in the face of her sensual lure. He was tempted by her in a way he found irresistible, and thus, allowed her to guide their friendship beyond the intercourse of mind and spirit, until finally, she revealed to him the pleasures of the flesh.

Newland lingered before an open fire in his library, reading the summons he had received from his paramour earlier that evening. He drew on his cigar, and then dropped the perfumed Parisian paper, scripted with her elegant penmanship, into the fire. He watched the flames consume the white parchment. What had once been pristine no longer possessed even a remnant of purity.

An hour later, he arrived at the entrance to a magnificent home, which spared no amount of money in its finery. Before he could lift a hand to knock, a butler opened the door and greeted him.

"This way sir," the butler said, and then showed Newland to an upstairs chamber. The butler opened the door to reveal a darkened boudoir, and stepped aside to let Newland enter the room. Though he might have hesitated had he allowed his rational mind to control his actions, this was not to be. His manly urges forced him to set reason aside. He stepped through the door, sauntered across the room, and stopped near the fireplace mantle.

"You have kept me waiting," the woman said. She rose from the bed and walked to him. Her dark crimson hair flowed down the length of her back. She was dressed only in her dark emerald peignoir trimmed in gold braid, the fabric so thin that she might not have been wearing anything at all.

"We've been through this," he said. "I wasn't to come again."

"I had to see you one last time." She stood before her lover, her face turned to his, her expression sultry, her lips irresistible. Newland's thoughts of resistance diminished, and the heat from the fire melted his restraint.

He raised a hand to her cheek and slowly stroked the length of her face, considering. The woman standing before him had been his one and only mistress. From her, he had learned the ways a man might please a woman. Though he appreciated her charms and cared for her, he did not love her. Nor she him. In his mind, the affair was over, bittersweet as the ending was, but time had closed in upon them.

Newland was torn. He realized it would be best for all, including those not present who were weighing upon his sensibilities, if he simply departed. Yet, the urge to ravish this woman was exceedingly strong—no, overwhelming. Her eyes danced madly, anticipating his move. He did not kiss her, but grasped the cloth that clung to her otherwise naked body. He pulled it from her with such violence that it tore off completely, exposing her fully to him. He clasped her hand and brought it close to his mouth. He turned her wrist to admire the creamy tone of her flesh and then brought her wrist to his lips, slowly kissing the delicate skin above her palm.

"Come," she whispered, urging him toward the bed.

But he resisted, holding her back. Not there. Not this time.

"Newland?" He had never before resisted her wiles. "It will be the last time. Then I will release you."

He seemed to relax, knowing that she had given him leave to pursue that which was pressing upon his spirit, the favor that decent society was urging upon him. Instead of taking her, he stood waiting for her to understand what he was offering her this evening.

She nodded sensuously and encouraged him to sit down on the settee. She eased him down and he reclined, lying against the seat-back. She kneeled between his thighs, and with ease and experience, freed his manhood to the night. With gentle fingers, she grasped his member, slid her hands down the length of it, and began to stroke. She slowly ran her hands upward to envelop the crown. She pulled his member toward her, and with the fingers of the other hand, began circling the sensitive flesh until he melted into her touch. From the beginning of their companionship, she had always known how to relax him, and though this evening was different, her touch was as familiar as his own. He had always succumbed to the desires of the flesh, though not the heart. But he knew that he had done her a great favor with his company.

He felt his heart pounding as he anticipated her deeper touch. He leaned forward and grasped her hair with his fingers, guiding her closer. He felt the tension in his body yielding to her demands.

When she drew her lips to his crown and began gliding them softly over his flesh, he closed his eyes, finding himself lost in lust. When she opened her mouth and touched him with her tongue, an electrical impulse shot through his limbs. Her tongue was like velvet. She began to swirl it, lightly at first, but the harder she licked, the greater his manly desires grew.

Unable to help himself, he groaned, as though suffering the agony of loss. A series of immeasurably deep sighs were expelled one after another, blending into the crackle of the wood burning in the fireplace.

The lady did not yield. She slid her tongue underneath his crown and along its tender flesh. His skin rippled with erotic sensations, and he felt his member arching with the need to be released. However, she took her time, working her tongue upward again and through the divided folds of his crown, licking and probing the tip. There, she began to dab lightly with her tongue around the opening, an erotic dance of a sensuous pair.

She had captured Newland's breath with her touch. She controlled him, his movement, his every desire, and she seemed to want to torture him with the anticipation of being released. She teased him with that delicious tongue of hers, making him wait, circling it around, stimulating his appetite. Finally, she drew the crown into her mouth and gently pulled against its flesh, suckling, drinking as if savoring the finest wine.

He released her hair and fell back, letting her have her way. She engulfed a great length of his member, drawing him all the way into her mouth and deep into her throat. She moved him in and out. His rampant member throbbed, arching more urgently as she suckled more and more vigorously, until his jewels, which were gathered in one of her hands, tightened, his release imminent.

"Ah-h," he groaned repeatedly, his arousal heightening. He panted audibly as she drove him toward the moment. He lost all control. Fire raced through his loins, and finally in a reckless burst, he was overcome and released the fruit of his seed in her mouth.

"My God, woman, your charms," he said, gasping for breath, his member still throbbing against the continued suction of her mouth.

He rose and took his paramour into his arms, kissing her gently. "How may I please you tonight?"

"Come to the bed with me." She rose and led him to the bed.

Though their last night together was brief, she did not complain. They both knew that once Newland was married, the affair might become too public. Prancing around while married tainted reputations in a new regard. After he brought his lover to her own passionate heights, he bid her a final farewell and found his way to the Opera House, where the best of society gathered.

As to be expected, the conversation of those seated above in the privacy of their club boxes was dull. Though there was already talk of the erection, in remote metropolitan distances "above the Forties," of a new Opera House which should compete in costliness and splendour with those of the great European capitals, the world of fashion was still content to reassemble every winter in the shabby red and gold boxes of the sociable old Academy. Conservatives cherished it for being small and inconvenient, and thus keeping out the "new people" whom New York was beginning to dread and yet be drawn to; and the sentimental clung to it for its historic associations, and the musical for its excellent acoustics, always so problematic a quality in halls built for the hearing of music.

It was Madame Nilsson's first appearance that winter, and what the daily press had already learned to describe as "an exceptionally brilliant audience" had gathered to hear her, transported through the slippery, snowy streets in private broughams, in the spacious family landau, or in the humbler but more convenient "Brown coupe." To come to the Opera in a Brown coupe was almost as honourable a way of arriving as in one's own carriage; and departure by the same means had the immense advantage of enabling one (with a playful allusion to democratic principles) to scramble into the first Brown conveyance in the line, instead of waiting till the cold-and-gin congested nose of one's own coachman gleamed under the portico of the Academy. It was one of the great livery-stableman's most masterly intuitions to have discovered that Americans want to get away from amusement even more quickly than they want to get to it.

When Newland Archer opened the door at the back of the club box the curtain had just gone up on the garden scene. There was no reason why the young man should not have come earlier, for he had dined at seven, alone with his mother and sister, and had lingered afterward over a cigar in the Gothic library with glazed black-walnut bookcases and finial-topped chairs which was the only room in the house where Mrs. Archer allowed smoking, and then there was the perfumed letter to consider. But, in the first place, and much to Newland's delight, New York was a metropolis, and perfectly aware that in metropolises it was "not the thing" to arrive early at the opera; and what was or was not "the thing" played a part as important in Newland Archer's New York as the inscrutable totem terrors that had ruled the destinies of his forefathers thousands of years ago.

The second reason for his delay was a personal one. He had dawdled over his cigar and then partaken in the more pleasurable company of his lady friend for one last time, because he was at heart a dilettante, and thinking over a pleasure to come often gave him a subtler satisfaction than its realisation. This was especially the case when the pleasure was a delicate one, as his pleasures mostly were; and on this occasion, when he felt satisfied with life itself, the moment he looked forward to was so rare and exquisite in quality that—well, if he had timed his arrival in accord with the prima donna's stage-manager he could not have entered the Academy at a more significant moment than just as she was singing: "He loves me—he loves me not—HE LOVES ME!—" and sprinkling the falling daisy petals with notes as clear as dew.

She sang, of course, "M'ama!" and not "he loves me," since an unalterable and unquestioned law of the musical world required that the German text of French operas sung by Swedish artists should be translated into Italian for the clearer understanding of English-speaking audiences. This seemed as natural to Newland Archer as all the other conventions on which his life was moulded: such as the duty of using two silver-backed brushes with his monogram in blue enamel to part his hair, and of never appearing in society without a flower (preferably a gardenia) in his buttonhole.

"M'ama ... non m'ama ... " the prima donna sang, and "M'ama!", with a final burst of love triumphant, as she pressed the dishevelled daisy to her lips and lifted her large eyes to the sophisticated countenance of the little brown Faust-Capoul, who was vainly trying, in a tight purple velvet doublet and plumed cap, to look as pure and true as his artless victim.

Newland Archer, leaning against the wall at the back of the club box, turned his eyes from the stage and scanned the opposite side of the house. Directly facing him was the box of old Mrs. Manson Mingott, whose monstrous obesity had long since made it impossible for her to attend the Opera, but who was always represented on fashionable nights by some of the younger members of the family. On this occasion, the front of the box was filled by her daughter-in-law, Mrs. Lovell Mingott, and her daughter, Mrs. Welland; and slightly withdrawn behind these brocaded matrons sat a young girl in white with eyes ecstatically fixed on the stagelovers. As Madame Nilsson's "M'ama!" thrilled out above the silent house (the boxes always stopped talking during the Daisy Song) a warm pink mounted to the girl's cheek, mantled her brow to the roots of her fair braids, and suffused the young slope of her breast to the line where it met a modest tulle tucker fastened with a single gardenia. She dropped her eyes to the immense bouquet of lilies-of-the-valley on her knee, and Newland Archer saw her white-gloved finger-tips touch the flowers softly. He drew a breath of satisfied vanity and his eyes returned to the stage.

No expense had been spared on the setting, which was acknowledged to be very beautiful even by people who shared his acquaintance with the Opera houses of Paris and Vienna. The foreground, to the footlights, was covered with emerald green cloth. In the middle distance symmetrical mounds of woolly green moss bounded by croquet hoops formed the base of shrubs shaped like orange-trees but studded with large pink and red roses. Gigantic pansies, considerably larger than the roses, and closely resembling the floral pen-wipers made by female parishioners for fashionable clergymen, sprang from the moss beneath the rose-trees; and here and there a daisy grafted on a rose-branch flowered with a luxuriance prophetic of Mr. Luther Burbank's far-off prodigies.

In the centre of this enchanted garden Madame Nilsson, in white cashmere slashed with pale blue satin, a reticule dangling from a blue girdle, and large yellow braids carefully disposed on each side of her muslin chemisette, listened with downcast eyes to M. Capoul's impassioned wooing, and affected a guileless incomprehension of his designs whenever, by word or glance, he persuasively indicated the ground floor window of the neat brick villa projecting obliquely from the right wing.

"The darling!" thought Newland Archer, his glance flitting back to the young girl with the lilies-of-the-valley. "She doesn't even guess what it's all about." And he contemplated her absorbed young face with a thrill of possessorship in which pride in his own masculine initiation was mingled with a tender reverence for her abysmal purity. "We'll read Faust together … by the Italian lakes … " he thought, somewhat hazily confusing the scene of his projected honey-moon with the masterpieces of literature which it would be his manly privilege to reveal to his bride. Newland was thrilled at the idea that the young girl was untouched, virginal—unlike the mistress whom he had kept. May Welland represented all that was pure and wholesome, and it was he alone who would sculpt her into his own creation. The day would soon be upon them. It was only that afternoon that May Welland had let him guess that she "cared" (New York's consecrated phrase of maiden avowal), and already his imagination, leaping ahead of the engagement ring, the betrothal kiss and the march from Lohengrin, pictured her at his side in some scene of old European witchery. Moreover, he pictured embracing her tightly in his arms as he made passionate love to her; imagined her sighs and moans and undulations as she gave herself to him completely, enthralled by his masculinity, his power.

He did not in the least wish the future Mrs. Newland Archer to be a simpleton. He meant her (thanks to his enlightening companionship) to develop a social tact and readiness of wit enabling her to hold her own with the most popular married women of the "younger set," in which it was the recognised custom to attract masculine homage while playfully discouraging it. If he had probed to the bottom of his vanity (as he sometimes nearly did) he would have found there the wish that his wife should be as worldly-wise and as eager to please as the married lady whose charms had held his fancy through two mildly agitated years; without, of course, any hint of the frailty which had so nearly marred that unhappy being's life, and had disarranged his own plans for a whole winter. This evening was most assuredly the last of his clandestine and illicit encounters, as Newland was now ready to accept the obligation of a wife, which polite society prevailed upon him to take. In his case, he would accede to society's demand that he marry with the utmost pleasure.

How this miracle of fire and ice was to be created, and to sustain itself in a harsh world, he had never taken the time to think out; but he was content to hold his view without analysing it, since he knew it was that of all the carefully-brushed, white-waistcoated, button- hole-flowered gentlemen who succeeded each other in the club box, exchanged friendly greetings with him, and turned their opera-glasses critically on the circle of ladies who were the product of the system. In matters intellectual and artistic Newland Archer felt himself distinctly the superior of these chosen specimens of old New York gentility; he had probably read more, thought more, and even seen a good deal more of the world, than any other man of the number. Singly they betrayed their inferiority; but grouped together they represented "New York," and the habit of masculine solidarity made him accept their doctrine on all the issues called moral. He instinctively felt that in this respect it would be troublesome—and also rather bad form—to strike out for himself, or reveal any of his past indulgences.

"Well—upon my soul!" exclaimed Lawrence Lefferts, turning his opera-glass abruptly away from the stage. Lawrence Lefferts was, on the whole, the foremost authority on "form" in New York. He had probably devoted more time than any one else to the study of this intricate and fascinating question; but study alone could not account for his complete and easy competence. One had only to look at him, from the slant of his bald forehead and the curve of his beautiful fair moustache to the long patent-leather feet at the other end of his lean and elegant person, to feel that the knowledge of "form" must be congenital in any one who knew how to wear such good clothes so carelessly and carry such height with so much lounging grace. As a young admirer had once said of him: "If anybody can tell a fellow just when to wear a black tie with evening clothes and when not to, it's Larry Lefferts." And on the question of pumps versus patent-leather "Oxfords" his authority had never been disputed.

"My God!" he said; and silently handed his glass to old Sillerton Jackson.

Newland Archer, following Lefferts's glance, saw with surprise that his exclamation had been occasioned by the entry of a new figure into old Mrs. Mingott's box. It was that of a slim young woman, a little less tall than May Welland, with brown hair growing in close curls about her temples and held in place by a narrow band of diamonds. The suggestion of this headdress, which gave her what was then called a "Josephine look," was carried out in the cut of the dark blue velvet gown rather theatrically caught up under her bosom by a girdle with a large old-fashioned clasp. The wearer of this unusual dress, who seemed quite unconscious of the attention it was attracting, stood a moment in the centre of the box, discussing with Mrs. Welland the propriety of taking the latter's place in the front right-hand corner; then she yielded with a slight smile, and seated herself in line with Mrs. Welland's sister-in-law, Mrs. Lovell Mingott, who was installed in the opposite corner.

Mr. Sillerton Jackson had returned the opera-glass to Lawrence Lefferts. The whole of the club turned instinctively, waiting to hear what the old man had to say; for old Mr. Jackson was as great an authority on "family" as Lawrence Lefferts was on "form." He knew all the ramifications of New York's cousinships; and could not only elucidate such complicated questions as that of the connection between the Mingotts (through the Thorleys) with the Dallases of South Carolina, and that of the relationship of the elder branch of Philadelphia Thorleys to the Albany Chiverses (on no account to be confused with the Manson Chiverses of University Place), but could also enumerate the leading characteristics of each family: as, for instance, the fabulous stinginess of the younger lines of Leffertses (the Long Island ones); or the fatal tendency of the Rushworths to make foolish matches; or the insanity recurring in every second generation of the Albany Chiverses, with whom their New York cousins had always refused to intermarry—with the disastrous exception of poor Medora Manson, who, as everybody knew ... but then her mother was a Rushworth.

In addition to this forest of family trees, Mr. Sillerton Jackson carried between his narrow hollow temples, and under his soft thatch of silver hair, a register of most of the scandals and mysteries that had smouldered under the unruffled surface of

New York society within the last fifty years. So far indeed did his information extend, and so acutely retentive was his memory, that he was supposed to be the only man who could have told you who Julius Beaufort, the banker, really was, and what had become of handsome Bob Spicer, old Mrs. Manson Mingott's father, who had disappeared so mysteriously (with a large sum of trust money) less than a year after his marriage, on the very day that a beautiful Spanish dancer who had been delighting thronged audiences in the old Opera-house on the Battery had taken ship for Cuba. But these mysteries, and many others, were closely locked in Mr. Jackson's breast; for not only did his keen sense of honour forbid his repeating anything privately imparted, but he was fully aware that his reputation for discretion increased his opportunities of finding out what he wanted to know.

The club box, therefore, waited in visible suspense while Mr. Sillerton Jackson handed back Lawrence Lefferts's opera-glass. For a moment he silently scrutinised the attentive group out of his filmy blue eyes overhung by old veined lids; then he gave his moustache a thoughtful twist, and said simply: "I didn't think the Mingotts would have tried it on."

# Chapter 2

Newland Archer, during this brief episode, had been thrown into a strange state of embarrassment.

It was annoying that the box which was thus attracting the undivided attention of masculine New York should be that in which his betrothed was seated between her mother and aunt; and for a moment he could not identify the lady in the Empire dress, nor imagine why her presence created such excitement among the initiated. Then light dawned on him, and with it came a momentary rush of indignation. No, indeed; no one would have thought the Mingotts would have tried it on!

But they had; they undoubtedly had; for the low- toned comments behind him left no doubt in Archer's mind that the young woman was May Welland's cousin, the cousin always referred to in the family as "poor Ellen Olenska." Archer knew that she had suddenly arrived from Europe a day or two previously; he had even heard from Miss Welland (not disapprovingly) that she had been to see poor Ellen, who was staying with old Mrs. Mingott. Archer entirely approved of family solidarity, and one of the qualities he most admired in the Mingotts was their resolute championship of the few black sheep that their blameless stock had produced. There was nothing mean or ungenerous in the young man's heart, and he was glad that his future wife should not be restrained by false prudery from being kind (in private) to her unhappy cousin; but to receive Countess Olenska in the family circle was a different thing from producing her in public, at the Opera of all places, and in the very box with the young girl whose engagement to him, Newland Archer, was to be announced within a few weeks. No, he felt as old Sillerton Jackson felt; he did not think the Mingotts would have tried it on!

He knew, of course, that whatever man dared (within Fifth Avenue's limits) that old Mrs. Manson Mingott, the Matriarch of the line, would dare. He had always admired the high and mighty old lady, who, in spite of having been only Catherine Spicer of Staten Island, with a father mysteriously discredited, and neither money nor position enough to make people forget it, had allied herself with the head of the wealthy Mingott line, married two of her daughters to "foreigners" (an Italian marquis and an English banker), and put the crowning touch to her audacities by building a large house of pale cream-coloured stone (when brown sandstone seemed as much the only wear as a frock-coat in the afternoon) in an inaccessible wilderness near the Central Park.

Old Mrs. Mingott's foreign daughters had become a legend. They never came back to see their mother, and the latter being, like many persons of active mind and dominating will, sedentary and corpulent in her habit, had philosophically remained at home. But the cream- coloured house (supposed to be modelled on the private hotels of the Parisian aristocracy) was there as a visible proof of her moral courage; and she throned in it, among pre-Revolutionary furniture and souvenirs of the Tuileries of Louis Napoleon (where she had shone in her middle age), as placidly as if there were nothing peculiar in living above Thirty-fourth Street, or in having French windows that opened like doors instead of sashes that pushed up.

Every one (including Mr. Sillerton Jackson) was agreed that old Catherine had never had beauty—a gift which, in the eyes of New York, justified every success, and excused a certain number of failings. Unkind people said that, like her Imperial namesake, she had won her way to success by strength of will and hardness of heart, and a kind of haughty effrontery that was somehow justified by the extreme decency and dignity of her private life. Mr. Manson Mingott had died when she was only twenty-eight, and had "tied up" the money with an additional caution born of the general distrust of the Spicers; but his bold young widow went her way fearlessly, mingled freely in foreign society, married her daughters in heaven knew what corrupt and fashionable circles, hobnobbed with Dukes and Ambassadors, associated familiarly with Papists, entertained Opera singers, and was the intimate friend of Mme. Taglioni; and all the while (as Sillerton Jackson was the first to proclaim) there had never been a breath on her reputation; the only respect, he always added, in which she differed from the earlier Catherine.

Mrs. Manson Mingott had long since succeeded in untying her husband's fortune, and had lived in affluence for half a century; but memories of her early straits had made her excessively thrifty, and though, when she bought a dress or a piece of furniture, she took care that it should be of the best, she could not bring herself to spend much on the transient pleasures of the table. Therefore, for totally different reasons, her food was as poor as Mrs. Archer's, and her wines did nothing to redeem it. Her relatives considered that the penury of her table discredited the Mingott name, which had always been associated with good living; but people continued to come to her in spite of the "made dishes" and flat champagne, and in reply to the remonstrances of her son Lovell (who tried to retrieve the family credit by having the best chef in New York) she used to say laughingly: "What's the use of two good cooks in one family, now that I've married the girls and can't eat sauces?"

Newland Archer, as he mused on these things, had once more turned his eyes toward the Mingott box. He saw that Mrs. Welland and her sister-in-law were facing their semicircle of critics with the Mingottian APLOMB which old Catherine had inculcated in all her tribe, and that only May Welland betrayed, by a heightened colour (perhaps due to the knowledge that he was watching her) a sense of the gravity of the situation. As for the cause of the commotion, she sat gracefully in her corner of the box, her eyes fixed on the stage, and revealing, as she leaned forward, a little more shoulder and bosom than New York was accustomed to seeing, at least in ladies who had reasons for wishing to pass unnoticed.

Few things seemed to Newland Archer more awful than an offence against "Taste," that far-off divinity of whom "Form" was the mere visible representative and vicegerent. Madame Olenska's pale and serious face appealed to his fancy as suited to the occasion and to her unhappy situation; but the way her dress (which had no tucker) sloped away from her thin shoulders shocked and troubled him. He hated to think of May Welland's being exposed to the influence of a young woman so careless of the dictates of Taste.

"After all," he heard one of the younger men begin behind him (everybody talked through the Mephistopheles- and-Martha scenes), "after all, just WHAT happened?"

"Well—she left him; nobody attempts to deny that."

"He's an awful brute, isn't he?" continued the young enquirer, a candid Thorley, who was evidently preparing to enter the lists as the lady's champion.

"The very worst; I knew him at Nice," said Lawrence Lefferts with authority. "A half-paralysed white sneering fellow—rather handsome head, but eyes with a lot of lashes. Well, I'll tell you the sort: when he wasn't with women he was collecting china. Paying any price for both, I understand."

There was a general laugh, and the young champion said: "Well, then——?"

"Well, then; she bolted with his secretary."

"Oh, I see." The champion's face fell.

"It didn't last long, though: I heard of her a few months later living alone in Venice. I believe Lovell Mingott went out to get her. He said she was desperately unhappy. That's all right—but this parading her at the Opera's another thing."

"Perhaps," young Thorley hazarded, "she's too unhappy to be left at home."

This was greeted with an irreverent laugh, and the youth blushed deeply, and tried to look as if he had meant to insinuate what knowing people called a "double entendre."

"Well—it's queer to have brought Miss Welland, anyhow," some one said in a low tone, with a side- glance at Archer.

"Oh, that's part of the campaign: Granny's orders, no doubt," Lefferts laughed. "When the old lady does a thing she does it thoroughly."

The act was ending, and there was a general stir in the box. Suddenly Newland Archer felt himself impelled to decisive action. The desire to be the first man to enter Mrs. Mingott's box, to proclaim to the waiting world his engagement to May Welland, and to see her through whatever difficulties her cousin's anomalous situation might involve her in; this impulse had abruptly overruled all scruples and hesitations, and sent him hurrying through the red corridors to the farther side of the house.

As he entered the box his eyes met Miss Welland's, and he saw that she had instantly understood his motive, though the family dignity which both considered so high a virtue would not permit her to tell him so. The persons of their world lived in an atmosphere of faint implications and pale delicacies, and the fact that he and she understood each other without a word seemed to the young man to bring them nearer than any explanation would have done. Her eyes said: "You see why Mamma brought me," and his answered: "I would not for the world have had you stay away."

When he saw May's singular look, Newland was overcome with the desire to touch the flesh of his soon to be bride. His mind began to wander, and he imagined that only the two of them were present...

He held out his hand to her. She placed her own hand, slender but strong, in his. He lifted her from the chair and drew her near.

They stared longingly into one another's eyes, hers unsure, his filled with certainty.

"Newland," she whispered, her voice quavering.

He hushed her and took her face in his hands. He drew near her and stopped before touching his lips to her soft skin. Her breath hastened and her body fell limp against the weight of his arms. He braced her body and, hesitating no longer, pressed his lips to hers and took what belonged to him.

He would have her, all of her. He would ravish her, he would complete her. He slid his tongue between her satiny lips and found her velvety tongue, which was waiting to discover the unknown. She sighed at his touch and allowed him to take the lead. He rubbed the tip of his tongue against hers, slowly at first. But it wasn't long before she placed her arms around his neck and followed with great enthusiasm.

When the kiss ended and they drew away from each other, she sighed. "Oh, Newland, my darling."

He did not give her a chance to speak. Instead, he closed the gap and kissed her some more. Their lips touched and withdrew several times before he slid his mouth away from hers and then glided his lips across her cheeks and down her neck. He almost felt the patter of her heart ripple against her décolletage. He slid his mouth lower to her bosom, where he felt her heart beating through her chest.

"Newland, please, I don't think … " Her voice faded against the growing storm of his desire.

He eased down the tulle tucker of her dress, which was fastened with only a single gardenia. Then he lowered the dress to reveal the creamy complexion of her bare breasts. Her nipples protruded like tender cherries waiting for the first taste. He slid his fingers across the supple texture of her delicate skin and circled the tips of her nipples until the flesh stood on end.

She released a pleasurable sigh, and her head lolled in ecstasy.

He lowered his mouth to the blossom and began consuming her flesh with his tongue. He circled one of the tips, while he delicately thrummed the other nipple between the pads of his fingers.

"I want you," he said.

She lifted her head as though awakening from a deep sleep. "Oh, Newland, my love."

He rose to his feet, took a step back, and sat down in a chair. When she stood in front of him without moving, he grasped her waist and pulled her near. As if frightened by his gaze, she quickly drew her hands to her exposed bosom and looked down into his eyes. Her lips parted, as if trying to form words.

"Don't speak," he said. He took her hands in his, so that her breasts were once again exposed to his eyes.

"But I'm a . . ."

"Kiss me," he said and quieted her by covering her lips with his. When he pulled away from her, he grasped her full breasts and began to massage.

Her body began to sway with desire. "Oh, Newland," she whispered.

She leaned forward and touched her lips to his. This time it was she who found his tongue and kissed him with fiery passion. But when she broke the kiss and opened her eyes, she once again had a look of apprehension.

"Close your eyes," he said at once. And when she did as he asked, he released her breasts and ran his hands along the length of her form, feeling the curves of her body. As soon as he reached her ankles, he slipped his hands underneath the dress and grasped her ankles. Then he raised his hands along the outer line of her legs to the soft, firm flesh of her bottom and squeezed. She moaned, and he slowly returned his hands down the length of her legs to her ankles. He brought both hands to one of her legs and slowly raised them again, one inside her leg, the other outside. When he passed her knee, he moved the other hand toward her inner thigh. Her legs quivered, but he would not yield.

"Place your hands on my shoulders," he said.

"Oh, Newland, we really shouldn't … " But any protest quickly waned and she did as he asked.

He slid his hands higher up her legs, feeling her skin ripple as he neared her feminine delta. Then he touched the fabric of her undergarment and slid his fingers around the edge near her sheath, urging her to part her legs. When she opened herself to him, he slipped a finger through the lace fabric and found her moist petals awaiting his deeper touch.

"Newland … Newland," she said, her voice catching as he slipped more fingers inside the lace garment.

Slowly and ever so gently, he began sliding his fingers back and forth through her delicate intimate folds. "Do I please you?" he whispered as he looked into her pristine, yet flushed face.

Her eyelids fluttered, although she kept them closed. "Oh, Newland," she said, her voice hoarse, her words almost unintelligible. "Yes," she hissed. "My dearest." Then she began to move her body in rhythm with his loving touch.

He withdrew his fingers and lowered the elegant lace undergarment. Then he raised her dress and placed her skirts in one of her hands to hold them up, while leaving her other hand on his shoulder in case she swooned. Newland Archer knew that May Welland was his to do with as he pleased. The thought sent a hot sensation shooting through his loins. His member throbbed. His head swelled with euphoria. But he would restrain himself. Soon enough, the pleasure would be his. And soon enough, she would learn the many ways of pleasing him. But tonight, he would act solely for her pleasure.

He studied her form, from her ankles to the shapely curves of her muscular thighs, and up to the curls that masked her feminine form. Her pureness stemmed not only from her fair complexion, but also from her sweet naivety. He parted her feminine folds to reveal her inner petals and lovely pink pearl. Then he began to massage that precious jewel of hers, round and round, sliding his fingers from the firmness of it to the richness of her passion. She sighed. She moved without inhibition. She let him have his way because his experienced hand energized her, excited her. And after she was fully aroused, he slipped a finger inside the entrance to her sheath—to be sure, she was chaste.

He hesitated before sliding in deeper. Perhaps he should wait. Then he slid his finger back to her pearl. And with the other hand, he grasped her breast, where he found the tip of her nipple and squeezed. He played without boundaries, without strictures, until she was completely undone.

"Newland, what is happening?" she asked, speaking at once, her breath catching. "I'm … I …"

And when he whispered his reassurances, she allowed herself to crest, crying his name aloud . . .

Indeed, Newland Archer and May Welland understood each other without words. When he gazed upon his betrothed, he knew this must be true. With the comfort of that thought, he dismissed his fantasies of what it would be like for the two of them to be alone, completely free, and returned his attention to the matter at hand.

"You know my niece Countess Olenska?" Mrs. Welland enquired as she shook hands with her future son- in-law. Archer bowed without extending his hand, as was the custom on being introduced to a lady; and Ellen Olenska bent her head slightly, keeping her own pale-gloved hands clasped on her huge fan of eagle feathers. Having greeted Mrs. Lovell Mingott, a large blonde lady in creaking satin, he sat down beside his betrothed, and said in a low tone: "I hope you've told Madame Olenska that we're engaged? I want everybody to know—I want you to let me announce it this evening at the ball."

Miss Welland's face grew rosy as the dawn, and she looked at him with radiant eyes. "If you can persuade Mamma," she said; "but why should we change what is already settled?" He made no answer but that which his eyes returned, and she added, still more confidently smiling: "Tell my cousin yourself: I give you leave. She says she used to play with you when you were children."

She made way for him by pushing back her chair, and promptly, and a little ostentatiously, with the desire that the whole house should see what he was doing, Archer seated himself at the Countess Olenska's side.

"We DID use to play together, didn't we?" she asked, turning her grave eyes to his. "You were a horrid boy, and kissed me once behind a door; but it was your cousin Vandie Newland, who never looked at me, that I was in love with." Her glance swept the horseshoe curve of boxes. "Ah, how this brings it all back to me—I see everybody here in knickerbockers and pantalettes," she said, with her trailing slightly foreign accent, her eyes returning to his face.

Agreeable as their expression was, the young man was shocked that they should reflect so unseemly a picture of the august tribunal before which, at that very moment, her case was being tried. Nothing could be in worse taste than misplaced flippancy; and he answered somewhat stiffly: "Yes, you have been away a very long time."

"Oh, centuries and centuries; so long," she said, "that I'm sure I'm dead and buried, and this dear old place is heaven;" which, for reasons he could not define, struck Newland Archer as an even more disrespectful way of describing New York society.

# Chapter 3

It invariably happened in the same way.

Mrs. Julius Beaufort, on the night of her annual ball, never failed to appear at the Opera; indeed, she always gave her ball on an Opera night in order to emphasise her complete superiority to household cares, and her possession of a staff of servants competent to organise every detail of the entertainment in her absence.

The Beauforts' house was one of the few in New York that possessed a ball-room (it antedated even Mrs. Manson Mingott's and the Headly Chiverses'); and at a time when it was beginning to be thought "provincial" to put a "crash" over the drawing-room floor and move the furniture upstairs, the possession of a ball-room that was used for no other purpose, and left for three-hundred-and-sixty-four days of the year to shuttered darkness, with its gilt chairs stacked in a corner and its chandelier in a bag; this undoubted superiority was felt to compensate for whatever was regrettable in the Beaufort past.

Mrs. Archer, who was fond of coining her social philosophy into axioms, had once said: "We all have our pet common people—" and though the phrase was a daring one, its truth was secretly admitted in many an exclusive bosom. But the Beauforts were not exactly common; some people said they were even worse. Mrs. Beaufort belonged indeed to one of America's most honoured families; she had been the lovely Regina Dallas (of the South Carolina branch), a penniless beauty introduced to New York society by her cousin, the imprudent Medora Manson, who was always doing the wrong thing from the right motive. When one was related to the Mansons and the Rushworths one had a "droit de cite" (as Mr. Sillerton Jackson, who had frequented the

Tuileries, called it) in New York society; but did one not forfeit it in marrying Julius Beaufort?

The question was: who was Beaufort? He passed for an Englishman, was agreeable, handsome, ill-tempered, hospitable and witty. He had come to America with letters of recommendation from old Mrs. Manson Mingott's English son-in-law, the banker, and had speedily made himself an important position in the world of affairs; but his habits were dissipated, his tongue was bitter, his antecedents were mysterious; and when Medora Manson announced her cousin's engagement to him it was felt to be one more act of folly in poor Medora's long record of imprudences.

But folly is as often justified of her children as wisdom, and two years after young Mrs. Beaufort's marriage it was admitted that she had the most distinguished house in New York. No one knew exactly how the miracle was accomplished. She was indolent, passive, the caustic even called her dull; but dressed like an idol, hung with pearls, growing younger and blonder and more beautiful each year, she throned in Mr. Beaufort's heavy brown-stone palace, and drew all the world there without lifting her jewelled little finger. The knowing people said it was Beaufort himself who trained the servants, taught the chef new dishes, told the gardeners what hot-house flowers to grow for the dinner-table and the drawing-rooms, selected the guests, brewed the after-dinner punch and dictated the little notes his wife wrote to her friends. If he did, these domestic activities were privately performed, and he presented to the world the appearance of a careless and hospitable millionaire strolling into his own drawing-room with the detachment of an invited guest, and saying: "My wife's gloxinias are a marvel, aren't they? I believe she gets them out from Kew."

Mr. Beaufort's secret, people were agreed, was the way he carried things off. It was all very well to whisper that he had been "helped" to leave England by the international banking-house in which he had been employed; he carried off that rumour as easily as the rest—though New York's business conscience was no less sensitive than its moral standard—he carried everything before him, and all New York into his drawing- rooms, and for over twenty years now people had said they were "going to the Beauforts'" with the same tone of security as if they had said they were going to Mrs. Manson Mingott's, and with the added satisfaction of knowing they would get hot canvas-back ducks and vintage wines, instead of tepid Veuve Clicquot without a year and warmed-up croquettes from Philadelphia.

Mrs. Beaufort, then, had as usual appeared in her box just before the Jewel Song; and when, again as usual, she rose at the end of the third act, drew her opera cloak about her lovely shoulders, and disappeared, New York knew that meant that half an hour later the ball would begin.

The Beaufort house was one that New Yorkers were proud to show to foreigners, especially on the night of the annual ball. The Beauforts had been among the first people in New York to own their own red velvet carpet and have it rolled down the steps by their own footmen, under their own awning, instead of hiring it with the supper and the ball-room chairs. They had also inaugurated the custom of letting the ladies take their cloaks off in the hall, instead of shuffling up to the hostess's bedroom and recurling their hair with the aid of the gas-burner; Beaufort was understood to have said that he supposed all his wife's friends had maids who saw to it that they were properly coiffees when they left home.

Then the house had been boldly planned with a ball-room, so that, instead of squeezing through a narrow passage to get to it (as at the Chiverses') one marched solemnly down a vista of enfiladed drawing- rooms (the sea-green, the crimson and the bouton d'or), seeing from afar the many-candled lustres reflected in the polished parquetry, and beyond that the depths of a conservatory where camellias and tree-ferns arched their costly foliage over seats of black and gold bamboo.

Newland Archer, as became a young man of his position, strolled in somewhat late. He had left his overcoat with the silk-stockinged footmen (the stockings were one of Beaufort's few fatuities), had dawdled a while in the library hung with Spanish leather and furnished with Buhl and malachite, where a few men were chatting and putting on their dancing-gloves, and had finally joined the line of guests whom Mrs. Beaufort was receiving on the threshold of the crimson drawing-room.

Archer was distinctly nervous. He had not gone back to his club after the Opera (as the young bloods usually did), but, the night being fine, had walked for some distance up Fifth Avenue before turning back in the direction of the Beauforts' house. He was definitely afraid that the Mingotts might be going too far; that, in fact, they might have Granny Mingott's orders to bring the Countess Olenska to the ball.

From the tone of the club box he had perceived how grave a mistake that would be; and, though he was more than ever determined to "see the thing through," he felt less chivalrously eager to champion his betrothed's cousin than before their brief talk at the Opera.

Wandering on to the bouton d'or drawing-room (where Beaufort had had the audacity to hang "Love Victorious," the much-discussed nude of Bouguereau) Archer found Mrs. Welland and her daughter standing near the ball-room door. Couples were already gliding over the floor beyond: the light of the wax candles fell on revolving tulle skirts, on girlish heads wreathed with modest blossoms, on the dashing aigrettes and ornaments of the young married women's coiffures, and on the glitter of highly glazed shirt-fronts and fresh glace gloves.

Miss Welland, evidently about to join the dancers, hung on the threshold, her lilies-of-the-valley in her hand (she carried no other bouquet), her face a little pale, her eyes burning with a candid excitement. A group of young men and girls were gathered about her, and there was much hand-clasping, laughing and pleasantry on which Mrs. Welland, standing slightly apart, shed the beam of a qualified approval. It was evident that Miss Welland was in the act of announcing her engagement, while her mother affected the air of parental reluctance considered suitable to the occasion.

Archer paused a moment. It was at his express wish that the announcement had been made, and yet it was not thus that he would have wished to have his happiness known. To proclaim it in the heat and noise of a crowded ball-room was to rob it of the fine bloom of privacy which should belong to things nearest the heart. His joy was so deep that this blurring of the surface left its essence untouched; but he would have liked to keep the surface pure too. It was something of a satisfaction to find that May Welland shared this feeling. Her eyes fled to his beseechingly, and their look said: "Remember, we're doing this because it's right."

No appeal could have found a more immediate response in Archer's breast; but he wished that the necessity of their action had been represented by some ideal reason, and not simply by poor Ellen Olenska. The group about Miss Welland made way for him with significant smiles, and after taking his share of the felicitations he drew his betrothed into the middle of the ball-room floor and put his arm about her waist.

"Now we shan't have to talk," he said, smiling into her candid eyes, as they floated away on the soft waves of the Blue Danube.

She made no answer. Her lips trembled into a smile, but the eyes remained distant and serious, as if bent on some ineffable vision. "Dear," Archer whispered, pressing her to him: it was borne in on him that the first hours of being engaged, even if spent in a ball-room, had in them something grave and sacramental. What a new life it was going to be, with this whiteness, radiance, goodness at one's side!

The dance over, the two, as became an affianced couple, wandered into the conservatory; and sitting behind a tall screen of tree-ferns and camellias Newland pressed her gloved hand to his lips. His chest swelled with pride.

"You see I did as you asked me to," she said.

"Yes: I couldn't wait," he answered smiling. After a moment he added: "Only I wish it hadn't had to be at a ball." But he could not be disappointed, for his fondest wish had been realized this evening, and he was now free to share with the world his love for his betrothed, May Welland.

"Yes, I know." She met his glance comprehendingly. "But after all—even here we're alone together, aren't we?"

"Oh, dearest—always!" Archer cried. Her innocence dazzled him, kindling lustful urges within his loins, an insatiable desire to ravage her flesh. But he refrained and considered what she had said.

Evidently she was always going to understand; she was always going to say the right thing. The discovery made the cup of his bliss overflow, and he went on gaily: "The worst of it is that I want to kiss you and I can't." As he spoke he took a swift glance about the conservatory, assured himself of their momentary privacy, and catching her to him laid a fugitive pressure on her lips. To counteract the audacity of this proceeding he led her to a bamboo sofa in a less elaborate, but more secluded part of the conservatory, and sitting down beside her broke a lily-of-the-valley from her bouquet. He took the lily from the bouquet, brought it to his lips, and breathed in its subtle, but elegant fragrance. He considered the broken stem of the flower and how delicate the plant seemed. Beads of liquid seeped from it. He touched the wetness and then looked into his beloved's eyes. Any restraint that he might have felt moments ago was lost. He was suddenly spurred on to taste what was his alone—May Welland. She sat silent, and the world lay like a sunlit valley at their feet. He could wait no longer.

He took her face in his hands and looked longingly into her eyes.

"We mustn't," she whispered nervously.

He kissed her gently and then sensuously licked her bottom lip. When she sighed, he pressed his mouth to hers and probed inside. Her body quivered, and he knew that she had not expected such boldness. And yet, she did not withdraw her affection, but reciprocated by beginning to swirl her velvety tongue with great enthusiasm.

Then he withdrew from the kiss. "Slowly," he said, knowing this was her first time.

She acquiesced to his request, letting him guide her, show her the way of love, moaning as he slowly and gently built the rhythm.

His experienced hands fell naturally to her bosom, not out of habit, but out of desire to touch her as he kissed her. The moment his hands touched her breasts, she trembled and reflexively tried to pull back. "Oh, you shouldn't," she demurred. But, his touch was too powerful. She might have offered greater resistance, but from the moment his fingers brushed across her nipples, which were protruding hard and ripe against the fabric of her dress, he knew that he held her captive.

When he massaged the tips of her breasts with his thumbs, she sighed with such pleasure that he was driven to satisfy more of her needs. He squeezed the tips of her nipples, gently at first, but when she responded enthusiastically with a lustful moan, he increased the pressure. Her body moved insistently to his touch, and he knew that she wanted even more.

He slipped his hands inside her dress and grasped a bare breast in each. She did not hesitate, but moved to encourage him. He massaged the entirety of her breasts first and then moved his fingers to the hard tips of her nipples. He circled his thumbs around them and then clasped the tips between his fingers and squeezed, causing her to shudder and squeal with delight.

He broke from the kiss and slid his lips across her cheeks and down her neck, lingering at the hollow of her neck, all the while, tracing his fingers across her breasts. Then he moved his lips lower until he found her bosom. He ran his tongue across one of her nipples, exploring its curves. She moaned in pleasure, and did so again and when he moved his tongue to the other nipple. And after he had explored both nipples with his lips and tongue, he took her breast inside his mouth and began to suck, spinning his tongue.

She tasted sweet, like morning dew, and smelled of lilies. He thought of the flower with the broken stem and the moisture oozing from the breakage. How could something so pure ever be broken? His mind meandered to more lascivious thoughts. Never again would Newland Archer be able to look at May Welland and view her as anything other than the pure virgin whose stem he had broken.

He pulled his mouth forward to find the erect tip of her nipple. He swirled his tongue around it, feeling the firm, but soft texture of her flesh. Her pure complexion, complemented by the pale pink of her nipples, aroused his manly desires so much that if they were completely alone, he would have stripped the clothes from her body and ravished her at once. But their circumstances were tenuous, and if nothing more, he would taste the dew from her well. That she could not deny him, not now, not when she moved so desirously.

He lowered his hands, outlining her form as he fell lower to her waist, where he stopped and surrounded her body with his hands. Though he continued to kiss her breasts, nuzzling his face between them, rolling his tongue from one nipple to the next, he held her torso firmly so that she would know his strength. Then he moved his hands lower. When he could go no further, he slid from his seated position to the floor. He took the bottom edge of her dress in his hands and slowly lifted her skirts. He placed the fabric across her knees, looked up to meet her eyes, and eased her legs apart.

"Newland, don't!" she whispered, feigning resistance. But though her words said no, her body yielded to his desires.

He brought a hand to one of her breasts, taking the tip between his fingers, and tenderly rolled the delicate flesh between his fingers. Her breath caught in her throat, and as before, her eyelids fluttered, and then she closed them tightly.

Newland knew that the opportunity had presented itself. He slipped her lace undergarment from her body and then encouraged her to lie back against the bench. He slipped the undergarment in his pocket and grasped her lower legs. He slid his hands along the smoothness of her skin, and then opened her legs so that he might revel in what his virgin bride-to-be offered him.

May brought her hands to her breasts and began massaging in a manner similar to the one her lover had shown her. She sighed as he slowly, but firmly, moved his hands up the length of her inner thighs, separating them. He dipped underneath her bottom, and then lifted her legs to place them over his shoulders. When she was positioned as he wanted her, he drew in a deep breath, inhaling all of her passionate perfume.

"Oh, my heavens, yes!" she said, her body quivering with desire.

"I will pleasure you, my love."

Then he touched his tongue to her intimate flesh, rolling it from her moist well of passion to the upper reaches of her form where he found her pearl. He stopped to circle his tongue around her protruding gem, and she trembled with pleasure. And the more he pleasured her, the more she moaned, surrendering completely to his touch. He was so overcome with desire from tasting her fruit and inhaling her fragrance that, had they not been at a crowded ball, he would have lain upon her—the formalities of marriage be damned. However, he restrained himself with difficulty and continued to please his young bride-to-be until he brought her to the pinnacle of desire. Her hips moved to his every touch; she needed release. Swooping his tongue downward, he tasted her rich cream and then returned to her pearl, on which his tongue began to dance lightly, swirling round and round, stroking it more insistently until she reached the summit of her pleasure.

"Oh, my goodness, I have never … " Her words were lost when he inhaled deeply. Her body quaked, and when she exhaled, she crested, her body giving way to lust.

Newland drew away from her body, certain that he had shown his fair love the pleasures a man might offer his bride. He was pleased with himself for taking what was his when he so chose.

Suddenly, Newland heard the sound of others approaching. Making haste, he quickly returned to May's intimate flower to consume the fruit of her creamy release. Her entire body shuddered, as if she was experiencing a second climax. He ran his tongue along the length of her folds, and then covered her legs with her dress. Then he rose and seated himself upon the settee, making sure to position himself a foot apart from her.

When the couple who had ventured into the room passed by, May began conversing with Newland about a new topic as though their passionate love scene had never happened. It was not her nature to acknowledge what had occurred.

"Did you tell my cousin Ellen?" she asked presently, as if she spoke through a dream.

He roused himself, and remembered that he had not done so. Some invincible repugnance to speak of such things to the strange foreign woman had checked the words on his lips.

"No—I hadn't the chance after all," he said, fibbing hastily.

"Ah." She looked disappointed, but gently resolved on gaining her point. "You must, then, for I didn't either; and I shouldn't like her to think—"

"Of course not. But aren't you, after all, the person to do it?"

She pondered on this. "If I'd done it at the right time, yes: but now that there's been a delay I think you must explain that I'd asked you to tell her at the Opera, before our speaking about it to everybody here. Otherwise she might think I had forgotten her. You see, she's one of the family, and she's been away so long that she's rather—sensitive."

Archer looked at her glowingly. "Dear and great angel! Of course I'll tell her." He glanced a trifle apprehensively toward the crowded ball-room. "But I haven't seen her yet. Has she come?"

"No; at the last minute she decided not to."

"At the last minute?" he echoed, betraying his surprise that she should ever have considered the alternative possible.

"Yes. She's awfully fond of dancing," the young girl answered simply. "But suddenly she made up her mind that her dress wasn't smart enough for a ball, though we thought it so lovely; and so my aunt had to take her home."

"Oh, well—" said Archer with happy indifference. Nothing about his betrothed pleased him more than her resolute determination to carry to its utmost limit that ritual of ignoring the "unpleasant" in which they had both been brought up.

"She knows as well as I do," he reflected, "the real reason of her cousin's staying away; but I shall never let her see by the least sign that I am conscious of there being a shadow of a shade on poor Ellen Olenska's reputation."

# Chapter 4

In the course of the next day the first of the usual betrothal visits were exchanged. The New York ritual was precise and inflexible in such matters; and in conformity with it Newland Archer first went with his mother and sister to call on Mrs. Welland, after which he and Mrs. Welland and May drove out to old Mrs. Manson Mingott's to receive that venerable ancestress's blessing.

A visit to Mrs. Manson Mingott was always an amusing episode to the young man. The house in itself was already an historic document, though not, of course, as venerable as certain other old family houses in University Place and lower Fifth Avenue. Those were of the purest 1830, with a grim harmony of cabbage- rose-garlanded carpets, rosewood consoles, round-arched fire-places with black marble mantels, and immense glazed book-cases of mahogany; whereas old Mrs. Mingott, who had built her house later, had bodily cast out the massive furniture of her prime, and mingled with the Mingott heirlooms the frivolous upholstery of the Second Empire. It was her habit to sit in a window of her sitting-room on the ground floor, as if watching calmly for life and fashion to flow northward to her solitary doors. She seemed in no hurry to have them come, for her patience was equalled by her confidence. She was sure that presently the hoardings, the quarries, the one-story saloons, the wooden green-houses in ragged gardens, and the rocks from which goats surveyed the scene, would vanish before the advance of residences as stately as her own—perhaps (for she was an impartial woman) even statelier; and that the cobble- stones over which the old clattering omnibuses bumped would be replaced by smooth asphalt, such as people reported having seen in Paris. Meanwhile, as every one she cared to see came to HER (and she could fill her rooms as easily as the Beauforts, and without adding a single item to the menu of her suppers), she did not suffer from her geographic isolation.

The immense accretion of flesh which had descended on her in middle life like a flood of lava on a doomed city had changed her from a plump active little woman with a neatly-turned foot and ankle into something as vast and august as a natural phenomenon. She had accepted this submergence as philosophically as all her other trials, and now, in extreme old age, was rewarded by presenting to her mirror an almost unwrinkled expanse of firm pink and white flesh, in the centre of which the traces of a small face survived as if awaiting excavation. A flight of smooth double chins led down to the dizzy depths of a still-snowy bosom veiled in snowy muslins that were held in place by a miniature portrait of the late Mr. Mingott; and around and below, wave after wave of black silk surged away over the edges of a capacious armchair, with two tiny white hands poised like gulls on the surface of the billows.

The burden of Mrs. Manson Mingott's flesh had long since made it impossible for her to go up and down stairs, and with characteristic independence she had made her reception rooms upstairs and established herself (in flagrant violation of all the New York proprieties) on the ground floor of her house; so that, as you sat in her sitting-room window with her, you caught (through a door that was always open, and a looped- back yellow damask portiere) the unexpected vista of a bedroom with a huge low bed upholstered like a sofa, and a toilet-table with frivolous lace flounces and a gilt-framed mirror.

Her visitors were startled and fascinated by the foreignness of this arrangement, which recalled scenes in French fiction, and architectural incentives to immorality such as the simple American had never dreamed of. That was how women with lovers lived in the wicked old societies, in apartments with all the rooms on one floor, and all the indecent propinquities that their novels described.

It amused Newland Archer (who had secretly situated the love-scenes of "Monsieur de Camors" in Mrs. Mingott's bedroom) to picture her blameless life led in the stage-setting of adultery; but he said to himself, with considerable admiration, that if a lover had been what she wanted, the intrepid woman would have had him too.

Newland allowed his imagination to roam through the pages of such an illicit novel. And whom should he find, but the ancestress herself in her boudoir.

"Send in the footman," old Mrs. Mingott said in a loud voice.

The butler appeared from behind the yellow damask portiere and bowed. "Madame?"

"I told you to send in the footman," she said. "Are you becoming deaf, my good man?"

"No, ma'am. I mean, yes, ma'am. I mean … I shall call in the footman."

"And tell him to leave his trousers at the door. I won't have him undressing before me."

"Very well, Madame."

"And he need not dally, for I have needs."

Some moments later, the footman, a man half the age of the ancestress, slunk around the heavy fabric of the curtain door and presented himself to her. His long mousey-colored hair, which he tied behind his head, fell like the scraggly strands of a horse's tail. His face was structurally long, with a bony appearance that rendered a blank, but obedient, expression. As instructed, he had removed his trousers and left them at the door. However, he had not entirely undressed. He kept on a bright red jacket with a stiff white-collared shirt underneath it, with shirttails covering his loins. And then there were his boots. As a rule, he was to leave them on to cover anything unsightly.

Footie, the pet name Mrs. Mingott had given him long ago, was familiar with the duties his mistress required of him. He was not only to attend to the horses and carriages, but he was also to service her every passionate, lustful whim. How he came to be the Chosen One was no mystery. He was the only servant thin enough to squeeze between her expanse of firm pink and white flesh. But that was not all—it also pleased her to no end that he was greatly endowed; or as more simply said by the other servants, he was hung. The ancestress had long been partial to long, thin members. Rumors had it that her late husband had been puny.

"Well, don't just stand there," she said. "I have needs good fellow."

The quavering footman took gangly, reluctant, strides toward his mistress and stopped once he stood before her massive person. "What is your pleasure today?" he asked.

"Show me your cock."

"As you wish, Madame." The footman lifted his shirttails to reveal his shaft and a magnificent pair of baubles. Both member and jewels were of a prodigious size and proportion, especially compared to that of his bony legs and knocked knees. And remarkably, Footie's member was of great length even soft.

"Very well," she said. "I see you need encouragement today."

The man's face flushed red.

"Turn around," she said.

The man smiled rather sheepishly, though the ancestress knew that he could hardly wait for what was to come next. Without delay, he turned clumsily, and as always bent over without request, practically taking himself down to the floor.

She grasped a riding crop resting alongside her massive mounds of thighs, a region of her body that was no longer distinct, but rather existed as a vast, conjoined mountain range of delicacies and hidden delights. "Grasp your knees," she said forcefully, as though she might actually rise from the comfort of her armchair if he even thought to hesitate. She lifted the whip and with great force and precision lashed the footman's backside. The poor man took a hop from the whip's sting and belted out an animalistic whimper.

"Come back, you devil," she demanded, and then she proceeded to spank the young man mercilessly. The man's whimpers soon turned to combined moans of pleasure and pain, and before long, his cock stood on end to great soaring heights. The ancestress laughed hysterically because she so enjoyed watching her subject and his member dance.

And once they had had their preliminary fun, she licked her lips slowly and said, "Now lift my skirts. In the manner I prefer."

The young man bent down and yanked up his mistress's skirts to reveal the creamy skin of her legs. Then he rose and stretched himself across her immense and pillowed accretion of flesh to reach the cloth of her lace undergarment. There, he tugged and struggled to free the garment from her mass, but finally gave up and ripped the cloth from her loins.

"Ah, you devil," she said, and began to laugh heartily.

The footman gave her a lascivious smile. As old and as corpulent as the ancestress was, she was quite a woman, and he made no secret of the fact that he enjoyed this game. "Shall I pleasure you, Madame?" Not waiting her reply, he went to work to separate the mountain range of her flesh to find her vast valley of lust.

The ancestress shivered, feeling an electricity surge through her loins, as the young man worked her thighs apart to reveal her dense forest of pleasure. "Do hurry, Footie," she said, lavishing him with words of endearment.

The footman stood before her and squeezed his thin body between her delectable, titanic thighs, and then ran his fingers through her heavenly passion, stroking tenderly. She moaned softly at first, but soon uttered impassioned symphonic cries, not unlike the Franz Liszt's Hungarian Rhapsody No. 2 that was played on the gramophone.

"Now, Footie, now!" she commanded, grinding her hips to him, urging him to enter her sheath.

However, he did not enter her with his massive and rampant member, no, not yet. Instead, he slowly filled her sheath with one of his long slender fingers, and then added another, and another, slowly dipping in and out, as he circled her pearl with the thumb of his other hand.

The ancestress moaned loudly. "Now, Footie, do it!" she cried, her voice desperate with desire, begging him to enter. But she was his prisoner now and he held her captive until he choose to enter. When she began to pant relentlessly, he finally drove his member through the opening of her sheath. He slowly negotiated her vessel, teasing the crown of his staff in and out of it, while she painstakingly urged him to enter more fully.

She was nearly undone and moaned incessantly, emitting loud shrieks that sounded more animalistic than human. Footie continued to tease her at some length. She rolled her head from side to side, but there was nothing she could do until he chose to enter. Then finally, Footie was overcome and thrust his member deep inside her well. In a gallop, he began pumping in and out of her as though he were a wild horse set free to roam across the untamed fields of passion.

And somewhere along the way, their voices united in a harmonious choir of fervent symphonic cries. Not a nook, crook, or cranny of the ground floor of the stately house was devoid of their performance. And before they finished their lovemaking, the ancestress, more than once, raised her whip and gently lashed the backside of her stud, and he responded to her urging. He went from a gallop to a sprint, performed enthusiastically, squealed with delight, and thrust ever harder.

Rounding the bend, the finish line was in sight. The ancestress thrust her hips forward with such violence that when she climaxed, she brought Footie right along with her, and together they crested with the utmost of pleasure . . .

Newland Archer gave his head a stout jerk to clear his mind, and then gazed at the old Mrs. Mingott perched in one of her frivolous Second Empire upholstered chairs. She had quite a peculiar look in her eyes. It was as if Newland Archer had magically unveiled one of her secrets; more truth than the matronly woman had ever cared to reveal. And at that moment in time, Newland decided he was clairvoyant.

"Are you quite all right, young man?" Mrs. Mingott said to Newland, forcing him to return his attention to the present conversation.

When he nodded respectfully, brief pleasantries were exchanged among the parties, and then the ancestress explained the absence of her granddaughter, Countess Olenska. To the general relief the Countess Olenska was not present in her grandmother's drawing-room during the visit of the betrothed couple. Mrs. Mingott said she had gone out; which, on a day of such glaring sunlight, and at the "shopping hour," seemed in itself an indelicate thing for a compromised woman to do. But at any rate it spared them the embarrassment of her presence, and the faint shadow that her unhappy past might seem to shed on their radiant future. The visit went off successfully, as was to have been expected. Old Mrs. Mingott was delighted with the engagement, which, being long foreseen by watchful relatives, had been carefully passed upon in family council; and the engagement ring, a large thick sapphire set in invisible claws, met with her unqualified admiration.

"It's the new setting: of course it shows the stone beautifully, but it looks a little bare to old-fashioned eyes," Mrs. Welland had explained, with a conciliatory side-glance at her future son-in-law.

"Old-fashioned eyes? I hope you don't mean mine, my dear? I like all the novelties," said the ancestress, lifting the stone to her small bright orbs, which no glasses had ever disfigured. "Very handsome," she added, returning the jewel; "very liberal. In my time a cameo set in pearls was thought sufficient. But it's the hand that sets off the ring, isn't it, my dear Mr. Archer?" and she waved one of her tiny hands, with small pointed nails and rolls of aged fat encircling the wrist like ivory bracelets. "Mine was modelled in Rome by the great Ferrigiani. You should have May's done: no doubt he'll have it done, my child. Her hand is large—it's these modern sports that spread the joints—but the skin is white.—And when's the wedding to be?" she broke off, fixing her eyes on Archer's face.

"Oh—" Mrs. Welland murmured, while the young man, smiling at his betrothed, replied: "As soon as ever it can, if only you'll back me up, Mrs. Mingott."

"We must give them time to get to know each other a little better, mamma," Mrs. Welland interposed, with the proper affectation of reluctance; to which the ancestress rejoined: "Know each other? Fiddlesticks! Everybody in New York has always known everybody. Let the young man have his way, my dear; don't wait till the bubble's off the wine. Marry them before Lent; I may catch pneumonia any winter now, and I want to give the wedding-breakfast."

These successive statements were received with the proper expressions of amusement, incredulity and gratitude; and the visit was breaking up in a vein of mild pleasantry when the door opened to admit the Countess Olenska, who entered in bonnet and mantle followed by the unexpected figure of Julius Beaufort.

There was a cousinly murmur of pleasure between the ladies, and Mrs. Mingott held out Ferrigiani's model to the banker. "Ha! Beaufort, this is a rare favour!" (She had an odd foreign way of addressing men by their surnames.)

"Thanks. I wish it might happen oftener," said the visitor in his easy arrogant way. "I'm generally so tied down; but I met the

Countess Ellen in Madison Square, and she was good enough to let me walk home with her."

"Ah—I hope the house will be gayer, now that Ellen's here!" cried Mrs. Mingott with a glorious effrontery. "Sit down—sit down, Beaufort: push up the yellow armchair; now I've got you I want a good gossip. I hear your ball was magnificent; and I understand you invited Mrs. Lemuel Struthers? Well—I've a curiosity to see the woman myself."

She had forgotten her relatives, who were drifting out into the hall under Ellen Olenska's guidance. Old Mrs. Mingott had always professed a great admiration for Julius Beaufort, and there was a kind of kinship in their cool domineering way and their short-cuts through the conventions. Now she was eagerly curious to know what had decided the Beauforts to invite (for the first time) Mrs. Lemuel Struthers, the widow of Struthers's Shoe-polish, who had returned the previous year from a long initiatory sojourn in Europe to lay siege to the tight little citadel of New York. "Of course if you and Regina invite her the thing is settled. Well, we need new blood and new money—and I hear she's still very good-looking," the carnivorous old lady declared.

In the hall, while Mrs. Welland and May drew on their furs, Archer saw that the Countess Olenska was looking at him with a faintly questioning smile.

"Of course you know already—about May and me," he said, answering her look with a shy laugh. "She scolded me for not giving you the news last night at the Opera: I had her orders to tell you that we were engaged—but I couldn't, in that crowd."

The smile passed from Countess Olenska's eyes to her lips: she looked younger, more like the bold brown Ellen Mingott of his boyhood. "Of course I know; yes. And I'm so glad. But one doesn't tell such things first in a crowd." The ladies were on the threshold and she held out her hand.

"Good-bye; come and see me some day," she said, still looking at Archer.

In the carriage, on the way down Fifth Avenue, they talked pointedly of Mrs. Mingott, of her age, her spirit, and all her wonderful attributes. No one alluded to Ellen Olenska; but Archer knew that Mrs. Welland was thinking: "It's a mistake for Ellen to be seen, the very day after her arrival, parading up Fifth Avenue at the crowded hour with Julius Beaufort—" and the young man himself mentally added: "And she ought to know that a man who's just engaged doesn't spend his time calling on married women. But I daresay in the set she's lived in they do— they never do anything else." And, in spite of the cosmopolitan views on which he prided himself, he thanked heaven that he was a New Yorker, and about to ally himself with one of his own kind.

# Chapter 5

The next evening old Mr. Sillerton Jackson came to dine with the Archers.

Mrs. Archer was a shy woman and shrank from society; but she liked to be well-informed as to its doings. Her old friend Mr. Sillerton Jackson applied to the investigation of his friends' affairs the patience of a collector and the science of a naturalist; and his sister, Miss Sophy Jackson, who lived with him, and was entertained by all the people who could not secure her much-sought-after brother, brought home bits of minor gossip that filled out usefully the gaps in his picture.

Therefore, whenever anything happened that Mrs. Archer wanted to know about, she asked Mr. Jackson to dine; and as she honoured few people with her invitations, and as she and her daughter Janey were an excellent audience, Mr. Jackson usually came himself instead of sending his sister. If he could have dictated all the conditions, he would have chosen the evenings when Newland was out; not because the young man was uncongenial to him (the two got on capitally at their club) but because the old anecdotist sometimes felt, on Newland's part, a tendency to weigh his evidence that the ladies of the family never showed.

Mr. Jackson, if perfection had been attainable on earth, would also have asked that Mrs. Archer's food should be a little better. But then New York, as far back as the mind of man could travel, had been divided into the two great fundamental groups of the Mingotts and Mansons and all their clan, who cared about eating and clothes and money, and the Archer-Newland- van-der-Luyden tribe, who were devoted to travel, horticulture and the best fiction, and looked down on the grosser forms of pleasure.

You couldn't have everything, after all. If you dined with the Lovell Mingotts you got canvas-back and terrapin and vintage wines; at Adeline Archer's you could talk about Alpine scenery and "The Marble Faun"; and luckily the Archer Madeira had gone round the Cape. Therefore when a friendly summons came from Mrs. Archer, Mr. Jackson, who was a true eclectic, would usually say to his sister: "I've been a little gouty since my last dinner at the Lovell Mingotts'—it will do me good to diet at Adeline's."

Mrs. Archer, who had long been a widow, lived with her son and daughter in West Twenty-eighth Street. An upper floor was dedicated to Newland, and the two women squeezed themselves into narrower quarters below. In an unclouded harmony of tastes and interests they cultivated ferns in Wardian cases, made macrame lace and wool embroidery on linen, collected American revolutionary glazed ware, subscribed to "Good Words," and read Ouida's novels for the sake of the Italian atmosphere. (They preferred those about peasant life, because of the descriptions of scenery and the pleasanter sentiments, though in general they liked novels about people in society, whose motives and habits were more comprehensible, spoke severely of Dickens, who "had never drawn a gentleman," and considered Thackeray less at home in the great world than Bulwer—who, however, was beginning to be thought old-fashioned.) Mrs. and Miss Archer were both great lovers of scenery. It was what they principally sought and admired on their occasional travels abroad; considering architecture and painting as subjects for men, and chiefly for learned persons who read Ruskin. Mrs. Archer had been born a Newland, and mother and daughter, who were as like as sisters, were both, as people said, "true Newlands"; tall, pale, and slightly round-shouldered, with long noses, sweet smiles and a kind of drooping distinction like that in certain faded Reynolds portraits. Their physical resemblance would have been complete if an elderly embonpoint had not stretched Mrs. Archer's black brocade, while Miss Archer's brown and purple poplins hung, as the years went on, more and more slackly on her virgin frame.

Mentally, the likeness between them, as Newland was aware, was less complete than their identical mannerisms often made it appear. The long habit of living together in mutually dependent intimacy had given them the same vocabulary, and the same habit of beginning their phrases "Mother thinks" or "Janey thinks," according as one or the other wished to advance an opinion of her own; but in reality, while Mrs. Archer's serene unimaginativeness rested easily in the accepted and familiar, Janey was subject to starts and aberrations of fancy welling up from springs of suppressed romance.

Mother and daughter adored each other and revered their son and brother; and Archer loved them with a tenderness made compunctious and uncritical by the sense of their exaggerated admiration, and by his secret satisfaction in it. After all, he thought it a good thing for a man to have his authority respected in his own house, even if his sense of humour sometimes made him question the force of his mandate.

On this occasion the young man was very sure that Mr. Jackson would rather have had him dine out; but he had his own reasons for not doing so.

Of course old Jackson wanted to talk about Ellen Olenska, and of course Mrs. Archer and Janey wanted to hear what he had to tell. All three would be slightly embarrassed by Newland's presence, now that his prospective relation to the Mingott clan had been made known; and the young man waited with an amused curiosity to see how they would turn the difficulty.

They began, obliquely, by talking about Mrs. Lemuel Struthers.

"It's a pity the Beauforts asked her," Mrs. Archer said gently. "But then Regina always does what he tells her; and BEAUFORT—"

"Certain nuances escape Beaufort," said Mr. Jackson, cautiously inspecting the broiled shad, and wondering for the thousandth time why Mrs. Archer's cook always burnt the roe to a cinder. (Newland, who had long shared his wonder, could always detect it in the older man's expression of melancholy disapproval.)

"Oh, necessarily; Beaufort is a vulgar man," said Mrs. Archer. "My grandfather Newland always used to say to my mother: 'Whatever you do, don't let that fellow Beaufort be introduced to the girls.' But at least he's had the advantage of associating with gentlemen; in England too, they say. It's all very mysterious—" She glanced at Janey and paused. She and Janey knew every fold of the Beaufort mystery, but in public Mrs. Archer continued to assume that the subject was not one for the unmarried.

"But this Mrs. Struthers," Mrs. Archer continued; "what did you say SHE was, Sillerton?"

"Out of a mine: or rather out of the saloon at the head of the pit. Then with Living Wax-Works, touring New England. After the police broke THAT up, they say she lived—" Mr. Jackson in his turn glanced at Janey, whose eyes began to bulge from under her prominent lids. There were still hiatuses for her in Mrs. Struthers's past.

"Then," Mr. Jackson continued (and Archer saw he was wondering why no one had told the butler never to slice cucumbers with a steel knife), "then Lemuel Struthers came along. They say his advertiser used the girl's head for the shoe-polish posters; her hair's intensely black, you know—the Egyptian style. Anyhow, he—eventually—married her." There were volumes of innuendo in the way the "eventually" was spaced, and each syllable given its due stress.

"Oh, well—at the pass we've come to nowadays, it doesn't matter," said Mrs. Archer indifferently. The ladies were not really interested in Mrs. Struthers just then; the subject of Ellen Olenska was too fresh and too absorbing to them. Indeed, Mrs. Struthers's name had been introduced by Mrs. Archer only that she might presently be able to say: "And Newland's new cousin—Countess Olenska? Was SHE at the ball too?"

There was a faint touch of sarcasm in the reference to her son, and Archer knew it and had expected it. Even Mrs. Archer, who was seldom unduly pleased with human events, had been altogether glad of her son's engagement. ("Especially after that silly business with Mrs. Rushworth," as she had remarked to Janey, alluding to what had once seemed to Newland a tragedy of which his soul would always bear the scar.)

There was no better match in New York than May Welland, look at the question from whatever point you chose. Of course such a marriage was only what Newland was entitled to; but young men are so foolish and incalculable—and some women so ensnaring and unscrupulous—that it was nothing short of a miracle to see one's only son safe past the Siren Isle and in the haven of a blameless domesticity.

All this Mrs. Archer felt, and her son knew she felt; but he knew also that she had been perturbed by the premature announcement of his engagement, or rather by its cause; and it was for that reason—because on the whole he was a tender and indulgent master—that he had stayed at home that evening. "It's not that I don't approve of the Mingotts' esprit de corps; but why Newland's engagement should be mixed up with that Olenska woman's comings and goings I don't see," Mrs. Archer grumbled to Janey, the only witness of her slight lapses from perfect sweetness.

She had behaved beautifully—and in beautiful behaviour she was unsurpassed—during the call on Mrs. Welland; but Newland knew (and his betrothed doubtless guessed) that all through the visit she and Janey were nervously on the watch for Madame Olenska's possible intrusion; and when they left the house together she had permitted herself to say to her son: "I'm thankful that Augusta Welland received us alone."

These indications of inward disturbance moved Archer the more that he too felt that the Mingotts had gone a little too far. But, as it was against all the rules of their code that the mother and son should ever allude to what was uppermost in their thoughts, he simply replied: "Oh, well, there's always a phase of family parties to be gone through when one gets engaged, and the sooner it's over the better." At which his mother merely pursed her lips under the lace veil that hung down from her grey velvet bonnet trimmed with frosted grapes.

Her revenge, he felt—her lawful revenge—would be to "draw" Mr. Jackson that evening on the Countess Olenska; and, having publicly done his duty as a future member of the Mingott clan, the young man had no objection to hearing the lady discussed in private—except that the subject was already beginning to bore him.

Mr. Jackson had helped himself to a slice of the tepid filet which the mournful butler had handed him with a look as sceptical as his own, and had rejected the mushroom sauce after a scarcely perceptible sniff. He looked baffled and hungry, and Archer reflected that he would probably finish his meal on Ellen Olenska.

Mr. Jackson leaned back in his chair, and glanced up at the candlelit Archers, Newlands and van der Luydens hanging in dark frames on the dark walls.

"Ah, how your grandfather Archer loved a good dinner, my dear Newland!" he said, his eyes on the portrait of a plump full-chested young man in a stock and a blue coat, with a view of a white-columned country-house behind him. "Well—well—well ... I wonder what he would have said to all these foreign marriages!"

Mrs. Archer ignored the allusion to the ancestral cuisine and Mr. Jackson continued with deliberation: "No, she was NOT at the ball."

"Ah—" Mrs. Archer murmured, in a tone that implied: "She had that decency."

"Perhaps the Beauforts don't know her," Janey suggested, with her artless malice.

Mr. Jackson gave a faint sip, as if he had been tasting invisible Madeira. "Mrs. Beaufort may not—but Beaufort certainly does, for she was seen walking up Fifth Avenue this afternoon with him by the whole of New York."

"Mercy—" moaned Mrs. Archer, evidently perceiving the uselessness of trying to ascribe the actions of foreigners to a sense of delicacy.

"I wonder if she wears a round hat or a bonnet in the afternoon," Janey speculated. "At the Opera I know she had on dark blue velvet, perfectly plain and flat—like a night-gown."

"Janey!" said her mother; and Miss Archer blushed and tried to look audacious.

"It was, at any rate, in better taste not to go to the ball," Mrs. Archer continued.

A spirit of perversity moved her son to rejoin: "I don't think it was a question of taste with her. May said she meant to go, and then decided that the dress in question wasn't smart enough."

Mrs. Archer smiled at this confirmation of her inference. "Poor Ellen," she simply remarked; adding compassionately: "We must always bear in mind what an eccentric bringing-up Medora Manson gave her. What can you expect of a girl who was allowed to wear black satin at her coming-out ball?"

"Ah—don't I remember her in it!" said Mr. Jackson; adding: "Poor girl!" in the tone of one who, while enjoying the memory, had fully understood at the time what the sight portended.

"It's odd," Janey remarked, "that she should have kept such an ugly name as Ellen. I should have changed it to Elaine." She glanced about the table to see the effect of this.

Her brother laughed. "Why Elaine?"

"I don't know; it sounds more—more Polish," said Janey, blushing.

"It sounds more conspicuous; and that can hardly be what she wishes," said Mrs. Archer distantly.

"Why not?" broke in her son, growing suddenly argumentative. "Why shouldn't she be conspicuous if she chooses? Why should she slink about as if it were she who had disgraced herself? She's 'poor Ellen' certainly, because she had the bad luck to make a wretched marriage; but I don't see that that's a reason for hiding her head as if she were the culprit."

"That, I suppose," said Mr. Jackson, speculatively, "is the line the Mingotts mean to take."

The young man reddened. "I didn't have to wait for their cue, if that's what you mean, sir. Madame Olenska has had an unhappy life: that doesn't make her an outcast."

"There are rumours," began Mr. Jackson, glancing at Janey.

"Oh, I know: the secretary," the young man took him up. "Nonsense, mother; Janey's grown-up. They say, don't they," he went on, "that the secretary helped her to get away from her brute of a husband, who kept her practically a prisoner? Well, what if he did? I hope there isn't a man among us who wouldn't have done the same in such a case."

Mr. Jackson glanced over his shoulder to say to the sad butler: "Perhaps ... that sauce ... just a little, after all—"; then, having helped himself, he remarked: "I'm told she's looking for a house. She means to live here."

"I hear she means to get a divorce," said Janey boldly.

"I hope she will!" Archer exclaimed.

The word had fallen like a bombshell in the pure and tranquil atmosphere of the Archer dining-room. Mrs. Archer raised her delicate eye-brows in the particular curve that signified: "The butler—" and the young man, himself mindful of the bad taste of discussing such intimate matters in public, hastily branched off into an account of his visit to old Mrs. Mingott.

After dinner, according to immemorial custom, Mrs. Archer and Janey trailed their long silk draperies up to the drawing-room, where, while the gentlemen smoked below stairs, they sat beside a Carcel lamp with an engraved globe, facing each other across a rosewood work-table with a green silk bag under it, and stitched at the two ends of a tapestry band of field-flowers destined to adorn an "occasional" chair in the drawing- room of young Mrs. Newland Archer.

While this rite was in progress in the drawing-room, Archer settled Mr. Jackson in an armchair near the fire in the Gothic library and handed him a cigar. Mr. Jackson sank into the armchair with satisfaction, lit his cigar with perfect confidence (it was Newland who bought them), and stretching his thin old ankles to the coals, said: "You say the secretary merely helped her to get away, my dear fellow? Well, he was still helping her a year later, then; for somebody met 'em living at Lausanne together."

Newland reddened. "Living together? Well, why not? Who had the right to make her life over if she hadn't? I'm sick of the hypocrisy that would bury alive a woman of her age if her husband prefers to live with harlots."

He stopped and turned away angrily to light his cigar. "Women ought to be free—as free as we are," he declared, making a discovery of which he was too irritated to measure the terrific consequences.

Newland's mind began to reel. He wondered if she had been sexually subjugated, forced to participate in orgies and sexual perversions against her will like a common slattern. It seemed likely, given her husband's reputation, that the Count regarded her as no more than another one of his harlots; a woman to exploit when he so fancied. Was it any wonder the poor woman had escaped with her husband's secretary? But to live with the secretary as his mistress, that was entirely another matter. That was certainly living freely.

Newland considered the Countess. The dress she wore at the opera gave her more than a Josephine look; it daringly revealed her feminine lines. And her sultry eyes—they spoke of carnal knowledge, tempted men to lose control. The woman was beguiling.

Newland began to picture himself with the Countess. His imagination transported him back to the first night he saw her at the Opera House right after she told him that he kissed her when they were children. In his mind's eye, he saw the Countess unexpectedly rise from her chair.

"If you will excuse me," she said, staring at him intensely.

He got up from his seat to let her pass, nodding his head politely.

She stopped to speak quietly with May and then turned to leave. He noticed when he sat back down that the Countess had dropped her handkerchief. He dipped a hand to the floor and quickly retrieved the article. Then he turned to May. "Your cousin, will she return?"

"No, I think she's not well," May said.

"She left her handkerchief."

"Be a dear, would you Newland, and return it to her. And see that she finds a Brown Coupe before long."

"Yes, of course, dear. I won't be long." He stood up and excused himself from the club box. Then he raced down the corridor to find the Countess. But she was nowhere in sight. He continued down a flight of stairs, but there was no sign of her. Just as he was about to give up hope of finding her, he turned and caught a glimpse of her blue dress as she disappeared through a closed door. He hurried to the door, opened it, and saw that it hid a concealed staircase. He rushed down the stairs, and when he circled around, he saw the back of her blue velvet dress.

"Countess Olenska?"

She stopped, a frightened expression on her face. "Oh, Mr. Archer." She brought her hands to her chest. "I must say, you quite startled me."

"I'm sorry. It was not my intention to frighten you."

She flashed a flirtatious smile. "Have you come to steal another kiss then?"

"Lest you forget, May and I—"

"No, of course not I haven't forgotten. I saw the way you looked at her."

He lifted his hand. "Your handkerchief, Countess."

She laughed softly. "Surely that cannot be the only reason you have followed me."

Newland was dumbfounded. She had divined his intentions. He could easily have turned back when he failed to find her at the first landing, but he did not. He had pursued her with determination.

The Countess advanced on Newland, stopping perilously close to him. She lifted her head, letting her eyes meet his. "Call me Ellen," she said softly.

"Ellen, your . . ." He lowered his arm when he realized she wasn't interested in the handkerchief.

Her lips were pursed and ready to be kissed. She was toying with his affections, testing his loyalty to May. He studied her face and then lowered his gaze to her creamy breasts. Her chest rose and fell quickly, and he felt her breath flowing against his cheeks. The next moment, his head began to spin; the woman was intoxicating, completely hypnotic. He suddenly felt a strong desire to throw his arms around her end make love to her.

Something snapped. Newland lost all sense of reason. He grasped the Countess's arms and pulled her near. His mind told him to stop, he admonished himself to release her and return to

May, but his manly desires forced him to act impetuously. He lunged forward and kissed her.

She did not fight him, but joined him with greater enthusiasm, more than he expected. Taking the initiative, she slipped her tongue into his mouth and began to swirl hers around his. She freed her arms and threw them around his neck. Then she pressed her body firmly against his and began to move her hips across his manhood.

Newland felt a fire surge from his chest to his loins. Her touch aroused him. And when he broke from the kiss, he stared intently into her eyes. She had rendered him speechless.

"Is that what you really wanted to give me?" she whispered, her voice sultry and expectant.

Newland did not answer her. He spun her around so that she faced the wall. Disregarding all sense of decency, he lifted her dress and placed it into one of her arms to hold up. He forced her to the wall and placed her free hand against it. Almost viciously, he ripped her undergarment free from her bottom and tossed it aside. Rather than resist, she looked over her shoulder, smiled at him, and then slowly licked her lips. He grasped her firm backside and gave her cheeks a squeeze, and then slid a hand through her intimate folds. She was moist and ready.

She moaned, moving her hips desirously.

Newland freed his member, stiffer than it had ever been in his life. He stepped forward and grasped her hips, pulling them toward him. He took a deep breath, inhaling her intimate fragrance, and then plunged his member inside her sheath. She emitted a high-pitched gasp, but moved eagerly to meet his rhythm. Then he slid a hand in front of her and lowered it, finding her inflamed pearl.

"Yes, there," she said, and stroked his hand. He compliantly began massaging and stimulating her jewel. The more he massaged, the more impassioned she grew, writhing and undulating to the rhythm of his strokes. When the Countess exhaled a long breath, her loins tightening, he could delay no longer. He was beyond the point of return. When she cried out as she climaxed, he released his seed into her slick vessel. Their timing had been perfect.

The door opened a flight above them.

"Quickly," he whispered in her ear.

She lowered her dress as he refastened his trousers. Then he grasped her hand, and together they flew down the length of the staircase, exiting a side-door, which led them outside of the Opera House. Without looking back, Newland promptly led her to the line for a Brown Coupe and returned to May's side.

And that was how Newland mentally recast the scene the first night he saw the Countess at the Opera House. "Yes, women ought to be free—as free as we are," he now thought, having considered the wonderful consequences.

Mr. Sillerton Jackson stretched his ankles nearer the coals and emitted a sardonic whistle.

"Well," he said after a pause, "apparently Count Olenska takes your view; for I never heard of his having lifted a finger to get his wife back."

# Chapter 6

That evening, after Mr. Jackson had taken himself away, and the ladies had retired to their chintz- curtained bedroom, Newland Archer mounted thoughtfully to his own study. A vigilant hand had, as usual, kept the fire alive and the lamp trimmed; and the room, with its rows and rows of books, its bronze and steel statuettes of "The Fencers" on the mantelpiece and its many photographs of famous pictures, looked singularly home-like and welcoming.

As he dropped into his armchair near the fire his eyes rested on a large photograph of May Welland, which the young girl had given him in the first days of their romance, and which had now displaced all the other portraits on the table. With a new sense of awe he looked at the frank forehead, serious eyes and gay innocent mouth of the young creature whose soul's custodian he was to be. That terrifying product of the social system he belonged to and believed in, the young girl who knew nothing and expected everything, looked back at him like a stranger through May Welland's familiar features; and once more it was borne in on him that marriage was not the safe anchorage he had been taught to think, but a voyage on uncharted seas. He thought marriage would make him faithful, but now he was uncertain.

The case of the Countess Olenska had stirred up old settled convictions and set them drifting dangerously through his mind. His own exclamation: "Women should be free—as free as we are," struck to the root of a problem that it was agreed in his world to regard as non-existent. "Nice" women, however wronged, would never claim the kind of freedom he meant, and generous- minded men like himself were therefore—in the heat of argument—the more chivalrously ready to concede it to them.

Such verbal generosities were in fact only a humbugging disguise of the inexorable conventions that tied things together and bound people down to the old pattern. But here he was pledged to defend, on the part of his betrothed's cousin, conduct that, on his own wife's part, would justify him in calling down on her all the thunders of Church and State. Of course the dilemma was purely hypothetical; since he wasn't a blackguard Polish nobleman, it was absurd to speculate what his wife's rights would be if he WERE. But Newland Archer was too imaginative not to feel that, in his case and May's, the tie might gall for reasons far less gross and palpable. What could he and she really know of each other, since it was his duty, as a "decent" fellow, to conceal his past from her, and hers, as a marriageable girl, to have no past to conceal? What if, for some one of the subtler reasons that would tell with both of them, they should tire of each other, misunderstand or irritate each other? He reviewed his friends' marriages—the supposedly happy ones—and saw none that answered, even remotely, to the passionate and tender comradeship which he pictured as his permanent relation with May Welland. He perceived that such a picture presupposed, on her part, the experience, the versatility, the freedom of judgment, which she had been carefully trained not to possess; and with a shiver of foreboding he saw his marriage becoming what most of the other marriages about him were: a dull association of material and social interests held together by ignorance on the one side and hypocrisy on the other. Lawrence Lefferts occurred to him as the husband who had most completely realised this enviable ideal. As became the high-priest of form, he had formed a wife so completely to his own convenience that, in the most conspicuous moments of his frequent love-affairs with other men's wives, she went about in smiling unconsciousness, saying that "Lawrence was so frightfully strict"; and had been known to blush indignantly, and avert her gaze, when some one alluded in her presence to the fact that Julius Beaufort (as became a "foreigner" of doubtful origin) had what was known in New York as "another establishment."

Archer tried to console himself with the thought that he was not quite such an ass as Larry Lefferts, nor May such a simpleton as poor Gertrude; but the difference was after all one of intelligence and not of standards. In reality they all lived in a kind of hieroglyphic world, where the real thing was never said or done or even thought, but only represented by a set of arbitrary signs; as when Mrs. Welland, who knew exactly why Archer had pressed her to announce her daughter's engagement at the Beaufort ball (and had indeed expected him to do no less), yet felt obliged to simulate reluctance, and the air of having had her hand forced, quite as, in the books on Primitive Man that people of advanced culture were beginning to read, the savage bride is dragged with shrieks from her parents' tent.

The result, of course, was that the young girl who was the centre of this elaborate system of mystification remained the more inscrutable for her very frankness and assurance. She was frank, poor darling, because she had nothing to conceal, assured because she knew of nothing to be on her guard against; and with no better preparation than this, she was to be plunged overnight into what people evasively called "the facts of life."

The young man was sincerely but placidly in love. He delighted in the radiant good looks of his betrothed, in her health, her horsemanship, her grace and quickness at games, and the shy interest in books and ideas that she was beginning to develop under his guidance. (She had advanced far enough to join him in ridiculing the Idyls of the King, but not to feel the beauty of Ulysses and the Lotus Eaters.) She was straightforward, loyal and brave; she had a sense of humour (chiefly proved by her laughing at HIS jokes); and he suspected, in the depths of her innocently-gazing soul, a glow of feeling that it would be a joy to waken. But when he had gone the brief round of her he returned discouraged by the thought that all this frankness and innocence were only an artificial product. Untrained human nature was not frank and innocent; it was full of the twists and defences of an instinctive guile. And he felt himself oppressed by this creation of factitious purity, so cunningly manufactured by a conspiracy of mothers and aunts and grandmothers and long-dead ancestresses, because it was supposed to be what he wanted, what he had a right to, in order that he might exercise his lordly pleasure in smashing it like an image made of snow.

There was a certain triteness in these reflections: they were those habitual to young men on the approach of their wedding day. But they were generally accompanied by a sense of compunction and self-abasement of which Newland Archer felt no trace. He could not deplore (as Thackeray's heroes so often exasperated him by doing) that he had not a blank page to offer his bride in exchange for the unblemished one she was to give to him. He could not get away from the fact that if he had been brought up as she had they would have been no more fit to find their way about than the Babes in the Wood; nor could he, for all his anxious cogitations, see any honest reason (any, that is, unconnected with his own momentary pleasure, and the passion of masculine vanity) why his bride should not have been allowed the same freedom of experience as himself.

Such questions, at such an hour, were bound to drift through his mind; but he was conscious that their uncomfortable persistence and precision were due to the inopportune arrival of the Countess Olenska. Here he was, at the very moment of his betrothal—a moment for pure thoughts and cloudless hopes—pitchforked into a coil of scandal which raised all the special problems he would have preferred to let lie. "Hang Ellen Olenska!" he grumbled, as he covered his fire and began to undress. How had he allowed her to seduce him, capture his affection, his manly affection? He could not really see why her fate should have the least bearing on his; yet he dimly felt that he had only just begun to measure the risks of the championship which his engagement had forced upon him.

A light tap sounded on the back hallway door.

Newland thought it might be best to ignore it this evening because he felt perplexed and conflicted. The knock repeated.

"Hang it all," he thought. He slipped on his robe and headed for the door. When he unlatched it, two female servants stood waiting.

"It's our evening, sir," the chambermaid Miranda said. "We're here to serve you."

Newland considered the women. He had known Miranda for some years now. She had been his faithful and loyal servant, attending to his every need. She was a dark-haired woman with a mousey face and had little in the way of bosoms, but her hips were full and her body a pleasurable form, comforting to lie upon. The other woman—a pert, blonde-haired girl, really—was many years younger and was new to the household. She had an eager look about her. Her breasts spilled from her maid's uniform, and when he saw them, Newland instantly felt an intense arousal. He had wondered what his commitment to May would do to these interludes. That was why he had broken off the affair with the society woman. But satisfying his manly needs with loyal chambermaids was not the same as having a love affair, or acting like an ass. On the contrary, cavorting with the servants to satisfy his desires would only ensure that he would remain faithful to May, that he would not fall in love with a woman of her stature. And Miranda was most discrete, and would not bring another girl who would not exercise the same discretion. His decision was made.

He stepped forward, clasped the bib of the young woman's dress, and pulled it forward, exposing her naked breasts. Her large, full nipples stood on end like buttons that needed attention. She wriggled her body enticingly. Without asking her leave, he slipped his hand inside the dress and pulled one of her breasts free to have a closer look and feel.

At his touch, the young chambermaid sucked in a strong, quivering breath. It might have been a sigh of pleasure, it might have been a moan of pain. Unmindful of her reaction, Newland placed his thumb and forefingers around the magnificent nipple, and then rolled and squeezed it between his fingers. She purred this time.

"And who might you be, Miss?" he asked the young woman.

"Oh, my," the chambermaid said, her speech labored. "My name … oh, my name is … Anne, Mr. Archer."

Newland gave the nipple one last squeeze, causing Anne to throw her head back and moan in pleasure. "Yes, Anne and Miranda, do come in," he said. Anne smiled and squeezed her own breasts, and Miranda licked her lips saucily. He stepped to the side and allowed the two chambermaids to enter, making sure to squeeze Miranda's voluptuous bottom as she wriggled past him in a teasing sort of manner. At his touch, Miranda was sure to shriek with pleasure.

Newland shut the door and approached Anne from behind. "The first thing we'll need to do is take these clothes off of you."

Miranda gleefully helped Newland undress the young woman, and once Anne stood naked, Newland quickly led her to the bed and gently lowered her down to the mattress. "Open your legs wide," he said, and helped her spread them. Miranda slid the robe from her master's back, and then began to undress herself.

Seeing the young Anne's intimate form, Newland felt his member jump and quickly stand fully erect. "So delicate," he said, the words rushing out of his lungs in anticipation of deflowering her.

"She's pure, to be sure, Mr. Archer," Miranda said, coming alongside of him to see for herself. "Ready to become a woman."

Newland faced Miranda. "And this is her pleasure?"

Anne answered herself, "Yes, of course, Mr. Archer." She smiled, and then cupped one of her breasts, lifted it to her mouth, and used her long tongue to slowly lick the magnificent nipple.

"Well then, if you're sure," he said, grinning and reveling in her nakedness. He once again ran his fingers gently over her erect nipple.

"Oh, yes," Anne hissed, beginning to undulate to his gentle touch. "More, Mr. Archer."

Newland began massaging Anne's intimate folds, thumbing a finger around her protruding pearl. Miranda, now fully naked, took her place on the bed above Anne. She propped herself on her hands and knees with her bottom and intimate form facing Newland, and she began shaking her bottom in lustful invitation. Newland reached to touch Miranda's pearl and began massaging both of the women at once, slithering his hands through their moist petals and folds. Then he slipped a finger inside of Miranda's sheath and began thrumming it in rhythm to his manipulations of Anne's pearl. He was careful not to compromise Anne's hymen—not yet.

Miranda rocked and moaned, begging for more, and so Newland pushed her forward so that she rested on her forearms, exposing more of her intimate form. He leaned forward and tasted her cream as he continued to play with Anne. Then he slid his tongue from her well of passion to her pearl, where he began to swirl. Miranda danced and undulated uninhibitedly. She was hot, moist, and ready for more. But she would have to wait. Newland pressed his member against Anne's female folds and slowly slid it through her cream. Anne moaned with pleasure, and began moving her hips more desirously toward him.

Newland could wait no longer. He leveled his member at the opening of her sheath and began to gently probe. She was tight, so tight, never having been opened or touched before. Newland felt the rush of his desires taking over him, so he pushed a little more insistently. Anne moaned louder as he attempted to enter her tight vessel. Since she was a virgin, he was not yet able to enter—she was too tight. So he grasped her erect nipple and squeezed until she was overflowing with a rich, creamy pool of passion. With a forceful push, he finally split her flesh and pushed his crown inside of her, and she was no longer a virgin.

Anne gasped at his entry, and then cried, "OH!" Her voice hinted at painful pleasure.

"Are you quite enjoying it, Anne?" Newland asked.

"Yes, yes, Mr. Archer, it's just … oh!" She arched her neck. "So good, so good," she repeated over and over. It was as though she were speaking to no one, that she was lost in a dream of perfect pleasure.

Not stopping, Newland slowly, but firmly, pushed his member deeper inside, filling her vessel to its end, and then he stopped to savor the moment.

"OH! My God," Anne said, gasping for breath. "I can't … I … I . . ."

"Take my breast," Miranda said to her.

Anne quickly grasped one of Miranda's breasts and began to suckle a nipple with great enthusiasm, and then she grasped Miranda's other breast and began massaging it with great fervor, rubbing her fingers across its erect tip. Miranda smiled wickedly and groaned in pleasure. And the more Anne sucked, the more she seemed to relax for Newland, making it easier for him to begin stroking in and out of her. With each passing minute, Newland's enthusiasm grew more pronounced. He began groaning wildly as he thrust in and out of Anne, while also enjoying the fruits of Miranda's cream with his tongue. Miranda moaned uninhibitedly, and before long, Anne joined in moaning just as excitedly, as though she had known carnal knowledge her whole life. The three moved as one, locked in passion.

"Oh, yes, yes," Anne said, continuing to suckle Miranda's breast. "I … I," she said, and a moment later, her hips thrust forward. "My God!"

Newland felt Anne's vessel contract and squeeze. Her entire body convulsed, and she thrashed her limbs uncontrollably. It was all that Newland could do to keep his member buried inside her. He had satisfied her completely. He continued to thrust in and out of her and then pulled his erection from her once she lay satisfied.

"Come closer," he said, patting Miranda's full bottom.

"Oh, Mr. Archer, I thought you'd never ask," Miranda said, and she placed herself at the edge of the bed and lifted her bottom in the air, so that he could access her forbidden door. "I've waited so long."

Newland grasped her breasts and squeezed. Then he returned his hands to her bottom cheeks, holding them firmly apart. "Brace yourself, my dear," he said. Wet with Anne's cream, he slowly pushed inside Miranda's forbidden door, grunting as he worked.

"Ah-h, my God!" she exclaimed. "Oh-h, Mr. Archer!"

Anne rose and stood behind Newland. There, she grasped his firm buttocks and began massaging as he rocked in and out of Miranda, groaning with utmost pleasure. Newland reached for Miranda's pearl and began massaging her to intensify her pleasure. A moment later, Anne moved one of her hands between Newland's fold and with her fingers began strumming the opening to his forbidden door. Newland groaned at her deeper touch, encouraging her to explore more, so Anne dipped a finger deep inside of him, and soon began moving it in and out to match his strokes in and out of Miranda.

At Anne's touch, Newland found himself completely overwhelmed. Unable to control himself, he thrust heartily a few more times, until with great tumult and satisfaction, his loins tightened and he released his seed within Miranda's cavity with such vigor that his body shook thunderously. His convulsions ignited Miranda fully, and she exploded with him.

"My God!" he exclaimed. "Why shouldn't women have the same freedom of experience?"

"Beg your pardon, Sir?" Anne said.

But Newland did not answer her. Overcome, he and Miranda collapsed onto the bed, gasping for breath. It took some time for them to recover, but once they did, Newland promptly dismissed the chambermaids. He kissed both women and squeezed Anne's breast and Miranda's bottom as they left his quarters, and before long, he soon found himself situated in bed, feeling satisfied and content, while thinking that he was glad that at least there were some women in this world who were not afraid to live life without hypocrisy.

A few days later the bolt fell.

The Lovell Mingotts had sent out cards for what was known as "a formal dinner" (that is, three extra footmen, two dishes for each course, and a Roman punch in the middle), and had headed their invitations with the words "To meet the Countess Olenska," in accordance with the hospitable American fashion, which treats strangers as if they were royalties, or at least as their ambassadors.

The guests had been selected with a boldness and discrimination in which the initiated recognised the firm hand of Catherine the Great. Associated with such immemorial standbys as the Selfridge Merrys, who were asked everywhere because they always had been, the Beauforts, on whom there was a claim of relationship, and Mr. Sillerton Jackson and his sister Sophy (who went wherever her brother told her to), were some of the most fashionable and yet most irreproachable of the dominant "young married" set; the Lawrence Leffertses, Mrs. Lefferts Rushworth (the lovely widow), the Harry Thorleys, the Reggie Chiverses and young Morris Dagonet and his wife (who was a van der Luyden). The company indeed was perfectly assorted, since all the members belonged to the little inner group of people who, during the long New York season, disported themselves together daily and nightly with apparently undiminished zest.

Forty-eight hours later the unbelievable had happened; every one had refused the Mingotts' invitation except the Beauforts and old Mr. Jackson and his sister. The intended slight was emphasised by the fact that even the Reggie Chiverses, who were of the Mingott clan, were among those inflicting it; and by the uniform wording of the notes, in all of which the writers "regretted that they were unable to accept," without the mitigating plea of a "previous engagement" that ordinary courtesy prescribed.

New York society was, in those days, far too small, and too scant in its resources, for every one in it (including livery-stable-keepers, butlers and cooks) not to know exactly on which evenings people were free; and it was thus possible for the recipients of Mrs. Lovell Mingott's invitations to make cruelly clear their determination not to meet the Countess Olenska.

The blow was unexpected; but the Mingotts, as their way was, met it gallantly. Mrs. Lovell Mingott confided the case to Mrs. Welland, who confided it to Newland Archer; who, aflame at the outrage, appealed passionately and authoritatively to his mother; who, after a painful period of inward resistance and outward temporising, succumbed to his instances (as she always did), and immediately embracing his cause with an energy redoubled by her previous hesitations, put on her grey velvet bonnet and said: "I'll go and see Louisa van der Luyden."

The New York of Newland Archer's day was a small and slippery pyramid, in which, as yet, hardly a fissure had been made or a foothold gained. At its base was a firm foundation of what Mrs. Archer called "plain people"; an honourable but obscure majority of respectable families who (as in the case of the Spicers or the Leffertses or the Jacksons) had been raised above their level by marriage with one of the ruling clans. People, Mrs. Archer always said, were not as particular as they used to be; and with old Catherine Spicer ruling one end of Fifth Avenue, and Julius Beaufort the other, you couldn't expect the old traditions to last much longer.

Firmly narrowing upward from this wealthy but inconspicuous substratum was the compact and dominant group which the Mingotts, Newlands, Chiverses and Mansons so actively represented. Most people imagined them to be the very apex of the pyramid; but they themselves (at least those of Mrs. Archer's generation) were aware that, in the eyes of the professional genealogist, only a still smaller number of families could lay claim to that eminence.

"Don't tell me," Mrs. Archer would say to her children, "all this modern newspaper rubbish about a New York aristocracy. If there is one, neither the Mingotts nor the Mansons belong to it; no, nor the Newlands or the Chiverses either. Our grandfathers and great-grandfathers were just respectable English or Dutch merchants, who came to the colonies to make their fortune, and stayed here because they did so well. One of your great-grandfathers signed the Declaration, and another was a general on Washington's staff, and received General Burgoyne's sword after the battle of Saratoga. These are things to be proud of, but they have nothing to do with rank or class. New York has always been a commercial community, and there are not more than three families in it who can claim an aristocratic origin in the real sense of the word."

Mrs. Archer and her son and daughter, like every one else in New York, knew who these privileged beings were: the Dagonets of Washington Square, who came of an old English county family allied with the Pitts and Foxes; the Lannings, who had intermarried with the descendants of Count de Grasse, and the van der Luydens, direct descendants of the first Dutch governor of Manhattan, and related by pre-revolutionary marriages to several members of the French and British aristocracy.

The Lannings survived only in the person of two very old but lively Miss Lannings, who lived cheerfully and reminiscently among family portraits and Chippendale; the Dagonets were a considerable clan, allied to the best names in Baltimore and Philadelphia; but the van der Luydens, who stood above all of them, had faded into a kind of super-terrestrial twilight, from which only two figures impressively emerged; those of Mr. and Mrs. Henry van der Luyden.

Mrs. Henry van der Luyden had been Louisa Dagonet, and her mother had been the granddaughter of Colonel du Lac, of an old Channel Island family, who had fought under Cornwallis and had settled in Maryland, after the war, with his bride, Lady Angelica Trevenna, fifth daughter of the Earl of St. Austrey. The tie between the Dagonets, the du Lacs of Maryland, and their aristocratic Cornish kinsfolk, the Trevennas, had always remained close and cordial. Mr. and Mrs. van der Luyden had more than once paid long visits to the present head of the house of Trevenna, the Duke of St. Austrey, at his country-seat in Cornwall and at St. Austrey in Gloucestershire; and his Grace had frequently announced his intention of some day returning their visit (without the Duchess, who feared the Atlantic).

Mr. and Mrs. van der Luyden divided their time between Trevenna, their place in Maryland, and Skuytercliff, the great estate on the Hudson which had been one of the colonial grants of the Dutch government to the famous first Governor, and of which Mr. van der Luyden was still "Patroon." Their large solemn house in Madison Avenue was seldom opened, and when they came to town they received in it only their most intimate friends.

"I wish you would go with me, Newland," his mother said, suddenly pausing at the door of the Brown coupe. "Louisa is fond of you; and of course it's on account of dear May that I'm taking this step—and also because, if we don't all stand together, there'll be no such thing as Society left."

# Chapter 7

Mrs. Henry van der Luyden listened in silence to her cousin Mrs. Archer's narrative.

It was all very well to tell yourself in advance that Mrs. van der Luyden was always silent, and that, though non-committal by nature and training, she was very kind to the people she really liked. Even personal experience of these facts was not always a protection from the chill that descended on one in the high-ceilinged white-walled Madison Avenue drawing-room, with the pale brocaded armchairs so obviously uncovered for the occasion, and the gauze still veiling the ormolu mantel ornaments and the beautiful old carved frame of Gainsborough's "Lady Angelica du Lac."

Mrs. van der Luyden's portrait by Huntington (in black velvet and Venetian point) faced that of her lovely ancestress. It was generally considered "as fine as a Cabanel," and, though twenty years had elapsed since its execution, was still "a perfect likeness." Indeed the Mrs. van der Luyden who sat beneath it listening to Mrs. Archer might have been the twin-sister of the fair and still youngish woman drooping against a gilt armchair before a green rep curtain. Mrs. van der Luyden still wore black velvet and Venetian point when she went into society—or rather (since she never dined out) when she threw open her own doors to receive it. Her fair hair, which had faded without turning grey, was still parted in flat overlapping points on her forehead, and the straight nose that divided her pale blue eyes was only a little more pinched about the nostrils than when the portrait had been painted. She always, indeed, struck Newland Archer as having been rather gruesomely preserved in the airless atmosphere of a perfectly irreproachable existence, as bodies caught in glaciers keep for years a rosy life-in-death.

Like all his family, he esteemed and admired Mrs. van der Luyden; but he found her gentle bending sweetness less approachable than the grimness of some of his mother's old aunts, fierce spinsters who said "No" on principle before they knew what they were going to be asked.

Mrs. van der Luyden's attitude said neither yes nor no, but always appeared to incline to clemency till her thin lips, wavering into the shadow of a smile, made the almost invariable reply: "I shall first have to talk this over with my husband."

She and Mr. van der Luyden were so exactly alike that Archer often wondered how, after forty years of the closest conjugality, two such merged identities ever separated themselves enough for anything as controversial as a talking-over. But as neither had ever reached a decision without prefacing it by this mysterious conclave, Mrs. Archer and her son, having set forth their case, waited resignedly for the familiar phrase.

Mrs. van der Luyden, however, who had seldom surprised any one, now surprised them by reaching her long hand toward the bell-rope.

"I think," she said, "I should like Henry to hear what you have told me."

A footman appeared, to whom she gravely added: "If Mr. van der Luyden has finished reading the newspaper, please ask him to be kind enough to come."

She said "reading the newspaper" in the tone in which a Minister's wife might have said: "Presiding at a Cabinet meeting"—not from any arrogance of mind, but because the habit of a life-time, and the attitude of her friends and relations, had led her to consider Mr. van der Luyden's least gesture as having an almost sacerdotal importance.

Her promptness of action showed that she considered the case as pressing as Mrs. Archer; but, lest she should be thought to have committed herself in advance, she added, with the sweetest look:

"Henry always enjoys seeing you, dear Adeline; and he will wish to congratulate Newland. And on second thought, if you would excuse me, we will be with you presently."

Mrs. van der Luyden hurried to her husband's study and entered without stopping to knock as was her typical custom; she quietly opened the door and peered in. He was seated with his back to her in an oversized, tall chair that sat before a fire that was burning brightly. She started toward him, thinking he must be asleep, as his newspaper had fallen to the floor. Before circling around the chair, Mr. van der Luyden suddenly emitted a loud noise, not a snore that she might be accustomed to hearing, but a manly groan. Only then did she notice his arm pumping up and down in a locomotive rhythm.

She stopped, bringing her hands to her bosom, not sure what she ought to do, as she had never once caught her husband under these most peculiar and potentially humiliating circumstances. It wasn't her nature to be shy in the privacy of their quarters. But this was altogether quite different. Then it occurred to her that Mr. van der Luyden had been remiss in his marital duties to her, and with that thought in mind, she felt a spring give way in her loins.

"Henry," she said, walking around to greet him face to face.

He immediately opened his eyes and stopped stroking his member, the crown engorged a reddish purple. "My dear! You've caught me red-handed, as they say."

"You have rejected me, sir!"

"Not at all, my dear. Sometimes a man just needs to know himself." He gave her a devilish smile. "Well, it seems as though you've arrived at just the right moment. Raise your skirts, Louise, darling."

She lifted her skirts, exposing her feminine folds, for Mrs. van der Luyden was often in the habit of traversing her home without underwear so that she could be ready for a sensuous encounter with her once randy husband. She readied herself and straddled her husband's lap.

"We must be quick," she said.

"Ah," he said, nodding compliantly and then quickly ran his fingers through her feminine form to discover that she was indeed impassioned. "My dear, Mrs. van der Luyden. I see you have eschewed the encumbrance that would impede my entry."

She giggled suggestively. "Oh, my darling, how I've missed you."

"And I, you, though it has only been a few days."

"You should have saved yourself for this evening."

He slipped a finger inside her moist sheath and moved it in and out. "You needn't worry over such trivial matters. I will be delighted to pleasure you again, if it pleases you."

Mrs. van der Luyden giggled with delight, throwing her head back, enjoying his touch. "Oh, Henry." The air caught in her throat. "You-you … are a-a, oh yes, yes, Henry … you are a dear."

He rotated his finger around as he slid it inside and out of her sheath a few more times. Then he grasped her hips and slowly lowered her body so that the crown of his staff was at the entrance to her moist aperture.

"Take it inside you, my dear," he said softly, his breath hot, panting with desire.

Mrs. van der Luyden slowly lowered herself, swallowing his robust crown first as it slipped between her folds. Then she gently thrust down, taking in his rampant member, savoring the slow slid down as his member filled her sheath. When he was fully immersed to the hilt, she stopped and stared into her husband-lover's eyes. "Henry," she said, and then rolled her head around, embracing the moment of ecstasy.

"My love," he whispered, grasping her breasts and massaging them.

And then suddenly, like a tigress set loose on the prowl, Mrs. van der Luyden began thrusting her hips up and down, slowly at first, but then to a more enthusiastic beat, as if she had spotted her prey and the chase was on. She was wild, untamed, and bent on capturing her wildebeest. She moaned exceedingly loud and moved fluidly without any sense of reserve. "Oh, Henry, Henry," she cried.

There was nothing Mr. van der Luyden could do except enjoy the ride. His wife was wet with an appetite and passion so voracious that the hunt was worth the kill. And such was her passion and his pleasure that she was in danger of killing him with lust. He let her do the work, but matched her timing, as though he were a flank hunter, waiting to lunge the moment her teeth sunk into the wildebeest.

"Oh … oh," Mrs. van der Luyden cried aloud, her husband's snarls resonating in harmony with her shrieks of passion. Her body rose and fell, undulating and writhing until finally, the prey was at her fingertips. Her loins tightened, and then she leapt with all her body flying through the air. She had captured exactly what she sought, her release.

Mr. van der Luyden moved in to finish the kill. He groaned loudly as he moved his wife's hips up and down a few more strokes, and finally finished the task.

"Oh, Henry. How you do satisfy me, my love," she said.

He grasped her face and pulled her near. Their lips touched and he slipped a gentle tongue into her mouth, and together, their tongues began to swirl. The kiss was ever so gentle, a tender counterpoint to their passionate lovemaking. He grasped her breast, lowered the bodice of her dress to find the creamy flesh of her bosom. He licked her erect nipples and then began to suck one of them.

When a jolt of electricity shot through her loins, causing her to undulate anew, Mrs. van der Luyden began to moan. "Oh, Henry, my dear. That feels so … but we . . ."

He raised his mouth from her. "Yes, my dear?"

"I'm afraid we have guests."

He ignored her and began circling his tongue around her nipple again.

She sighed as he teased the tip of the nipple by stroking it gently with his tongue, and then she felt his remarkably resilient member beginning to arise anew. "Oh, Henry."

"You say we have guests?" he asked reluctantly.

She drew back and looked into his eyes. "Yes, unfortunately . . ."

He squeezed her bottom, and said, "Come, my dear. We'll continue this later."

Mrs. van der Luyden giggled girlishly. "Yes, my love, we certainly must."

The two readied themselves, and promptly left the privacy of Mr. van der Luyden's study.

The double doors had solemnly reopened and between them appeared Mrs. van der Luyden along with her husband, Mr. Henry van der Luyden, tall, spare and frock-coated, with faded fair hair, a straight nose like his wife's and the same look of frozen gentleness in eyes that were merely pale grey instead of pale blue.

Mr. van der Luyden greeted Mrs. Archer with cousinly affability, proffered to Newland low-voiced congratulations couched in the same language as his wife's, and seated himself in one of the brocade armchairs with the simplicity of a reigning sovereign.

"I had just finished reading the Times," he said, laying his long finger-tips together. "In town my mornings are so much occupied that I find it more convenient to read the newspapers after luncheon." Mr. van der Luyden cleared his throat and looked at his lovely tigress of a wife. Words were not necessary.

"Ah, there's a great deal to be said for that plan—indeed I think my uncle Egmont used to say he found it less agitating not to read the morning papers till after dinner," said Mrs. Archer responsively.

"Yes: my good father abhorred hurry. But now we live in a constant rush," said Mr. van der Luyden in measured tones, looking with pleasant deliberation about the large shrouded room which to Archer was so complete an image of its owners.

"But I hope you HAD finished your reading, Henry?" his wife interposed.

"Quite—quite," he reassured her.

"Then I should like Adeline to tell you—"

"Oh, it's really Newland's story," said his mother smiling; and proceeded to rehearse once more the monstrous tale of the affront inflicted on Mrs. Lovell Mingott.

"Of course," she ended, "Augusta Welland and Mary Mingott both felt that, especially in view of Newland's engagement, you and Henry OUGHT TO KNOW."

"Ah—" said Mr. van der Luyden, drawing a deep breath.

There was a silence during which the tick of the monumental ormolu clock on the white marble mantelpiece grew as loud as the boom of a minute-gun. Archer contemplated with awe the two slender faded figures, seated side by side in a kind of viceregal rigidity, mouthpieces of some remote ancestral authority which fate compelled them to wield, when they would so much rather have lived in simplicity and seclusion, digging invisible weeds out of the perfect lawns of Skuytercliff, and playing Patience together in the evenings.

Mr. van der Luyden was the first to speak.

"You really think this is due to some—some intentional interference of Lawrence Lefferts's?" he enquired, turning to Archer.

"I'm certain of it, sir. Larry has been going it rather harder than usual lately—if cousin Louisa won't mind my mentioning it—having rather a stiff affair with the postmaster's wife in their village, or some one of that sort; and whenever poor Gertrude Lefferts begins to suspect anything, and he's afraid of trouble, he gets up a fuss of this kind, to show how awfully moral he is, and talks at the top of his voice about the impertinence of inviting his wife to meet people he doesn't wish her to know. He's simply using Madame Olenska as a lightning-rod; I've seen him try the same thing often before."

"The LEFFERTSES!—" said Mrs. van der Luyden.

"The LEFFERTSES!—" echoed Mrs. Archer. "What would uncle Egmont have said of Lawrence Lefferts's pronouncing on anybody's social position? It shows what Society has come to."

"We'll hope it has not quite come to that," said Mr. van der Luyden firmly.

"Ah, if only you and Louisa went out more!" sighed Mrs. Archer.

But instantly she became aware of her mistake. The van der Luydens were morbidly sensitive to any criticism of their secluded existence. They were the arbiters of fashion, the Court of last Appeal, and they knew it, and bowed to their fate. But being shy and retiring persons, with no natural inclination for their part, they lived as much as possible in the sylvan solitude of Skuytercliff, and when they came to town, declined all invitations on the plea of Mrs. van der Luyden's health.

Newland Archer came to his mother's rescue. "Everybody in New York knows what you and cousin Louisa represent. That's why Mrs. Mingott felt she ought not to allow this slight on Countess Olenska to pass without consulting you."

Mrs. van der Luyden glanced at her husband, who glanced back at her.

"It is the principle that I dislike," said Mr. van der Luyden. "As long as a member of a well-known family is backed up by that family it should be considered—final."

"It seems so to me," said his wife, as if she were producing a new thought.

"I had no idea," Mr. van der Luyden continued, "that things had come to such a pass." He paused, and looked at his wife again. "It occurs to me, my dear, that the Countess Olenska is already a sort of relation—through Medora Manson's first husband. At any rate, she will be when Newland marries." He turned toward the young man. "Have you read this morning's Times, Newland?"

"Why, yes, sir," said Archer, who usually tossed off half a dozen papers with his morning coffee.

Husband and wife looked at each other again. Their pale eyes clung together in prolonged and serious consultation; then a faint smile fluttered over Mrs. van der Luyden's face. She had evidently guessed and approved.

Mr. van der Luyden turned to Mrs. Archer. "If Louisa's health allowed her to dine out—I wish you would say to Mrs. Lovell Mingott—she and I would have been happy to—er—fill the places of the Lawrence Leffertses at her dinner." He paused to let the irony of this sink in. "As you know, this is impossible." Mrs. Archer sounded a sympathetic assent. "But Newland tells me he has read this morning's Times; therefore he has probably seen that Louisa's relative, the Duke of St. Austrey, arrives next week on the Russia. He is coming to enter his new sloop, the Guinevere, in next summer's International Cup Race; and also to have a little canvasback shooting at Trevenna." Mr. van der Luyden paused again, and continued with increasing benevolence: "Before taking him down to Maryland we are inviting a few friends to meet him here—only a little dinner—with a reception afterward. I am sure Louisa will be as glad as I am if Countess Olenska will let us include her among our guests." He got up, bent his long body with a stiff friendliness toward his cousin, and added: "I think I have Louisa's authority for saying that she will herself leave the invitation to dine when she drives out presently: with our cards—of course with our cards."

Mrs. Archer, who knew this to be a hint that the seventeen-hand chestnuts which were never kept waiting were at the door, rose with a hurried murmur of thanks. Mrs. van der Luyden beamed on her with the smile of Esther interceding with Ahasuerus; but her husband raised a protesting hand.

"There is nothing to thank me for, dear Adeline; nothing whatever. This kind of thing must not happen in New York; it shall not, as long as I can help it," he pronounced with sovereign gentleness as he steered his cousins to the door.

Two hours later, every one knew that the great C-spring barouche in which Mrs. van der Luyden took the air at all seasons had been seen at old Mrs. Mingott's door, where a large square envelope was handed in; and that evening at the Opera Mr. Sillerton Jackson was able to state that the envelope contained a card inviting the Countess Olenska to the dinner which the van der Luydens were giving the following week for their cousin, the Duke of St. Austrey.

Some of the younger men in the club box exchanged a smile at this announcement, and glanced sideways at Lawrence Lefferts, who sat carelessly in the front of the box, pulling his long fair moustache, and who remarked with authority, as the soprano paused: "No one but Patti ought to attempt the Sonnambula."

# Chapter 8

It was generally agreed in New York that the Countess Olenska had "lost her looks."

She had appeared there first, in Newland Archer's boyhood, as a brilliantly pretty little girl of nine or ten, of whom people said that she "ought to be painted." Her parents had been continental wanderers, and after a roaming babyhood she had lost them both, and been taken in charge by her aunt, Medora Manson, also a wanderer, who was herself returning to New York to "settle down."

Poor Medora, repeatedly widowed, was always coming home to settle down (each time in a less expensive house), and bringing with her a new husband or an adopted child; but after a few months she invariably parted from her husband or quarrelled with her ward, and, having got rid of her house at a loss, set out again on her wanderings. As her mother had been a Rushworth, and her last unhappy marriage had linked her to one of the crazy Chiverses, New York looked indulgently on her eccentricities; but when she returned with her little orphaned niece, whose parents had been popular in spite of their regrettable taste for travel, people thought it a pity that the pretty child should be in such hands.

Every one was disposed to be kind to little Ellen Mingott, though her dusky red cheeks and tight curls gave her an air of gaiety that seemed unsuitable in a child who should still have been in black for her parents. It was one of the misguided Medora's many peculiarities to flout the unalterable rules that regulated American mourning, and when she stepped from the steamer her family were scandalised to see that the crape veil she wore for her own brother was seven inches shorter than those of her sisters-in-law, while little Ellen was in crimson merino and amber beads, like a gipsy foundling.

But New York had so long resigned itself to Medora that only a few old ladies shook their heads over Ellen's gaudy clothes, while her other relations fell under the charm of her high colour and high spirits. She was a fearless and familiar little thing, who asked disconcerting questions, made precocious comments, and possessed outlandish arts, such as dancing a Spanish shawl dance and singing Neapolitan love-songs to a guitar. Under the direction of her aunt (whose real name was Mrs. Thorley Chivers, but who, having received a Papal title, had resumed her first husband's patronymic, and called herself the Marchioness Manson, because in Italy she could turn it into Manzoni) the little girl received an expensive but incoherent education, which included "drawing from the model," a thing never dreamed of before, and playing the piano in quintets with professional musicians.

Of course no good could come of this; and when, a few years later, poor Chivers finally died in a mad- house, his widow (draped in strange weeds) again pulled up stakes and departed with Ellen, who had grown into a tall bony girl with conspicuous eyes. For some time no more was heard of them; then news came of Ellen's marriage to an immensely rich Polish nobleman of legendary fame, whom she had met at a ball at the Tuileries, and who was said to have princely establishments in Paris, Nice and Florence, a yacht at Cowes, and many square miles of shooting in Transylvania. She disappeared in a kind of sulphurous apotheosis, and when a few years later Medora again came back to New York, subdued, impoverished, mourning a third husband, and in quest of a still smaller house, people wondered that her rich niece had not been able to do something for her. Then came the news that Ellen's own marriage had ended in disaster, and that she was herself returning home to seek rest and oblivion among her kinsfolk.

These things passed through Newland Archer's mind a week later as he watched the Countess Olenska enter the van der Luyden drawing-room on the evening of the momentous dinner.

The occasion was a solemn one, and he wondered a little nervously how she would carry it off. She came rather late, one hand still ungloved, and fastening a bracelet about her wrist; yet she entered without any appearance of haste or embarrassment the drawing-room in which New York's most chosen company was somewhat awfully assembled.

In the middle of the room she paused, looking about her with a grave mouth and smiling eyes; and in that instant Newland Archer rejected the general verdict on her looks. It was true that her early radiance was gone. The red cheeks had paled; she was thin, worn, a little older-looking than her age, which must have been nearly thirty. But there was about her the mysterious authority of beauty, a sureness in the carriage of the head, the movement of the eyes, which, without being in the least theatrical, struck his as highly trained and full of a conscious power. At the same time she was simpler in manner than most of the ladies present, and many people (as he heard afterward from Janey) were disappointed that her appearance was not more "stylish"—for stylishness was what New York most valued. It was, perhaps, Archer reflected, because her early vivacity had disappeared; because she was so quiet—quiet in her movements, her voice, and the tones of her low- pitched voice. New York had expected something a good deal more reasonant in a young woman with such a history.

The dinner was a somewhat formidable business. Dining with the van der Luydens was at best no light matter, and dining there with a Duke who was their cousin was almost a religious solemnity. It pleased Archer to think that only an old New Yorker could perceive the shade of difference (to New York) between being merely a Duke and being the van der Luydens' Duke. New York took stray noblemen calmly, and even (except in the Struthers set) with a certain distrustful hauteur; but when they presented such credentials as these they were received with an old-fashioned cordiality that they would have been greatly mistaken in ascribing solely to their standing in Debrett. It was for just such distinctions that the young man cherished his old New York even while he smiled at it.

The van der Luydens had done their best to emphasise the importance of the occasion. The du Lac Sevres and the Trevenna George II plate were out; so was the van der Luyden "Lowestoft" (East India Company) and the Dagonet Crown Derby. Mrs. van der Luyden looked more than ever like a Cabanel, and Mrs. Archer, in her grandmother's seed-pearls and emeralds, reminded her son of an Isabey miniature. All the ladies had on their handsomest jewels, but it was characteristic of the house and the occasion that these were mostly in rather heavy old-fashioned settings; and old Miss Lanning, who had been persuaded to come, actually wore her mother's cameos and a Spanish blonde shawl.

The Countess Olenska was the only young woman at the dinner; yet, as Archer scanned the smooth plump elderly faces between their diamond necklaces and towering ostrich feathers, they struck him as curiously immature compared with hers. It frightened him to think what must have gone to the making of her eyes.

The Duke of St. Austrey, who sat at his hostess's right, was naturally the chief figure of the evening. But if the Countess Olenska was less conspicuous than had been hoped, the Duke was almost invisible. Being a well-bred man he had not (like another recent ducal visitor) come to the dinner in a shooting-jacket; but his evening clothes were so shabby and baggy, and he wore them with such an air of their being homespun, that (with his stooping way of sitting, and the vast beard spreading over his shirt-front) he hardly gave the appearance of being in dinner attire. He was short, round-shouldered, sunburnt, with a thick nose, small eyes and a sociable smile; but he seldom spoke, and when he did it was in such low tones that, despite the frequent silences of expectation about the table, his remarks were lost to all but his neighbours.

When the men joined the ladies after dinner the Duke went straight up to the Countess Olenska, and they sat down in a corner and plunged into animated talk. Neither seemed aware that the Duke should first have paid his respects to Mrs. Lovell Mingott and Mrs. Headly Chivers, and the Countess have conversed with that amiable hypochondriac, Mr. Urban Dagonet of Washington Square, who, in order to have the pleasure of meeting her, had broken through his fixed rule of not dining out between January and April. The two chatted together for nearly twenty minutes; then the Countess rose and, walking alone across the wide drawing-room, sat down at Newland Archer's side.

It was not the custom in New York drawing-rooms for a lady to get up and walk away from one gentleman in order to seek the company of another. Etiquette required that she should wait, immovable as an idol, while the men who wished to converse with her succeeded each other at her side. But the Countess was apparently unaware of having broken any rule; she sat at perfect ease in a corner of the sofa beside Archer, and looked at him with the kindest eyes.

"I want you to talk to me about May," she said.

Instead of answering her he asked: "You knew the Duke before?"

"Oh, yes—we used to see him every winter at Nice. He's very fond of gambling—he used to come to the house a great deal." She said it in the simplest manner, as if she had said: "He's fond of wild-flowers"; and after a moment she added candidly: "I think he's the dullest man I ever met."

This pleased her companion so much that he forgot the slight shock her previous remark had caused him. It was undeniably exciting to meet a lady who found the van der Luydens' Duke dull, and dared to utter the opinion. He longed to question her, to hear more about the life of which her careless words had given him so illuminating a glimpse; but he feared to touch on distressing memories, and before he could think of anything to say she had strayed back to her original subject.

"May is a darling; I've seen no young girl in New York so handsome and so intelligent. Are you very much in love with her?"

Newland Archer reddened and laughed. "As much as a man can be."

She continued to consider him thoughtfully, as if not to miss any shade of meaning in what he said, "Do you think, then, there is a limit?"

"To being in love? If there is, I haven't found it!"

She glowed with sympathy. "Ah—it's really and truly a romance?"

"The most romantic of romances!"

"How delightful! And you found it all out for yourselves—it was not in the least arranged for you?"

Archer looked at her incredulously. "Have you forgotten," he asked with a smile, "that in our country we don't allow our marriages to be arranged for us?"

A dusky blush rose to her cheek, and he instantly regretted his words.

"Yes," she answered, "I'd forgotten. You must forgive me if I sometimes make these mistakes. I don't always remember that everything here is good that was—that was bad where I've come from." She looked down at her Viennese fan of eagle feathers, and he saw that her lips trembled.

"I'm so sorry," he said impulsively; "but you ARE among friends here, you know."

"Yes—I know. Wherever I go I have that feeling. That's why I came home. I want to forget everything else, to become a complete American again, like the Mingotts and Wellands, and you and your delightful mother, and all the other good people here tonight."

Newland felt the inexplicable need to protect the Countess. She had no idea just how despised she was among polite society. And while the van der Luydens were waving their hands in approval, which no one would deign to challenge, the Countess was making matters exceedingly difficult by rejecting convention with her flagrant behavior. Yet, there was something naive and unassuming about her. How could she choose to seat herself beside him without any concern over the consequences of her actions? And then to engage him so freely as though he were a bosom chum? He had never met a woman quite like her. She shocked him, but he found himself stimulated by her boldness.

As she studied her Viennese fan of eagle feathers, Newland availed himself of the opportunity to consider her features. He did not mind that her cheeks had paled—there was certainly a mysterious authority in her beauty. Her lips were delicate, a pinkish red, and appeared supple like the finest of silks. Their fullness seemed as if they were made to be kissed. Newland Archer suddenly found himself overcome with desire. What struck him most about the Countess was that she seemed to have an uncanny ability to capture his attention in the most striking of ways. At that moment, Ellen Olenska was the most enticing woman he had ever met.

"I have missed the city," she said.

Newland rose and faced the veranda. "Before you join the others, perhaps I could show you the view ... from the window of course. I wouldn't want you to catch a chill."

"I would like that very much," she said.

"The view is quite remarkable," he said, waiting for her to rise. She placed her hand upon his arm and he escorted her to the window inside a private alcove where the others could not readily see them.

"I have always enjoyed the lights of New York City," she said.

"There is a certain magic in their sparkle."

"Sometimes I forget that they sparkle. I had rather thought of them as merely light in a dark place." The Countess laughed lightly. "I'm so sorry, I didn't mean to be so somber."

Newland faced the Countess. He was struck by her beauty in the dim light. He could only see her as sparkling.

The Countess gazed into his eyes. "Are you quite all right?" she asked, smiling up at him.

Newland was not all right; he was conflicted and torn. How could he be so happily engaged to May, and yet be standing there with a woman he barely knew and be filled with such a powerful desire to kiss her? The sorrowful look in her eyes said she wanted him to act spontaneously. And had they been the only two present in the drawing room, he would have acted.

He lifted the Countess's hand. With her glove removed, he felt her skin, which was soft as velvet. He studied the lines of her narrow hands and long fingers. Such a delicate and gentle a creature was she. He slowly lifted her hand and brought it to his lips. He gazed into her eyes for a moment and then gently kissed the back of her hand. The touch of his mouth against her flesh sent an electrical impulse racing from his chest to his loins. He stepped closer and grasped her elbow to support her arm, and then slowly began kissing the length of her arm.

She sighed quietly and then took a deep breath. Her chest began rising and falling as her breath hastened. He could almost hear her heart pattering. She did not try to fight him, not in the slightest, but let him continue making his way up the length of her smooth, delicate arm. He was enraptured by her fragrance, inflamed by her feminine allure.

He stopped at the inside of her elbow and rubbed his lips in small circles inside the crease of her arm. When she gasped, he knew that his touch excited her. He opened his mouth and gently sucked her skin. When he released, he dipped a tongue in the crease of her arm and circled slowly. He could feel the fine hairs on her arm raise, and her skin rippled.

She released an exquisite sigh of pleasure.

He lingered a moment more, and then moved his lips along the delicate inside of her arm. Her body quivered as he slowly and deliberately moved upward. When he reached her neck, he stopped and drew in a deep breath, absorbing her raw fragrance, the result of her excitement. He rolled his tongue deep between the folds of her arm, and continued to her bare shoulder blade. Her perfumed fragrance heightened his pleasure.

She exhaled, moaning softly, although she did not speak.

He tasted the flesh of her shoulder, and as he moved along, he stopped at the décolletage of her neck to bask in the fragrance of gardenia. His senses were overtaken by her feminine scent, and he was crazed with a desire that he had never known before this moment. He kissed her neck, tasting the salt of her flesh, and moved to kiss the line of her jaw. He brushed his lips across the velvety texture of her face, stopping to touch his nose to hers.

He wanted nothing more than to feel her lips against his. Would he deny himself this moment or would he continue and know her more intimately than if he had been making love to her? To make love was to bask in the pleasures that drove the desires of man, but to kiss was where the heart and passion of the man thrived. The kiss, unlike any other physical touch, defined romance between a man and woman. It told all. There were no secrets concealed from its beauty.

Newland dwelled blissfully in the moment. The anticipation thrilled him in a way that could not be expressed in words. For a moment, they gazed deeply into each other's eyes, and then, overcome with passion and desire, Newland closed his and gently pressed his lips to hers.

The spark of their touch sent a tidal wave through his body. He felt his body tense, quake. He took her in his arms and held her tight, all the while feeling his lips pressed against hers.

Passion overran his body and his desires leapt forward. He opened his mouth and slid a gentle tongue between the folds of her soft lips. Her tongue met his, and Newland could have sworn to the Almighty that heaven had sent him an angel. Their tongues began to swirl, gently at first, and before long, a full-fledged passion swept between them, and their tongues were circling as though they were dancing to the end beats of a Tango.

He wanted more, more. But the opportunity was not at hand. The murmuring of the other guests had become more prominent. Newland gently ended the kiss, taking a moment to study the heaven-sent face of the Countess. When she opened her eyes and looked deeply into his, words were neither possible nor necessary. He slowly drew away from her and held out his arm so that he might escort her back inside the drawing room.

Newland guided the Countess back to the party. "Well, we are back," the Countess said. "Ah, here's May arriving, and you will want to hurry away to her," she added, but without moving; and her eyes turned back from the door to rest on the young man's face.

The drawing-rooms were beginning to fill up with after-dinner guests, and following Madame Olenska's glance Archer saw May Welland entering with her mother. In her dress of white and silver, with a wreath of silver blossoms in her hair, the tall girl looked like a Diana just alight from the chase.

"Oh," said Archer, "I have so many rivals; you see she's already surrounded. There's the Duke being introduced."

"Then stay with me a little longer," Madame Olenska said in a low tone, just touching his knee with her plumed fan. It was the lightest touch, but it thrilled him like a caress.

"Yes, let me stay," he answered in the same tone, hardly knowing what he said; but just then Mr. van der Luyden came up, followed by old Mr. Urban Dagonet. The Countess greeted them with her grave smile, and Archer, feeling his host's admonitory glance on him, rose and surrendered his seat.

Madame Olenska held out her hand as if to bid him goodbye.

"Tomorrow, then, after five—I shall expect you," she said; and then turned back to make room for Mr. Dagonet.

"Tomorrow—" Archer heard himself repeating, though there had been no engagement, and during their talk she had given him no hint that she wished to see him again.

As he moved away he saw Lawrence Lefferts, tall and resplendent, leading his wife up to be introduced; and heard Gertrude Lefferts say, as she beamed on the Countess with her large unperceiving smile: "But I think we used to go to dancing-school together when we were children—." Behind her, waiting their turn to name themselves to the Countess, Archer noticed a number of the recalcitrant couples who had declined to meet her at Mrs. Lovell Mingott's. As Mrs. Archer remarked: when the van der Luydens chose, they knew how to give a lesson. The wonder was that they chose so seldom.

The young man felt a touch on his arm and saw Mrs. van der Luyden looking down on him from the pure eminence of black velvet and the family diamonds. "It was good of you, dear Newland, to devote yourself so unselfishly to Madame Olenska. I told your cousin Henry he must really come to the rescue."

He was aware of smiling at her vaguely, and she added, as if condescending to his natural shyness: "I've never seen May looking lovelier. The Duke thinks her the handsomest girl in the room."

# Chapter 9

The Countess Olenska had said "after five"; and at half after the hour Newland Archer rang the bell of the peeling stucco house with a giant wisteria throttling its feeble cast-iron balcony, which she had hired, far down West Twenty-third Street, from the vagabond Medora.

It was certainly a strange quarter to have settled in. Small dressmakers, bird-stuffers and "people who wrote" were her nearest neighbours; and further down the dishevelled street Archer recognised a dilapidated wooden house, at the end of a paved path, in which a writer and journalist called Winsett, whom he used to come across now and then, had mentioned that he lived. Winsett did not invite people to his house; but he had once pointed it out to Archer in the course of a nocturnal stroll, and the latter had asked himself, with a little shiver, if the humanities were so meanly housed in other capitals.

Madame Olenska's own dwelling was redeemed from the same appearance only by a little more paint about the window-frames; and as Archer mustered its modest front he said to himself that the Polish Count must have robbed her of her fortune as well as of her illusions.

The young man had spent an unsatisfactory day. He had lunched with the Wellands, hoping afterward to carry off May for a walk in the Park. He wanted to have her to himself, to tell her how enchanting she had looked the night before, and how proud he was of her, and to press her to hasten their marriage. But Mrs. Welland had firmly reminded him that the round of family visits was not half over, and, when he hinted at advancing the date of the wedding, had raised reproachful eye-brows and sighed out: "Twelve dozen of everything—hand-embroidered—"

Packed in the family landau they rolled from one tribal doorstep to another, and Archer, when the afternoon's round was over, parted from his betrothed with the feeling that he had been shown off like a wild animal cunningly trapped. He supposed that his readings in anthropology caused him to take such a coarse view of what was after all a simple and natural demonstration of family feeling; but when he remembered that the Wellands did not expect the wedding to take place till the following autumn, and pictured what his life would be till then, a dampness fell upon his spirit.

"Tomorrow," Mrs. Welland called after him, "we'll do the Chiverses and the Dallases"; and he perceived that she was going through their two families alphabetically, and that they were only in the first quarter of the alphabet.

He had meant to tell May of the Countess Olenska's request—her command, rather—that he should call on her that afternoon; but in the brief moments when they were alone he had had more pressing things to say. Besides, it struck him as a little absurd to allude to the matter. He knew that May most particularly wanted him to be kind to her cousin; was it not that wish which had hastened the announcement of their engagement? It gave him an odd sensation to reflect that, but for the Countess's arrival, he might have been, if not still a free man, at least a man less irrevocably pledged. But May had willed it so, and he felt himself somehow relieved of further responsibility—and therefore at liberty, if he chose, to call on her cousin without telling her. However, his mind was heavy with the thought of their kiss.

As he stood on Madame Olenska's threshold curiosity was his uppermost feeling. He was puzzled by the tone in which she had summoned him; after they looked at the city lights together he concluded that she was less simple than she seemed.

The door was opened by a swarthy foreign-looking maid, with a prominent bosom under a gay neckerchief, whom he vaguely fancied to be Sicilian. She welcomed him with all her white teeth, and answering his enquiries by a head-shake of incomprehension led him through the narrow hall into a low firelit drawing- room. The room was empty, and she left him, for an appreciable time, to wonder whether she had gone to find her mistress, or whether she had not understood what he was there for, and thought it might be to wind the clock—of which he perceived that the only visible specimen had stopped. He knew that the southern races communicated with each other in the language of pantomime, and was mortified to find her shrugs and smiles so unintelligible. At length she returned with a lamp; and Archer, having meanwhile put together a phrase out of Dante and Petrarch, evoked the answer: "La signora e fuori; ma verra subito"; which he took to mean: "She's out—but you'll soon see."

What he saw, meanwhile, with the help of the lamp, was the faded shadowy charm of a room unlike any room he had known. He knew that the Countess Olenska had brought some of her possessions with her—bits of wreckage, she called them—and these, he supposed, were represented by some small slender tables of dark wood, a delicate little Greek bronze on the chimney- piece, and a stretch of red damask nailed on the discoloured wallpaper behind a couple of Italian-looking pictures in old frames.

Newland Archer prided himself on his knowledge of Italian art. His boyhood had been saturated with Ruskin, and he had read all the latest books: John Addington Symonds, Vernon Lee's "Euphorion," the essays of P. G. Hamerton, and a wonderful new volume called "The Renaissance" by Walter Pater. He talked easily of Botticelli, and spoke of Fra Angelico with a faint condescension. But these pictures bewildered him, for they were like nothing that he was accustomed to look at (and therefore able to see) when he travelled in Italy; and perhaps, also, his powers of observation were impaired by the oddness of finding himself in this strange empty house, where apparently no one expected him. He was sorry that he had not told May Welland of Countess Olenska's request, and a little disturbed by the thought that his betrothed might come in to see her cousin. What would she think if she found him sitting there with the air of intimacy implied by waiting alone in the dusk at a lady's fireside?

But since he had come he meant to wait; and he sank into a chair and stretched his feet to the logs.

It was odd to have summoned him in that way, and then forgotten him; but Archer felt more curious than mortified. The atmosphere of the room was so different from any he had ever breathed that self-consciousness vanished in the sense of adventure. He had been before in drawing-rooms hung with red damask, with pictures "of the Italian school"; what struck him was the way in which Medora Manson's shabby hired house, with its blighted background of pampas grass and Rogers statuettes, had, by a turn of the hand, and the skilful use of a few properties, been transformed into something intimate, "foreign," subtly suggestive of old romantic scenes and sentiments. He tried to analyse the trick, to find a clue to it in the way the chairs and tables were grouped, in the fact that only two Jacqueminot roses (of which nobody ever bought less than a dozen) had been placed in the slender vase at his elbow, and in the vague pervading perfume that was not what one put on handkerchiefs, but rather like the scent of some far-off bazaar, a smell made up of Turkish coffee and ambergris and dried roses.

His mind wandered away to the question of what May's drawing-room would look like. He knew that Mr. Welland, who was behaving "very handsomely," already had his eye on a newly built house in East Thirty-ninth Street. The neighbourhood was thought remote, and the house was built in a ghastly greenish-yellow stone that the younger architects were beginning to employ as a protest against the brownstone of which the uniform hue coated New York like a cold chocolate sauce; but the plumbing was perfect. Archer would have liked to travel, to put off the housing question; but, though the Wellands approved of an extended European honeymoon (perhaps even a winter in Egypt), they were firm as to the need of a house for the returning couple. The young man felt that his fate was sealed: for the rest of his life he would go up every evening between the cast-iron railings of that greenish- yellow doorstep, and pass through a Pompeian vestibule into a hall with a wainscoting of varnished yellow wood. But beyond that his imagination could not travel. He knew the drawing-room above had a bay window, but he could not fancy how May would deal with it. She submitted cheerfully to the purple satin and yellow tuftings of the Welland drawing-room, to its sham Buhl tables and gilt vitrines full of modern Saxe. He saw no reason to suppose that she would want anything different in her own house; and his only comfort was to reflect that she would probably let him arrange his library as he pleased—which would be, of course, with "sincere" Eastlake furniture, and the plain new bookcases without glass doors.

The round-bosomed maid came in, drew the curtains, pushed back a log, and said consolingly: "Verra—verra." When she had gone Archer stood up and began to wander about. Should he wait any longer? His position was becoming rather foolish. Perhaps he had misunderstood Madame Olenska—perhaps she had not invited him after all.

Down the cobblestones of the quiet street came the ring of a stepper's hoofs; they stopped before the house, and he caught the opening of a carriage door. Parting the curtains he looked out into the early dusk. A street- lamp faced him, and in its light he saw Julius Beaufort's compact English brougham, drawn by a big roan, and the banker descending from it, and helping out Madame Olenska.

Beaufort stood, hat in hand, saying something which his companion seemed to negative; then they shook hands, and he jumped into his carriage while she mounted the steps.

When Newland saw Beaufort with the Countess, a fiery anger rose up inside. That scoundrel was the last person Newland expected to see with her. Newland turned away from the window, paced across the room, and forced himself to suppress his rage.

When she entered the room she showed no surprise at seeing Archer there; surprise seemed the emotion that she was least addicted to. The thought that she was so carefree reignited his irritation.

"How do you like my funny house?" she asked. "To me it's like heaven."

As she spoke she untied her little velvet bonnet and tossing it away with her long cloak stood looking at him with meditative eyes. Newland remembered how she had looked at him after they had kissed, how she was able to peer inside of him and touch a piece of his soul. And now looking into her eyes again, any discomfort that he felt only moments ago seemed to dissipate into thin air. What a remarkable effect she had on him.

"You've arranged it delightfully," he rejoined, alive to the flatness of the words, but imprisoned in the conventional by his consuming desire to be simple and striking.

"Oh, it's a poor little place. My relations despise it. But at any rate it's less gloomy than the van der Luydens'."

The words gave him an electric shock, for few were the rebellious spirits who would have dared to call the stately home of the van der Luydens gloomy. Those privileged to enter it shivered there, and spoke of it as "handsome." But suddenly he was glad that she had given voice to the general shiver.

"It's delicious—what you've done here," he repeated, thinking of how delicious she had tasted last night when he kissed her. He wondered if she would approach him and at least give him a peck on his cheek, but she kept her distance, playing coy, as though they had never shared the kiss. Perhaps she meant to forget that it had ever happened. He was, after all, engaged to her younger cousin. Perhaps he had startled her with his forwardness, although her body certainly revealed that she had enjoyed his advance.

"I like the little house," she admitted; "but I suppose what I like is the blessedness of its being here, in my own country and my own town; and then, of being alone in it." She spoke so low that he hardly heard the last phrase; but in his awkwardness he took it up.

"You like so much to be alone?"

"Yes; as long as my friends keep me from feeling lonely." She sat down near the fire, said: "Nastasia will bring the tea presently," and signed to him to return to his armchair, adding: "I see you've already chosen your corner."

Leaning back, she folded her arms behind her head, and looked at the fire under drooping lids.

"This is the hour I like best—don't you?"

A proper sense of his dignity caused him to answer: "I was afraid you'd forgotten the hour. Beaufort must have been very engrossing."

She looked amused. "Why—have you waited long? Mr. Beaufort took me to see a number of houses—since it seems I'm not to be allowed to stay in this one." She appeared to dismiss both Beaufort and himself from her mind, and went on: "I've never been in a city where there seems to be such a feeling against living in des quartiers excentriques. What does it matter where one lives? I'm told this street is respectable."

"It's not fashionable."

"Fashionable! Do you all think so much of that? Why not make one's own fashions? But I suppose I've lived too independently; at any rate, I want to do what you all do—I want to feel cared for and safe."

He was touched, as he had been the evening before when she spoke of her need of guidance.

"That's what your friends want you to feel. New York's an awfully safe place," he added with a flash of sarcasm.

"Yes, isn't it? One feels that," she cried, missing the mockery. "Being here is like—like—being taken on a holiday when one has been a good little girl and done all one's lessons."

The analogy was well meant, but did not altogether please him. He did not mind being flippant about New York, but disliked to hear any one else take the same tone. He wondered if she did not begin to see what a powerful engine it was, and how nearly it had crushed her. The Lovell Mingotts' dinner, patched up in extremis out of all sorts of social odds and ends, ought to have taught her the narrowness of her escape; but either she had been all along unaware of having skirted disaster, or else she had lost sight of it in the triumph of the van der Luyden evening. Archer inclined to the former theory; he fancied that her New York was still completely undifferentiated, and the conjecture nettled him.

"Last night," he said, "New York laid itself out for you. The van der Luydens do nothing by halves."

"No: how kind they are! It was such a nice party. Every one seems to have such an esteem for them."

The terms were hardly adequate; she might have spoken in that way of a tea-party at the dear old Miss Lannings'.

"The van der Luydens," said Archer, feeling himself pompous as he spoke, "are the most powerful influence in New York society. Unfortunately—owing to her health—they receive very seldom."

She unclasped her hands from behind her head, and looked at him meditatively.

"Isn't that perhaps the reason?"

"The reason—?"

"For their great influence; that they make themselves so rare."

He coloured a little, stared at her—and suddenly felt the penetration of the remark. At a stroke she had pricked the van der Luydens and they collapsed. He laughed, and sacrificed them.

Nastasia brought the tea, with handleless Japanese cups and little covered dishes, placing the tray on a low table.

"But you'll explain these things to me—you'll tell me all I ought to know," Madame Olenska continued, leaning forward to hand him his cup.

"It's you who are telling me; opening my eyes to things I'd looked at so long that I'd ceased to see them."

She detached a small gold cigarette-case from one of her bracelets, held it out to him, and took a cigarette herself. On the chimney were long spills for lighting them.

"Ah, then we can both help each other. But I want help so much more. You must tell me just what to do."

It was on the tip of his tongue to reply: "Don't be seen driving about the streets with Beaufort—" but he was being too deeply drawn into the atmosphere of the room, which was her atmosphere, and to give advice of that sort would have been like telling some one who was bargaining for attar-of-roses in Samarkand that one should always be provided with arctics for a New York winter. New York seemed much farther off than Samarkand, and if they were indeed to help each other she was rendering what might prove the first of their mutual services by making him look at his native city objectively. Viewed thus, as through the wrong end of a telescope, it looked disconcertingly small and distant; but then from Samarkand it would.

A flame darted from the logs and she bent over the fire, stretching her thin hands so close to it that a faint halo shone about the oval nails. The light touched to russet the rings of dark hair escaping from her braids, and made her pale face paler.

"There are plenty of people to tell you what to do," Archer rejoined, obscurely envious of them.

"Oh—all my aunts? And my dear old Granny?" She considered the idea impartially. "They're all a little vexed with me for setting up for myself—poor Granny especially. She wanted to keep me with her; but I had to be free—" He was impressed by this light way of speaking of the formidable Catherine, and moved by the thought of what must have given Madame Olenska this thirst for even the loneliest kind of freedom. But the idea of Beaufort gnawed him.

"I think I understand how you feel," he said. "Still, your family can advise you; explain differences; show you the way."

She lifted her thin black eyebrows. "Is New York such a labyrinth? I thought it so straight up and down—like Fifth Avenue. And with all the cross streets numbered!" She seemed to guess his faint disapproval of this, and added, with the rare smile that enchanted her whole face: "If you knew how I like it for just THAT—the straight-up-and-downness, and the big honest labels on everything!"

He saw his chance. "Everything may be labelled—but everybody is not."

"Perhaps. I may simplify too much—but you'll warn me if I do." She turned from the fire to look at him. "There are only two people here who make me feel as if they understood what I mean and could explain things to me: you and Mr. Beaufort."

Archer winced at the joining of the names, and then, with a quick readjustment, understood, sympathised and pitied. So close to the powers of evil she must have lived that she still breathed more freely in their air. But since she felt that he understood her also, his business would be to make her see Beaufort as he really was, with all he represented—and abhor it.

He answered gently: "I understand. But just at first don't let go of your old friends' hands: I mean the older women, your Granny Mingott, Mrs. Welland, Mrs. van der Luyden. They like and admire you—they want to help you."

She shook her head and sighed. "Oh, I know—I know! But on condition that they don't hear anything unpleasant. Aunt Welland put it in those very words when I tried... . Does no one want to know the truth here, Mr. Archer? The real loneliness is living among all these kind people who only ask one to pretend!" She lifted her hands to her face, and he saw her thin shoulders shaken by a sob.

"Madame Olenska!—Oh, don't, Ellen," he cried, starting up and bending over her. He drew down one of her hands, clasping and chafing it like a child's while he murmured reassuring words; but in a moment she freed herself, and looked up at him with wet lashes.

"Does no one cry here, either? I suppose there's no need to, in heaven," she said, straightening her loosened braids with a laugh, and bending over the tea- kettle. It was burnt into his consciousness that he had called her "Ellen"—called her so twice; and that she had not noticed it. Far down the inverted telescope he saw the faint white figure of May Welland—in New York. But he turned the telescope around and saw only Ellen.

He kneeled next to her, bringing her fingers to his lips.

"Dear Newland," she said. "How kind you are to me."

He kissed her hand. "My dear.

"But you must not worry over me. You have May to think of now."

"May asked me to look after you, to see that you are taken care of."

"I wouldn't think her kindness extended so far."

He brought her hand to his cheek, drew in her scent, and closed his eyes for a moment. No, he could not think of May now. Newland set her aside in his mind, and when he opened his eyes, he saw only the beautiful and free-spirited Countess.

"Let me comfort you," he said, and lowered himself to a relaxed position at her feet.

"No, you shouldn't." But she did not shrink away, in fact she made no move to resist.

Newland released her hand and grasped the hem of her dress. He began to slowly lift her skirts, bringing them to the Countess's lap. He caressed her legs, slowly working his hands down to her ankles. He grasped first one foot and then the other, and slipped off her dainty silk satin shoes. Returning to her, he massaged first the arches of her feet and then slowly moved his hands up the length of her legs. He reached her knees and passed them and then rested his hand on her inner thighs and squeezed.

"Newland, we shouldn't," she whispered, but there was no stopping him. He was intent on discovering her.

He gently drew her legs apart so that he might slide his hands higher. She feigned resistance for a moment and then relented, sighing as he opened her legs wider. Yielding fully to his insistent touch, she leaned into the back of her chair, closed her eyes, and let him continue. When he pulled her skirt up higher, he quickly realized that she wore no undergarment.

"Ellen?"

She opened her eyes and gazed into his, flashing a lascivious grin. "I enjoy the freedom."

Returning the smile, he said, "So I see." And when she closed her eyes again, he returned his gaze to her feminine fount of passion. He slipped his hands underneath her derrière, squeezed, and then gently pulled her body closer to him. All he could think about was kissing her and tasting from her well of passion. Opening her legs, her delicate flower unfolded to him. The view was exquisite. Her pearl was bulging, enticing him, but he would make her wait.

He placed his mouth on her thigh and began kissing her along the erogenous flesh of her inner leg. Her body quivered at his touch, and he felt her skin rippling when he tasted her flesh. Still, he would not claim his prize, but moved slowly and deliberately, lingering with his tongue as he slid higher toward her intimate orchid.

He raised one of her legs and placed it over his shoulder as he continued to kiss her inner thigh. When he reached her curls, he brushed his lips across her feminine petals and over to her other leg. Raising her leg, he slid a slow tongue down and back up her inner thigh, and then rested the leg on his shoulder.

He slid his hands underneath her derrière and regarded her crimson flower. With a deep breath, he filled his senses with her impassioned perfume. He groaned quietly as he exhaled. Then he rolled a light tongue across her feminine folds, stopping to twirl his tongue on her pearl.

She rolled her head from side to side, her breath quickening. "Yes, Newland, just that, right there," she whispered.

But he lowered his tongue to the opening of her sheath and swirled his tongue round and round, tasting the fruits of her rich cream, and then, sliding through the folds of her intimate form, he danced upward to her pearl again.

Her hips undulated with a slow heated grind, keeping rhythm with the touch of his tongue. She placed her hands upon his head and guided him downward, so his tongue moved slightly lower. She began to pant, slowly at first, but before long, her breath gave way and she began to moan, sometimes verbally instructing him how to enhance her pleasure, as if he had been her lover from the beginning of time. He had never known a woman so open about her desires, so willing to ask him to please her.

He reached to touch her flower and quickly slid a finger inside her sheath, where he began stroking the velvety upper wall. She began to move more ardently, and so he responded to her desire by sliding another finger inside her, which caused her to spread her legs wider.

He drew back to watch her move as he continued to pleasure her more. Then he glanced up to see her face. Her lips were pouted in a near kiss; her expression was one of pure heavenly pleasure.

"Make love to me, Newland. I need you inside of me."

He could not resist her. He eased himself from her, rose up, and unfastened his trousers. He brought his erect member to her folds, stroked it through her cream once or twice, and then slipped his crown inside her sheath. He hesitated, dipping in and out of her, not yet filling her.

She wrapped her legs around his back and pulled him toward her. "Make love to me."

Slowly, he began to slide the length of his shaft inside of her, both of them sighing harmoniously as he made his way toward filling her sheath. Once she was fully engaged, he stopped, and together they took another moment to savor the richness of their overflowing desire.

But when she moved her hips desirously toward him, Newland began to stroke his member in and out of her. No woman could compare to her, not the way she made him feel when he was inside of her. She enveloped him—mind, body, and soul. She embodied passion, elegance, and grace. She was a soft, tender creature unafraid to embrace her femininity, but also free and open about her desires. And he might have stayed right there, making soft, passionate love to her forever, except that his manly desires took over when she began squeezing and massaging his manhood with her vessel. Her mouth parted and her breath hastened. Her sighs turned to heated moans. Her hips began to thrust more urgently; she was tightening, tightening. Her breath caught and released several times, she was near, very close to cresting.

Undone by her passion, Newland closed his eyes and began the sprint, thrusting vigorously until he could last no longer.

"Deeper, Newland! Faster! Oh, yes, I'm going to . . ."

Her breath caught a final time as she crested, sighing with great resolution. Overwhelmed, he exploded at the same moment, releasing his seed and filling her vessel. A moment later, he took her into his arms and kissed her.

"You are the loveliest," he said, opening his eyes to meet hers. "The loveliest. How shall I ever . . .?"

"Dearest, sweetest man," she said. "Nothing has changed, it will be our secret."

He leaned forward and kissed her again. Both of them sighed with incomparable pleasure.

Suddenly Nastasia put her head inside the door to say something in her rich Italian. The Countess dismissed her servant for two minutes.

"We must be quick. It seems that I have more company," she said.

Newland quickly dressed himself as the Countess lowered her dress and smoothed her ruffled hair.

Madame Olenska, again with a hand at her hair, uttered an exclamation of assent—a flashing "Gia—gia"—and the Duke of St. Austrey entered, piloting a tremendous blackwigged and red-plumed lady in overflowing furs.

"My dear Countess, I've brought an old friend of mine to see you—Mrs. Struthers. She wasn't asked to the party last night, and she wants to know you."

The Duke beamed on the group, and Madame Olenska advanced with a murmur of welcome toward the queer couple. She seemed to have no idea how oddly matched they were, nor what a liberty the Duke had taken in bringing his companion— and to do him justice, as Archer perceived, the Duke seemed as unaware of it himself.

"Of course I want to know you, my dear," cried Mrs. Struthers in a round rolling voice that matched her bold feathers and her brazen wig. "I want to know everybody who's young and interesting and charming. And the Duke tells me you like music—didn't you, Duke? You're a pianist yourself, I believe? Well, do you want to hear Sarasate play tomorrow evening at my house? You know I've something going on every Sunday evening—it's the day when New York doesn't know what to do with itself, and so I say to it: 'Come and be amused.' And the Duke thought you'd be tempted by Sarasate. You'll find a number of your friends."

Madame Olenska's face grew brilliant with pleasure. "How kind! How good of the Duke to think of me!" She pushed a chair up to the tea-table and Mrs. Struthers sank into it delectably. "Of course I shall be too happy to come."

"That's all right, my dear. And bring your young gentleman with you." Mrs. Struthers extended a hail- fellow hand to Archer. "I can't put a name to you—but I'm sure I've met you—I've met everybody, here, or in Paris or London. Aren't you in diplomacy? All the diplomatists come to me. You like music too? Duke, you must be sure to bring him."

The Duke said "Rather" from the depths of his beard, and Archer withdrew with a stiffly circular bow that made him feel as full of spine as a self-conscious school-boy among careless and unnoticing elders.

He was not sorry for the denouement of his visit: he only wished it had come sooner, and spared him a certain waste of emotion. As he went out into the wintry night, New York again became vast and imminent, and May Welland the loveliest woman in it. He turned into his florist's to send her the daily box of lilies-of-the-valley which, to his confusion, he found he had forgotten that morning.

As he wrote a word on his card and waited for an envelope he glanced about the embowered shop, and his eye lit on a cluster of yellow roses. He had never seen any as sun-golden before, and his first impulse was to send them to May instead of the lilies. But they did not look like her—there was something too rich, too strong, in their fiery beauty. In a sudden revulsion of mood, and almost without knowing what he did, he signed to the florist to lay the roses in another long box, and slipped his card into a second envelope, on which he wrote the name of the Countess Olenska; then, just as he was turning away, he drew the card out again, and left the empty envelope on the box.

"They'll go at once?" he enquired, pointing to the roses.

The florist assured him that they would.

# Chapter 10

The next day he persuaded May to escape for a walk in the Park after luncheon. As was the custom in old-fashioned Episcopalian New York, she usually accompanied her parents to church on Sunday afternoons; but Mrs. Welland condoned her truancy, having that very morning won her over to the necessity of a long engagement, with time to prepare a hand-embroidered trousseau containing the proper number of dozens.

The day was delectable. The bare vaulting of trees along the Mall was ceiled with lapis lazuli, and arched above snow that shone like splintered crystals. It was the weather to call out May's radiance, and she burned like a young maple in the frost. Archer was proud of the glances turned on her, and the simple joy of possessorship cleared away his underlying perplexities.

"It's so delicious—waking every morning to smell lilies-of-the-valley in one's room!" she said.

"Yesterday they came late. I hadn't time in the morning—"

"But your remembering each day to send them makes me love them so much more than if you'd given a standing order, and they came every morning on the minute, like one's music-teacher—as I know Gertrude Lefferts's did, for instance, when she and Lawrence were engaged."

"Ah—they would!" laughed Archer, amused at her keenness. He looked sideways at her fruit-like cheek and felt rich and secure enough to add: "When I sent your lilies yesterday afternoon I saw some rather gorgeous yellow roses and packed them off to Madame Olenska. Was that right?"

"How dear of you! Anything of that kind delights her. It's odd she didn't mention it: she lunched with us today, and spoke of Mr. Beaufort's having sent her wonderful orchids, and cousin Henry van der Luyden a whole hamper of carnations from Skuytercliff. She seems so surprised to receive flowers. Don't people send them in Europe? She thinks it such a pretty custom."

"Oh, well, no wonder mine were overshadowed by Beaufort's," said Archer irritably. Then he remembered that he had not put a card with the roses, and was vexed at having spoken of them. He wanted to say: "I called on your cousin yesterday," but hesitated. If Madame Olenska had not spoken of his visit it might seem awkward that he should, although she had assured him that their moment of intimacy would remain their secret. Yet not to do so gave the affair an air of mystery that he disliked, and if May ever learned what happened, they would all be ruined. To shake off the question he began to talk of their own plans, their future, and Mrs. Welland's insistence on a long engagement.

"If you call it long! Isabel Chivers and Reggie were engaged for two years: Grace and Thorley for nearly a year and a half. Why aren't we very well off as we are?" she said.

It was the traditional maidenly interrogation, and he felt ashamed of himself for finding it singularly childish. No doubt she simply echoed what was said for her; but she was nearing her twenty-second birthday, and he wondered at what age "nice" women began to speak for themselves.

"Never, if we won't let them, I suppose," he mused, and recalled his mad outburst to Mr. Sillerton Jackson: "Women ought to be as free as we are—"

It would presently be his task to take the bandage from this young woman's eyes, and bid her look forth on the world. But how many generations of the women who had gone to her making had descended bandaged to the family vault? He shivered a little, remembering some of the new ideas in his scientific books, and the much-cited instance of the Kentucky cave-fish, which had ceased to develop eyes because they had no use for them. What if, when he had bidden May Welland to open hers, they could only look out blankly at blankness?

"We might be much better off," he said. "We might be altogether together—we might travel."

Her face lit up. "That would be lovely," she owned: she would love to travel. But her mother would not understand their wanting to do things so differently.

"As if the mere 'differently' didn't account for it!" the wooer insisted.

"Newland! You're so original!" she exulted.

His heart sank, for he saw that he was saying all the things that young men in the same situation were expected to say, and that she was making the answers that instinct and tradition taught her to make—even to the point of calling him original.

"Original!" he said. "We're all as like each other as those dolls cut out of the same folded paper. We're like patterns stencilled on a wall. Can't you and I strike out for ourselves, May?"

He had stopped and faced her in the excitement of their discussion, and her eyes rested on him with a bright unclouded admiration.

"Mercy—shall we elope?" she laughed.

"If you would—"

"You DO love me, Newland! I'm so happy."

"But then—why not be happier?"

"We can't behave like people in novels, though, can we?"

"Why not—why not—why not?"

She looked a little bored by his insistence. She knew very well that they couldn't, but it was troublesome to have to produce a reason. "I'm not clever enough to argue with you. But that kind of thing is rather—vulgar, isn't it?" she suggested, relieved to have hit on a word that would assuredly extinguish the whole subject.

"Are you so much afraid, then, of being vulgar?" he asked, knowing her answer, but waiting for her response nevertheless.

She had seemingly gotten the better of him with her claim of not being clever.

May drew near Newland and looked up and into his eyes. They were quite alone, tucked away under the Mall, ceiled with the lapis lazuli. "Kiss me, my darling man."

Newland took her in his arms and kissed her tender lips. When he broke the kiss, she said softly, "I do so want to please you, Newland. I'm sure you can understand that. It's not so long to wait."

He shrugged, continuing to hold her near.

"You would have us live as man and wife now," she said. "I certainly can appreciate that."

"Can you?"

"It is always more difficult for the man."

"Dearest May."

She slowly lowered her hands from the small of his back to his firm seat. "I could please you, my love."

"I wouldn't want you to . . ."

She squeezed his buttocks with her delicate hands; his body stiffened.

"May?"

"I'm not so opposed to pleasuring you my love, especially since we are to wait longer than you would prefer to be man and wife. There are ways to please a man other than the conventional manner. A woman needn't be so limited in her approach."

"You would do . . .?"

One of her hands slid around to the front of his trousers and grasped his jewels. "I think I understand simple pleasures."

He didn't speak, and without argument let her massage him.

"I do so want to know you, Newland," she said as she unfastened his trousers.

"May," he said, his voice quaking. "We're not alone."

She gazed around them. "Oh, I think we are quite alone, Newland. If you do recall, the others who might be here have all gone to church."

He relaxed after looking nervously around them. "Yes. Of course. " He smiled at her devilishly.

She reached inside his trousers and touched his suddenly erect manhood. Her fingers were gentle and slid the length of his staff and back up again, stopping to circle the tip of his crown with a dainty finger. She gazed over her shoulder one more time, and then turned her attention back to her task. With her gentle fingertips, she clasped his staff and pulled it free from his undergarment. With it standing in the open air, she giggled, and began to play with his crown as though she had been given a precious new toy for the first time in her life.

"May," he whispered. "Maybe you should not—"

"You don't mind, terribly, do you, Newland? You won't think I'm a . . ." She giggled again.

"No," he said, as she stroked the length of his staff and then grasped his jewels. "I must say, I am quite enjoying your … "

She brought her hand up to his crown again. "Then let me pleasure you more, my dear."

"Yes," he said, his tone hoarse with arousal.

She circled her soft fingertip around the edge of his crown, dipping underneath its umbrella. She slowly and quite deliberately took her time to know him completely.

"Come with me," she said. Gripping his engorged staff, she led him to the bench just behind them. She seated herself, all the while giggling as though she had just discovered a secret, hidden treasure. She brought both of her hands to his rampant, throbbing cock, and began to stroke him with a more animated, passionate rhythm.

"Oh, Newland," she said, as she worked harder to please him. "Do you like it?" She gazed up at him and looked into his face. "Do you, my love?"

Newland opened his eyes, looked down at her, and stared longingly into her eyes. "Yes, but ... I, well, I ... "

She continued stroking him. "But? Just tell me my love."

"I might find a greater pleasure if you, well, if you would ... swirl your lovely tongue around my manhood."

May looked down at his throbbing member in her hands. Newland could see that the thought of her placing a tongue on his manhood had never occurred to her. Yet, by her expression, he saw that the very idea, from the moment he uttered the words, suddenly appealed to her sensibilities. In fact, it struck her as fascinating, he realized. She looked at him as though his manhood was magical.

"Doing this for you makes me feel so tingly inside," she said. "Tingly in my . . ." She giggled, and overcome, lowered her face and touched her tongue to the tip of his crown, tasting him. When she licked the opening, he moaned in pleasure. Overwhelmed herself, she sighed, and then began to swirl her tongue as though heaven had descended upon her.

He began to grind his hips more insistently toward her sensuous and loving touch. And May, impassioned by his desire, swirled her tongue more earnestly, taking in every elegant curve of his anatomy. The act warmed her body and moistened her female folds as if he were touching her himself.

She lifted her head and smiled at him. I never imagined for all the world that I could experience such delectable pleasure." Then she resumed her licking and kissing of his member.

"May, I-I . . ." he said, uttering some incoherent sounds.

"Yes, my dear?"

"Take it inside, deeper."

May took his staff deeper into her mouth, bringing him farther and farther into her throat.

"Draw it in and out, slowly at first," he said.

When she reached the base of his staff, she began moving his member in and out of her succulent oral vessel. His body jerked and throbbed at first, and when she hastened the pace, he fell into beat with her controlling strokes. As she took him in and out, all the while bathing his staff with her tongue, circling his crown when she brought him to her lips, she seemed to revel in the sounds of his impassioned sighs and manly groans.

"Suckle me, dear May," he said, groaning.

She was relentless, and continued, suckling him harder and harder, until he was under her complete control.

"Oh, May, I'm about to . . ."

She broke for a moment. "Yes, dear?"

"It would so please me if you swallowed when I release."

She smiled at him devilishly, and then returned to pleasuring him.

She licked, and suckled, taking him deeper and deeper, until, finally, finally, when she took him deep into her throat, he released. And as she pulled forward, he spilled his seed onto her tongue. She slowly withdrew her mouth and swallowed. Then she lingered with her lips along the length of his staff and stopped at his crown. There, she delighted in circling the tip of his crown.

"My dear May," he said, as he recovered himself.

And then, without preamble, she stood with the utmost grace and looked into Newland's face. But all he could do was gaze at her awkwardly, as he covered himself. As if there had been no more than a breath of air inhaled and exchanged from her lungs, she returned her conversation to exactly where they had left off before she had satisfied him.

"You asked me a quession before," she said matter-of-factly. "You asked if I was so much afraid, then, of being vulgar?" She was evidently staggered by this notion. "Of course I should hate it—so would you," she rejoined, a trifle irritably, but certainly only to make her point.

He stood silent, after dressing himself, and beating his stick nervously against his boot-top; he hummed to himself feeling perplexed, and feeling also that she had indeed found the right way of closing the discussion whether he appreciated it or not. He thought she might not say more, but then, she went on light- heartedly, and said: "Oh, did I tell you that I showed Ellen my ring? She thinks it the most beautiful setting she ever saw. There's nothing like it in the rue de la Paix, she said. I do love you, Newland, for being so artistic!"

The next afternoon, as Archer, before dinner, sat smoking sullenly in his study, Janey wandered in on him. He had failed to stop at his club on the way up from the office where he exercised the profession of the law in the leisurely manner common to well-to-do New Yorkers of his class. He was out of spirits and slightly out of temper, and a haunting horror of doing the same thing every day at the same hour besieged his brain.

"Sameness—sameness!" he muttered, the word running through his head like a persecuting tune as he saw the familiar tall-hatted figures lounging behind the plate- glass; and because he usually dropped in at the club at that hour he had gone home instead. He knew not only what they were likely to be talking about, but the part each one would take in the discussion. The Duke of course would be their principal theme; though the appearance in Fifth Avenue of a golden-haired lady in a small canary-coloured brougham with a pair of black cobs (for which Beaufort was generally thought responsible) would also doubtless be thoroughly gone into. Such "women" (as they were called) were few in New York, those driving their own carriages still fewer, and the appearance of Miss Fanny Ring in Fifth Avenue at the fashionable hour had profoundly agitated society. Only the day before, her carriage had passed Mrs. Lovell Mingott's, and the latter had instantly rung the little bell at her elbow and ordered the coachman to drive her home. "What if it had happened to

Mrs. van der Luyden?" people asked each other with a shudder. Archer could hear Lawrence Lefferts, at that very hour, holding forth on the disintegration of society.

He raised his head irritably when his sister Janey entered, and then quickly bent over his book (Swinburne's "Chastelard"—just out) as if he had not seen her. She glanced at the writing-table heaped with books, opened a volume of the "Contes Drolatiques," made a wry face over the archaic French, and sighed: "What learned things you read!"

"Well—?" he asked, as she hovered Cassandra-like before him.

"Mother's very angry."

"Angry? With whom? About what?"

"Miss Sophy Jackson has just been here. She brought word that her brother would come in after dinner: she couldn't say very much, because he forbade her to: he wishes to give all the details himself. He's with cousin Louisa van der Luyden now."

"For heaven's sake, my dear girl, try a fresh start. It would take an omniscient Deity to know what you're talking about."

"It's not a time to be profane, Newland.... Mother feels badly enough about your not going to church ... "

With a groan he plunged back into his book.

"NEWLAND! Do listen. Your friend Madame Olenska was at Mrs. Lemuel Struthers's party last night: she went there with the Duke and Mr. Beaufort."

At the last clause of this announcement a senseless anger swelled the young man's breast. To smother it he laughed. How dare she go off to a party after he had made such passionate love to her! "Well, what of it? I knew she meant to."

Janey paled and her eyes began to project. "You knew she meant to—and you didn't try to stop her? To warn her?"

"Stop her? Warn her?" He laughed again. "I'm not engaged to be married to the Countess Olenska!" The words had a fantastic sound in his own ears.

"You're marrying into her family."

"Oh, family—family!" he jeered.

"Newland—don't you care about Family?"

"Not a brass farthing."

"Nor about what cousin Louisa van der Luyden will think?"

"Not the half of one—if she thinks such old maid's rubbish."

"Mother is not an old maid," said his virgin sister with pinched lips.

He felt like shouting back: "Yes, she is, and so are the van der Luydens, and so we all are, when it comes to being so much as brushed by the wing-tip of Reality." But he saw her long gentle face puckering into tears, and felt ashamed of the useless pain he was inflicting.

"Hang Countess Olenska! Don't be a goose, Janey—I'm not her keeper."

"No; but you DID ask the Wellands to announce your engagement sooner so that we might all back her up; and if it hadn't been for that cousin Louisa would never have invited her to the dinner for the Duke."

"Well—what harm was there in inviting her? She was the best-looking woman in the room; she made the dinner a little less funereal than the usual van der Luyden banquet."

"You know cousin Henry asked her to please you: he persuaded cousin Louisa. And now they're so upset that they're going back to Skuytercliff tomorrow. I think, Newland, you'd better come down. You don't seem to understand how mother feels."

In the drawing-room Newland found his mother. She raised a troubled brow from her needlework to ask: "Has Janey told you?"

"Yes." He tried to keep his tone as measured as her own. "But I can't take it very seriously."

"Not the fact of having offended cousin Louisa and cousin Henry?"

"The fact that they can be offended by such a trifle as Countess Olenska's going to the house of a woman they consider common."

"Consider—!"

"Well, who is; but who has good music, and amuses people on Sunday evenings, when the whole of New York is dying of inanition."

"Good music? All I know is, there was a woman who got up on a table and sang the things they sing at the places you go to in Paris. There was smoking and champagne."

"Well—that kind of thing happens in other places, and the world still goes on."

"I don't suppose, dear, you're really defending the French Sunday?"

"I've heard you often enough, mother, grumble at the English Sunday when we've been in London."

"New York is neither Paris nor London."

"Oh, no, it's not!" her son groaned.

"You mean, I suppose, that society here is not as brilliant? You're right, I daresay; but we belong here, and people should respect our ways when they come among us. Ellen Olenska especially: she came back to get away from the kind of life people lead in brilliant societies."

Newland made no answer, and after a moment his mother ventured: "I was going to put on my bonnet and ask you to take me to see cousin Louisa for a moment before dinner." He frowned, and she continued: "I thought you might explain to her what you've just said: that society abroad is different … that people are not as particular, and that Madame Olenska may not have realised how we feel about such things. It would be, you know, dear," she added with an innocent adroitness, "in Madame Olenska's interest if you did."

"Dearest mother, I really don't see how we're concerned in the matter. The Duke took Madame Olenska to Mrs. Struthers's—in fact he brought Mrs. Struthers to call on her. I was there when they came. If the van der Luydens want to quarrel with anybody, the real culprit is under their own roof."

"Quarrel? Newland, did you ever know of cousin Henry's quarrelling? Besides, the Duke's his guest; and a stranger too. Strangers don't discriminate: how should they? Countess Olenska is a New Yorker, and should have respected the feelings of New York."

"Well, then, if they must have a victim, you have my leave to throw Madame Olenska to them," cried her son, exasperated. "I don't see myself—or you either—offering ourselves up to expiate her crimes."

"Oh, of course you see only the Mingott side," his mother answered, in the sensitive tone that was her nearest approach to anger.

The sad butler drew back the drawing-room portieres and announced: "Mr. Henry van der Luyden."

Mrs. Archer dropped her needle and pushed her chair back with an agitated hand.

"Another lamp," she cried to the retreating servant, while Janey bent over to straighten her mother's cap.

Mr. van der Luyden's figure loomed on the threshold, and Newland Archer went forward to greet his cousin.

"We were just talking about you, sir," he said.

Mr. van der Luyden seemed overwhelmed by the announcement. He drew off his glove to shake hands with the ladies, and smoothed his tall hat shyly, while Janey pushed an arm-chair forward, and Archer continued: "And the Countess Olenska."

Mrs. Archer paled.

"Ah—a charming woman. I have just been to see her," said Mr. van der Luyden, complacency restored to his brow. He sank into the chair, laid his hat and gloves on the floor beside him in the old-fashioned way, and went on: "She has a real gift for arranging flowers. I had sent her a few carnations from Skuytercliff, and I was astonished. Instead of massing them in big bunches as our head-gardener does, she had scattered them about loosely, here and there ... I can't say how. The Duke had told me: he said: `Go and see how cleverly she's arranged her drawing-room.' And she has. I should really like to take Louisa to see her, if the neighbourhood were not so—unpleasant."

A dead silence greeted this unusual flow of words from Mr. van der Luyden. Mrs. Archer drew her embroidery out of the basket into which she had nervously tumbled it, and Newland, leaning against the chimney-place and twisting a humming-bird-feather screen in his hand, saw Janey's gaping countenance lit up by the coming of the second lamp.

"The fact is," Mr. van der Luyden continued, stroking his long grey leg with a bloodless hand weighed down by the Patroon's great signet-ring, "the fact is, I dropped in to thank her for the very pretty note she wrote me about my flowers; and also—but this is between ourselves, of course—to give her a friendly warning about allowing the Duke to carry her off to parties with him. I don't know if you've heard—"

Mrs. Archer produced an indulgent smile. "Has the Duke been carrying her off to parties?"

"You know what these English grandees are. They're all alike. Louisa and I are very fond of our cousin—but it's hopeless to expect people who are accustomed to the European courts to trouble themselves about our little republican distinctions. The Duke goes where he's amused." Mr. van der Luyden paused, but no one spoke. "Yes—it seems he took her with him last night to Mrs. Lemuel Struthers's. Sillerton Jackson has just been to us with the foolish story, and Louisa was rather troubled. So I thought the shortest way was to go straight to Countess Olenska and explain— by the merest hint, you know—how we feel in New York about certain things. I felt I might, without indelicacy, because the evening she dined with us she rather suggested ... rather let me see that she would be grateful for guidance. And she WAS."

Mr. van der Luyden looked about the room with what would have been self-satisfaction on features less purged of the vulgar passions. On his face it became a mild benevolence which Mrs. Archer's countenance dutifully reflected.

"How kind you both are, dear Henry—always! Newland will particularly appreciate what you have done because of dear May and his new relations."

She shot an admonitory glance at her son, who said: "Immensely, sir. But I was sure you'd like Madame Olenska."

Mr. van der Luyden looked at him with extreme gentleness. "I never ask to my house, my dear Newland," he said, "any one whom I do not like. And so I have just told Sillerton Jackson." With a glance at the clock he rose and added: "But Louisa will be waiting. We are dining early, to take the Duke to the Opera."

After the portieres had solemnly closed behind their visitor a silence fell upon the Archer family.

"Gracious—how romantic!" at last broke explosively from Janey. No one knew exactly what inspired her elliptic comments, and her relations had long since given up trying to interpret them.

Mrs. Archer shook her head with a sigh. "Provided it all turns out for the best," she said, in the tone of one who knows how surely it will not. "Newland, you must stay and see Sillerton Jackson when he comes this evening: I really shan't know what to say to him."

"Poor mother! But he won't come—" her son laughed, stooping to kiss away her frown.

# Chapter 11

Some two weeks later, Newland Archer, sitting in abstracted idleness in his private compartment of the office of Letterblair, Lamson and Low, attorneys at law, was summoned by the head of the firm.

Old Mr. Letterblair, the accredited legal adviser of three generations of New York gentility, throned behind his mahogany desk in evident perplexity. As he stroked his closeclipped white whiskers and ran his hand through the rumpled grey locks above his jutting brows, his disrespectful junior partner thought how much he looked like the Family Physician annoyed with a patient whose symptoms refuse to be classified.

"My dear sir—" he always addressed Archer as "sir"—"I have sent for you to go into a little matter; a matter which, for the moment, I prefer not to mention either to Mr. Skipworth or Mr. Redwood." The gentlemen he spoke of were the other senior partners of the firm; for, as was always the case with legal associations of old standing in New York, all the partners named on the office letter-head were long since dead; and Mr. Letterblair, for example, was, professionally speaking, his own grandson.

He leaned back in his chair with a furrowed brow. "For family reasons—" he continued.

Archer looked up.

"The Mingott family," said Mr. Letterblair with an explanatory smile and bow. "Mrs. Manson Mingott sent for me yesterday. Her grand-daughter the Countess Olenska wishes to sue her husband for divorce. Certain papers have been placed in my hands." He paused and drummed on his desk. "In view of your prospective alliance with the family I should like to consult you—to consider the case with you—before taking any farther steps."

Archer felt the blood in his temples. He had seen the Countess Olenska only once since his visit to her, and then at the Opera, in the Mingott box. During this interval she had become a less vivid and importunate image, receding from his foreground as May Welland resumed her rightful place in it. He had not heard her divorce spoken of since Janey's first random allusion to it, and had dismissed the tale as unfounded gossip. Theoretically, the idea of divorce was almost as distasteful to him as to his mother; and he was annoyed that Mr. Letterblair (no doubt prompted by old Catherine Mingott) should be so evidently planning to draw him into the affair. After all, there were plenty of Mingott men for such jobs, and as yet he was not even a Mingott by marriage.

He waited for the senior partner to continue. Mr. Letterblair unlocked a drawer and drew out a packet. "If you will run your eye over these papers—"

Archer frowned. "I beg your pardon, sir; but just because of the prospective relationship, I should prefer your consulting Mr. Skipworth or Mr. Redwood."

Mr. Letterblair looked surprised and slightly offended. It was unusual for a junior to reject such an opening.

He bowed. "I respect your scruple, sir; but in this case I believe true delicacy requires you to do as I ask. Indeed, the suggestion is not mine but Mrs. Manson Mingott's and her son's. I have seen Lovell Mingott; and also Mr. Welland. They all named you."

Archer felt his temper rising. He had been somewhat languidly drifting with events for the last fortnight, and letting May's fair looks and radiant nature obliterate the rather importunate pressure of the Mingott claims. But this behest of old Mrs. Mingott's roused him to a sense of what the clan thought they had the right to exact from a prospective son-in-law; and he chafed at the role.

"Her uncles ought to deal with this," he said.

"They have. The matter has been gone into by the family. They are opposed to the Countess's idea; but she is firm, and insists on a legal opinion."

The young man was silent: he had not opened the packet in his hand.

"Does she want to marry again?"

"I believe it is suggested; but she denies it."

"Then—"

"Will you oblige me, Mr. Archer, by first looking through these papers? Afterward, when we have talked the case over, I will give you my opinion."

Archer withdrew reluctantly with the unwelcome documents. Since their last meeting he had half-unconsciously collaborated with events in ridding himself of the burden of Madame Olenska. His hour alone with her by the firelight had drawn them into a momentary intimacy on which the Duke of St. Austrey's intrusion with Mrs. Lemuel Struthers, and the Countess's joyous greeting of them, had rather providentially broken. Two days later Archer had assisted at the comedy of her reinstatement in the van der Luydens' favour, and had said to himself, with a touch of tartness, that a lady who knew how to thank all-powerful elderly gentlemen to such good purpose for a bunch of flowers did not need either the private consolations or the public championship of a young man of his small compass. To look at the matter in this light simplified his own case and surprisingly furbished up all the dim domestic virtues. He could not picture May Welland, in whatever conceivable emergency, hawking about her private difficulties and lavishing her confidences on strange men; and she had never seemed to him finer or fairer than in the week that followed. He had even yielded to her wish for a long engagement, since she had found the one disarming answer to his plea for haste.

"You know, when it comes to the point, your parents have always let you have your way ever since you were a little girl," he argued; and she had answered, with her clearest look: "Yes; and that's what makes it so hard to refuse the very last thing they'll ever ask of me as a little girl."

That was the old New York note; that was the kind of answer he would like always to be sure of his wife's making. If one had habitually breathed the New York air there were times when anything less crystalline seemed stifling.

The papers he had retired to read did not tell him much in fact; but they plunged him into an atmosphere in which he choked and spluttered. They consisted mainly of an exchange of letters between Count Olenska's solicitors and a French legal firm to whom the Countess had applied for the settlement of her financial situation. There was also a short letter from the Count to his wife: after reading it, Newland Archer rose, jammed the papers back into their envelope, and reentered Mr. Letterblair's office.

"Here are the letters, sir. If you wish, I'll see Madame Olenska," he said in a constrained voice.

"Thank you—thank you, Mr. Archer. Come and dine with me tonight if you're free, and we'll go into the matter afterward: in case you wish to call on our client tomorrow."

Newland Archer walked straight home again that afternoon. It was a winter evening of transparent clearness, with an innocent young moon above the house- tops; and he wanted to fill his soul's lungs with the pure radiance, and not exchange a word with any one till he and Mr. Letterblair were closeted together after dinner. It was impossible to decide otherwise than he had done: he must see Madame Olenska himself rather than let her secrets be bared to other eyes. A great wave of compassion had swept away his indifference and impatience: she stood before him as an exposed and pitiful figure, to be saved at all costs from farther wounding herself in her mad plunges against fate.

He remembered what she had told him of Mrs. Welland's request to be spared whatever was "unpleasant" in her history, and winced at the thought that it was perhaps this attitude of mind which kept the New York air so pure. "Are we only Pharisees after all?" he wondered, puzzled by the effort to reconcile his instinctive disgust at human vileness with his equally instinctive pity for human frailty.

For the first time he perceived how elementary his own principles had always been. He passed for a young man who had not been afraid of risks, and he knew that his secret love-affair with poor silly Mrs. Thorley Rushworth had not been too secret to invest him with a becoming air of adventure. But Mrs. Rushworth was "that kind of woman"; foolish, vain, clandestine by nature, and far more attracted by the secrecy and peril of the affair than by such charms and qualities as he possessed. When the fact dawned on him it nearly broke his heart, but now it seemed the redeeming feature of the case. The affair, in short, had been of the kind that most of the young men of his age had been through, and emerged from with calm consciences and an undisturbed belief in the abysmal distinction between the women one loved and respected and those one enjoyed—and pitied. In this view they were sedulously abetted by their mothers, aunts and other elderly female relatives, who all shared Mrs. Archer's belief that when "such things happened" it was undoubtedly foolish of the man, but somehow always criminal of the woman. All the elderly ladies whom Archer knew regarded any woman who loved imprudently as necessarily unscrupulous and designing, and mere simple- minded man as powerless in her clutches. The only thing to do was to persuade him, as early as possible, to marry a nice girl, and then trust to her to look after him.

In the complicated old European communities, Archer began to guess, love-problems might be less simple and less easily classified. Rich and idle and ornamental societies must produce many more such situations; and there might even be one in which a woman naturally sensitive and aloof would yet, from the force of circumstances, from sheer defencelessness and loneliness, be drawn into a tie inexcusable by conventional standards.

Newland thought of his intimate encounter with Countess Ellen Olenska. Was she no more than a trollop, the type of woman that was only to be enjoyed, rather than loved and respected? At the time, he felt only lust for her, but now, upon considering her situation more closely, he was beginning to see her as more of a real person who deserved to be loved—a woman that could be both loved and enjoyed.

One thing was certain—Newland's attraction for the Countess was strong. Had their evening not been disrupted, he would have carried her to her bed and made passionate love to her into the late hours of the night. He could not help but imagine how he would make love to her.

He would have slowly undressed her, one button at a time, until she stood before him completely bare. He would have kissed each and every inch of her body, breathing in her fragrance and consuming her with all his senses. Then it occurred to Newland that he had not touched her breasts, not once. He had tasted her rich cream and made love to her in such haste, each still wearing their clothes, but they had not disrobed so that their bodies touched.

Newland was suddenly filled with a desire to touch her breasts, to grasp them in his hands, and bury his face between them. How he longed to suckle them, and to tease the tips with his tongue.

On reaching home he wrote a line to the Countess Olenska, asking at what hour of the next day she could receive him, and despatched it by a messenger-boy, who returned presently with a word to the effect that she was going to Skuytercliff the next morning to stay over Sunday with the van der Luydens, but that he would find her alone that evening after dinner. The note was written on a rather untidy half-sheet, without date or address, but her hand was firm and free. Newland drew the note to his nose and inhaled. The paper had a sweet smell, like gardenias—the very fragrance that defined her person. He was amused at the idea of her week-ending in the stately solitude of Skuytercliff, but immediately afterward felt that there, of all places, she would most feel the chill of minds rigorously averted from the "unpleasant." A sense of frustration swept over Newland. He had an insatiable desire to see the Countess.

"Sir?" It was the meek voice of that young chambermaid, Anne.

Newland set the note aside and turned to the young woman. Her blonde hair was neatly tied, her pretty face a rosy color, and more enticingly noticeable, her full bosom spilled from her dress.

"It's my evening, Mr. Archer."

He could not take his eyes from her breasts, remembering her button size nipples that he had suckled only nights ago. He had basked in their delight, nursing those nipples as he claimed her virginity, making her a woman.

"Mr. Archer?" she said in a quivering voice. "Shall I come to you later this evening when you return? I'd very much like to come to you. If . . ." She let out a girlish giggle.

He checked his timepiece, thinking that if he took comfort with Anne now, he might better be able to clear his mind. "No, I think now would do nicely."

She smiled, her face flushing a deeper shade.

He closed the door to his private quarters, turned, and saw Anne waiting at the foot of the bed. He approached her from behind, reached his arms around her, and grasped her full breasts. Closing his eyes, he imagined that he was touching the Countess and gently began massaging Anne's voluptuous breasts.

She moaned, lightly at first, and thrust her chest forward desirously.

Then he spun her around and gaped at her breasts spilling from her apron. He grasped the top edges of the dress and jerked the bodice down, exposing her breasts. Her large nipples were hard, beckoning him. Newland immediately sunk down, took one of her breasts into his mouth, and began to suck with great vigor. To increase her pleasure, he used a hand to massage the other.

Anne moaned harder and longer and began undulating her hips.

He rolled his head from one breast to the other, and then pulled them together so that he could lick both her nipples with a long slide of his tongue. He lingered between her bosoms, suckling and licking the tips, and then clasped one of her nipples between his teeth and bit lightly.

"Mr. Archer, oh yes," Anne hissed with urgent desire.

Newland rose up and quickly laid her on the bed. With haste, he raised her skirts and pulled her undergarment from her body. Once she lay exposed, he spread open her legs, and began massaging her intimate form, running his fingers through her moist petals and across her fully erect crimson pearl. When he felt how ready she was for his member, he first thrust a finger inside of her sheath, dipping it in and out of her several times. She writhed beneath him, turning her head from side to side with inflamed desire. Wet, her body called for his manhood. He removed his trousers and positioned himself between her legs. He clasped one of her breasts in his mouth and again began to suck, and then pushed his throbbing manhood inside of her sheath with one masterful stroke.

Anne moaned loudly as he began thrusting his cock.

"Faster, faster," she said. "Harder."

Newland closed his eyes and thought of the Countess. He would much rather have been making love to Ellen, but Anne's vessel was so tight and rich with cream that he soon found himself lost in the pleasure of Anne's sweet loins.

Anne grasped his buttocks, gave him a sweet squeeze, and then quite unexpectedly, began spanking him, keeping beat as he thrust inside of her.

"More, harder," she demanded, groaning and whining as she worked her hips like a madwoman, continuing to slap his buttocks.

Newland raised his head from her bosom and looked into her face. The young woman's eyes were closed. She was completely enraptured. For a moment, he thought he might reprimand her, although he didn't quite have the heart to spoil her pleasure. Her head rolled from side to side, her hips thrust to his every beat, and he actually found that he enjoyed the stings of her playful spanks, as his member grew harder with each successive strike.

"Oh, oh, Mr. Archer. Suck one of my breasts. Whichever one you like. And thrust harder! More, more . . ." She grasped his head with both hands and guided his mouth back to one of her breasts, and then resumed spanking him, delivering some of the blows to the cleft between his cheeks. "Harder, faster," she cried.

Now under the young woman's control, Newland obeyed, panting to keep pace with her. He was besieged by her wild and relentless passion, his desire heightened by her slaps to his backside. He was ready to explode, but the young woman beat him to it. Her body suddenly tightened, went absolutely stiff, and then began convulsing in pleasure. Anne screamed out that she was undone. Her vessel tightened, and Newland himself could wait no longer. He released his seed, filling her vessel, until it overflowed.

Exhausted, he collapsed upon her to catch his breath.

When he rose up and slid out of her vessel, Anne opened her eyes and looked at her master. "Sir?" she said.

"What is it Anne?"

As she lay back on the bed with her legs spread open, she grabbed hold of one of her mammoth breasts, brought it to her mouth, and circled a nipple with her tongue. Then she looked at Newland with a grin. "Again, sir?" she asked, curiously.

Newland looked down at his wilting member and sighed.

"No, no, alas, I think not. We've quite finished for the night."

He was at Mr. Letterblair's punctually at seven, glad of the pretext for excusing himself soon after dinner. He had formed his own opinion from the papers entrusted to him, and did not especially want to go into the matter with his senior partner. Mr. Letterblair was a widower, and they dined alone, copiously and slowly, in a dark shabby room hung with yellowing prints of "The Death of Chatham" and "The Coronation of Napoleon." On the sideboard, between fluted Sheraton knife-cases, stood a decanter of Haut Brion, and another of the old Lanning port (the gift of a client), which the wastrel Tom Lanning had sold off a year or two before his mysterious and discreditable death in San Francisco— an incident less publicly humiliating to the family than the sale of the cellar.

After a velvety oyster soup came shad and cucumbers, then a young broiled turkey with corn fritters, followed by a canvas-back with currant jelly and a celery mayonnaise. Mr. Letterblair, who lunched on a sandwich and tea, dined deliberately and deeply, and insisted on his guest's doing the same. Finally, when the closing rites had been accomplished, the cloth was removed, cigars were lit, and Mr. Letterblair, leaning back in his chair and pushing the port westward, said, spreading his back agreeably to the coal fire behind him: "The whole family are against a divorce. And I think rightly."

Archer instantly felt himself on the other side of the argument. "But why, sir? If there ever was a case—"

"Well—what's the use? SHE'S here—he's there; the Atlantic's between them. She'll never get back a dollar more of her money than what he's voluntarily returned to her: their damned heathen marriage settlements take precious good care of that. As things go over there, Olenska's acted generously: he might have turned her out without a penny."

The young man knew this and was silent.

"I understand, though," Mr. Letterblair continued, "that she attaches no importance to the money. Therefore, as the family say, why not let well enough alone?"

Archer had gone to the house an hour earlier in full agreement with Mr. Letterblair's view; but put into words by this selfish, well-fed and supremely indifferent old man it suddenly became the Pharisaic voice of a society wholly absorbed in barricading itself against the unpleasant.

"I think that's for her to decide."

"H'm—have you considered the consequences if she decides for divorce?"

"You mean the threat in her husband's letter? What weight would that carry? It's no more than the vague charge of an angry blackguard."

"Yes; but it might make some unpleasant talk if he really defends the suit."

"Unpleasant—!" said Archer explosively.

Mr. Letterblair looked at him from under enquiring eyebrows, and the young man, aware of the uselessness of trying to explain what was in his mind, bowed acquiescently while his senior continued: "Divorce is always unpleasant."

"You agree with me?" Mr. Letterblair resumed, after a waiting silence.

"Naturally," said Archer.

"Well, then, I may count on you; the Mingotts may count on you; to use your influence against the idea?"

Archer hesitated. "I can't pledge myself till I've seen the Countess Olenska," he said at length.

"Mr. Archer, I don't understand you. Do you want to marry into a family with a scandalous divorce-suit hanging over it?"

"I don't think that has anything to do with the case."

Mr. Letterblair put down his glass of port and fixed on his young partner a cautious and apprehensive gaze.

Archer understood that he ran the risk of having his mandate withdrawn, and for some obscure reason he disliked the prospect. Now that the job had been thrust on him he did not propose to relinquish it; and, to guard against the possibility, he saw that he must reassure the unimaginative old man who was the legal conscience of the Mingotts.

"You may be sure, sir, that I shan't commit myself till I've reported to you; what I meant was that I'd rather not give an opinion till I've heard what Madame Olenska has to say."

Mr. Letterblair nodded approvingly at an excess of caution worthy of the best New York tradition, and the young man, glancing at his watch, pleaded an engagement and took leave.

# Chapter 12

Old-fashioned New York dined at seven, and the habit of after-dinner calls, though derided in Archer's set, still generally prevailed. As the young man strolled up Fifth Avenue from Waverley Place, the long thoroughfare was deserted but for a group of carriages standing before the Reggie Chiverses' (where there was a dinner for the Duke), and the occasional figure of an elderly gentleman in heavy overcoat and muffler ascending a brownstone doorstep and disappearing into a gas-lit hall. Thus, as Archer crossed Washington Square, he remarked that old Mr. du Lac was calling on his cousins the Dagonets, and turning down the corner of West Tenth Street he saw Mr. Skipworth, of his own firm, obviously bound on a visit to the Miss Lannings. A little farther up Fifth Avenue, Beaufort appeared on his doorstep, darkly projected against a blaze of light, descended to his private brougham, and rolled away to a mysterious and probably unmentionable destination. It was not an Opera night, and no one was giving a party, so that Beaufort's outing was undoubtedly of a clandestine nature. Archer connected it in his mind with a little house beyond Lexington Avenue in which beribboned window curtains and flower-boxes had recently appeared, and before whose newly painted door the canary-coloured brougham of Miss Fanny Ring was frequently seen to wait.

Beyond the small and slippery pyramid which composed Mrs. Archer's world lay the almost unmapped quarter inhabited by artists, musicians and "people who wrote." These scattered fragments of humanity had never shown any desire to be amalgamated with the social structure. In spite of odd ways they were said to be, for the most part, quite respectable; but they preferred to keep to themselves. Medora Manson, in her prosperous days, had inaugurated a "literary salon"; but it had soon died out owing to the reluctance of the literary to frequent it.

Others had made the same attempt, and there was a household of Blenkers—an intense and voluble mother, and three blowsy daughters who imitated her—where one met Edwin Booth and Patti and William Winter, and the new Shakespearian actor George Rignold, and some of the magazine editors and musical and literary critics.

Mrs. Archer and her group felt a certain timidity concerning these persons. They were odd, they were uncertain, they had things one didn't know about in the background of their lives and minds. Literature and art were deeply respected in the Archer set, and Mrs. Archer was always at pains to tell her children how much more agreeable and cultivated society had been when it included such figures as Washington Irving, Fitz-Greene Halleck and the poet of "The Culprit Fay." The most celebrated authors of that generation had been "gentlemen"; perhaps the unknown persons who succeeded them had gentlemanly sentiments, but their origin, their appearance, their hair, their intimacy with the stage and the Opera, made any old New York criterion inapplicable to them.

"When I was a girl," Mrs. Archer used to say, "we knew everybody between the Battery and Canal Street; and only the people one knew had carriages. It was perfectly easy to place any one then; now one can't tell, and I prefer not to try."

Only old Catherine Mingott, with her absence of moral prejudices and almost parvenu indifference to the subtler distinctions, might have bridged the abyss; but she had never opened a book or looked at a picture, and cared for music only because it reminded her of gala nights at the Italiens, in the days of her triumph at the Tuileries. Possibly Beaufort, who was her match in daring, would have succeeded in bringing about a fusion; but his grand house and silk-stockinged footmen were an obstacle to informal sociability. Moreover, he was as illiterate as old Mrs.

Mingott, and considered "fellows who wrote" as the mere paid purveyors of rich men's pleasures; and no one rich enough to influence his opinion had ever questioned it.

Newland Archer had been aware of these things ever since he could remember, and had accepted them as part of the structure of his universe. He knew that there were societies where painters and poets and novelists and men of science, and even great actors, were as sought after as Dukes; he had often pictured to himself what it would have been to live in the intimacy of drawing-rooms dominated by the talk of Merimee (whose "Lettres a une Inconnue" was one of his inseparables), of Thackeray, Browning or William Morris. But such things were inconceivable in New York, and unsettling to think of. Archer knew most of the "fellows who wrote," the musicians and the painters: he met them at the Century, or at the little musical and theatrical clubs that were beginning to come into existence. He enjoyed them there, and was bored with them at the Blenkers', where they were mingled with fervid and dowdy women who passed them about like captured curiosities; and even after his most exciting talks with Ned Winsett he always came away with the feeling that if his world was small, so was theirs, and that the only way to enlarge either was to reach a stage of manners where they would naturally merge.

He was reminded of this by trying to picture the society in which the Countess Olenska had lived and suffered, and also—perhaps—tasted mysterious joys. He remembered with what amusement she had told him that her grandmother Mingott and the Wellands objected to her living in a "Bohemian" quarter given over to "people who wrote." It was not the peril but the poverty that her family disliked; but that shade escaped her, and she supposed they considered literature compromising.

She herself had no fears of it, and the books scattered about her drawing-room (a part of the house in which books were usually supposed to be "out of place"), though chiefly works of fiction, had whetted Archer's interest with such new names as those of Paul Bourget, Huysmans, and the Goncourt brothers. Ruminating on these things as he approached her door, he was once more conscious of the curious way in which she reversed his values, and of the need of thinking himself into conditions incredibly different from any that he knew if he were to be of use in her present difficulty.

Nastasia opened the door, smiling mysteriously. On the bench in the hall lay a sable-lined overcoat, a folded opera hat of dull silk with a gold J. B. on the lining, and a white silk muffler: there was no mistaking the fact that these costly articles were the property of Julius Beaufort.

Archer was angry: so angry that he came near scribbling a word on his card and going away; then he remembered that in writing to Madame Olenska he had been kept by excess of discretion from saying that he wished to see her privately. He had therefore no one but himself to blame if she had opened her doors to other visitors; and he entered the drawing-room with the dogged determination to make Beaufort feel himself in the way, and to outstay him.

The banker stood leaning against the mantelshelf, which was draped with an old embroidery held in place by brass candelabra containing church candies of yellowish wax. He had thrust his chest out, supporting his shoulders against the mantel and resting his weight on one large patent-leather foot. As Archer entered he was smiling and looking down on his hostess, who sat on a sofa placed at right angles to the chimney. A table banked with flowers formed a screen behind it, and against the orchids and azaleas which the young man recognised as tributes from the Beaufort hot-houses, Madame Olenska sat half-reclined, her head propped on a hand and her wide sleeve leaving the arm bare to the elbow.

It was usual for ladies who received in the evenings to wear what were called "simple dinner dresses": a close-fitting armour of whale-boned silk, slightly open in the neck, with lace ruffles filling in the crack, and tight sleeves with a flounce uncovering just enough wrist to show an Etruscan gold bracelet or a velvet band. But Madame Olenska, heedless of tradition, was attired in a long robe of red velvet bordered about the chin and down the front with glossy black fur. Archer remembered, on his last visit to Paris, seeing a portrait by the new painter, Carolus Duran, whose pictures were the sensation of the Salon, in which the lady wore one of these bold sheath-like robes with her chin nestling in fur. There was something perverse and provocative in the notion of fur worn in the evening in a heated drawing-room, and in the combination of a muffled throat and bare arms; but the effect was undeniably pleasing.

"Lord love us—three whole days at Skuytercliff!" Beaufort was saying in his loud sneering voice as Archer entered. "You'd better take all your furs, and a hot-water-bottle."

"Why? Is the house so cold?" she asked, holding out her left hand to Archer in a way mysteriously suggesting that she expected him to kiss it.

"No; but the missus is," said Beaufort, nodding carelessly to the young man.

"But I thought her so kind. She came herself to invite me. Granny says I must certainly go."

"Granny would, of course. And I say it's a shame you're going to miss the little oyster supper I'd planned for you at Delmonico's next Sunday, with Campanini and Scalchi and a lot of jolly people."

She looked doubtfully from the banker to Archer.

"Ah—that does tempt me! Except the other evening at Mrs. Struthers's I've not met a single artist since I've been here."

"What kind of artists? I know one or two painters, very good fellows, that I could bring to see you if you'd allow me," said Archer boldly.

"Painters? Are there painters in New York?" asked Beaufort, in a tone implying that there could be none since he did not buy their pictures; and Madame Olenska said to Archer, with her grave smile: "That would be charming. But I was really thinking of dramatic artists, singers, actors, musicians. My husband's house was always full of them."

She said the words "my husband" as if no sinister associations were connected with them, and in a tone that seemed almost to sigh over the lost delights of her married life. Archer looked at her perplexedly, wondering if it were lightness or dissimulation that enabled her to touch so easily on the past at the very moment when she was risking her reputation in order to break with it.

"I do think," she went on, addressing both men, "that the imprevu adds to one's enjoyment. It's perhaps a mistake to see the same people every day."

"It's confoundedly dull, anyhow; New York is dying of dullness," Beaufort grumbled. "And when I try to liven it up for you, you go back on me. Come—think better of it! Sunday is your last chance, for Campanini leaves next week for Baltimore and Philadelphia; and I've a private room, and a Steinway, and they'll sing all night for me."

"How delicious! May I think it over, and write to you tomorrow morning?"

She spoke amiably, yet with the least hint of dismissal in her voice. Beaufort evidently felt it, and being unused to dismissals, stood staring at her with an obstinate line between his eyes.

"Why not now?"

"It's too serious a question to decide at this late hour."

"Do you call it late?"

She returned his glance coolly. "Yes; because I have still to talk business with Mr. Archer for a little while."

"Ah," Beaufort snapped. There was no appeal from her tone, and with a slight shrug he recovered his composure, took her hand, which he kissed with a practised air, and calling out from the threshold: "I say, Newland, if you can persuade the Countess to stop in town of course you're included in the supper," left the room with his heavy important step.

For a moment Archer fancied that Mr. Letterblair must have told her of his coming; but the irrelevance of her next remark made him change his mind.

"You know painters, then? You live in their milieu?" she asked, her eyes full of interest.

"Oh, not exactly. I don't know that the arts have a milieu here, any of them; they're more like a very thinly settled outskirt."

"But you care for such things?"

"Immensely. When I'm in Paris or London I never miss an exhibition. I try to keep up."

She looked down at the tip of the little satin boot that peeped from her long draperies.

"I used to care immensely too: my life was full of such things. But now I want to try not to."

"You want to try not to?"

"Yes: I want to cast off all my old life, to become just like everybody else here."

Archer reddened. "You'll never be like everybody else," he said.

She raised her straight eyebrows a little. "Ah, don't say that. If you knew how I hate to be different!"

Her face had grown as sombre as a tragic mask. She leaned forward, clasping her knee in her thin hands, and looking away from him into remote dark distances.

"I want to get away from it all," she insisted.

He waited a moment and cleared his throat. "I know. Mr. Letterblair has told me."

"Ah?"

"That's the reason I've come. He asked me to—you see I'm in the firm."

She looked slightly surprised, and then her eyes brightened. "You mean you can manage it for me? I can talk to you instead of Mr. Letterblair? Oh, that will be so much easier!"

Her tone touched him, and his confidence grew with his self-satisfaction. He perceived that she had spoken of business to Beaufort simply to get rid of him; and to have routed Beaufort was something of a triumph.

"I am here to talk about it," he repeated.

She sat silent, her head still propped by the arm that rested on the back of the sofa. Her face looked pale and extinguished, as if dimmed by the rich red of her dress. She struck Archer, of a sudden, as a pathetic and even pitiful figure.

"Now we're coming to hard facts," he thought, conscious in himself of the same instinctive recoil that he had so often criticised in his mother and her contemporaries. How little practice he had had in dealing with unusual situations! Their very vocabulary was unfamiliar to him, and seemed to belong to fiction and the stage. In face of what was coming he felt as awkward and embarrassed as a boy.

After a pause Madame Olenska broke out with unexpected vehemence: "I want to be free; I want to wipe out all the past."

"I understand that."

Her face warmed. "Then you'll help me?"

"First—" he hesitated—"perhaps I ought to know a little more."

She seemed surprised. "You know about my husband—my life with him?"

He made a sign of assent.

"Well—then—what more is there? In this country are such things tolerated? I'm a Protestant—our church does not forbid divorce in such cases."

"Certainly not."

They were both silent again, and Archer felt the spectre of Count Olenska's letter grimacing hideously between them. The letter filled only half a page, and was just what he had described it to be in speaking of it to Mr. Letterblair: the vague charge of an angry blackguard. But how much truth was behind it? Only Count Olenska's wife could tell.

"I've looked through the papers you gave to Mr. Letterblair," he said at length.

"Well—can there be anything more abominable?"

"No."

She changed her position slightly, screening her eyes with her lifted hand.

"Of course you know," Archer continued, "that if your husband chooses to fight the case—as he threatens to—"

"Yes—?"

"He can say things—things that might be unpl—might be disagreeable to you: say them publicly, so that they would get about, and harm you even if—"

"If—?"

"I mean: no matter how unfounded they were."

She paused for a long interval; so long that, not wishing to keep his eyes on her shaded face, he had time to imprint on his mind the exact shape of her other hand, the one on her knee, and every detail of the three rings on her fourth and fifth fingers; among which, he noticed, a wedding ring did not appear.

"What harm could such accusations, even if he made them publicly, do me here?"

It was on his lips to exclaim: "My poor child—far more harm than anywhere else!" Instead, he answered, in a voice that sounded in his ears like Mr. Letterblair's: "New York society is a very small world compared with the one you've lived in. And it's ruled, in spite of appearances, by a few people with—well, rather old-fashioned ideas."

She said nothing, and he continued: "Our ideas about marriage and divorce are particularly old-fashioned. Our legislation favours divorce—our social customs don't."

"Never?"

"Well—not if the woman, however injured, however irreproachable, has appearances in the least degree against her, has exposed herself by any unconventional action to—to offensive insinuations—"

She drooped her head a little lower, and he waited again, intensely hoping for a flash of indignation, or at least a brief cry of denial. None came.

A little travelling clock ticked purringly at her elbow, and a log broke in two and sent up a shower of sparks. The whole hushed and brooding room seemed to be waiting silently with Archer.

"Yes," she murmured at length, "that's what my family tell me."

He winced a little. "It's not unnatural—"

"OUR family," she corrected herself; and Archer coloured. "For you'll be my cousin soon," she continued gently.

"I hope so."

"And you take their view?"

He stood up at this, wandered across the room, stared with void eyes at one of the pictures against the old red damask, and came back irresolutely to her side. How could he say: "Yes, if what your husband hints is true, or if you've no way of disproving it?"

"Sincerely—" she interjected, as he was about to speak.

He looked down into the fire. "Sincerely, then—what should you gain that would compensate for the possibility—the certainty—of a lot of beastly talk?"

"But my freedom—is that nothing?"

It flashed across him at that instant that the charge in the letter was true, and that she hoped to marry the partner of her guilt. How was he to tell her that, if she really cherished such a plan, the laws of the State were inexorably opposed to it? The mere suspicion that the thought was in her mind made him feel harshly and impatiently toward her. "But aren't you as free as air as it is?" he returned. "Who can touch you? Mr. Letterblair tells me the financial question has been settled—"

"Oh, yes," she said indifferently.

"Well, then: is it worth while to risk what may be infinitely disagreeable and painful? Think of the newspapers—their vileness! It's all stupid and narrow and unjust—but one can't make over society."

"No," she acquiesced; and her tone was so faint and desolate that he felt a sudden remorse for his own hard thoughts.

"The individual, in such cases, is nearly always sacrificed to what is supposed to be the collective interest: people cling to any convention that keeps the family together—protects the children, if there are any," he rambled on, pouring out all the stock phrases that rose to his lips in his intense desire to cover over the ugly reality which her silence seemed to have laid bare. Since she would not or could not say the one word that would have cleared the air, his wish was not to let her feel that he was trying to probe into her secret. Better keep on the surface, in the prudent old New York way, than risk uncovering a wound he could not heal.

"It's my business, you know," he went on, "to help you to see these things as the people who are fondest of you see them. The Mingotts, the Wellands, the van der Luydens, all your friends and relations: if I didn't show you honestly how they judge such questions, it wouldn't be fair of me, would it?" He spoke insistently, almost pleading with her in his eagerness to cover up that yawning silence.

She said slowly: "No; it wouldn't be fair."

The fire had crumbled down to greyness, and one of the lamps made a gurgling appeal for attention. Madame Olenska rose, wound it up and returned to the fire, but without resuming her seat.

Her remaining on her feet seemed to signify that there was nothing more for either of them to say, and Archer stood up also.

"Very well; I will do what you wish," she said abruptly. The blood rushed to his forehead; and, taken aback by the suddenness of her surrender, he caught her two hands awkwardly in his.

"I—I do want to help you," he said.

"You do help me. Good night, my cousin."

He bent and laid his lips on her hands, which were cold and lifeless. He looked into her eyes. "You're cold," he said.

"It's nothing."

"Let me put another log on the fire."

"Please don't trouble yourself, I'll ring for the help."

Newland walked to a stack of wood and placed a few more on the fire, poking and stirring the ambers. When the fire intensified, he turned and faced the Countess. She looked away. He walked over to her, took her hand, and seated her down next to him on the sofa. His feelings were mixed. He wanted her to be free of the Count, but he didn't want her to suffer humiliation.

Her perfume was sensuous, the sweet fragrance of gardenia. Whenever he smelled the gardenia flower, visions of her flooded his brain, and his body thrilled.

"You really should go. I'm suddenly so tired," she said.

Newland brought the back of her hand to his mouth and slowly placed his lips against it. Her skin was soft, so lovely, so quintessentially feminine. Touching her was intoxicating.

"Newland, we shouldn't, not again."

She said the words, but the look in her eyes said that she wanted more. He grasped her other hand and brought it to his lips.

"I want you," he said.

"We mustn't. You're—?"

"Don't," he said, drawing her into his arms. He never wanted a woman more in his life. She made him feel alive, feel like the man he had always wanted to be. He felt not only passion, but also a thirst for life, and she was his ever-flowing fountain.

"If you truly cared for me, you would leave now," she said. "You have May to think of."

"I'm going to look after you, Ellen."

"But you can't. You have obligations to—"

He took her face in his hands and stared longingly into her eyes. A log tumbled in the fireplace, making a sudden clatter. Ellen's eyes began to flutter as though she were swooning in response to his captivating stare. Newland had never looked so deeply into a woman's eyes. He'd never felt as though he touched the soul of another until this moment.

Her lips parted to speak. But all she could do was whisper his name.

He leaned forward, with eyes closed, and gently pressed his lips against hers. As he began to kiss her more, he felt a wetness fall from her cheeks to his mouth, and then he tasted the tears. After kissing them away, he drew back and said, "Ellen, don't cry. I'll always be here for you."

She began to shake her head no. "How could we live like this?"

"How could we not live?"

Presently, her weeping stopped, and she searched his eyes. Overwhelmed, she kissed him passionately. He slipped his tongue to her mouth, and together they tasted the sweetness of each other's devoted affection.

When he broke from the kiss, he brushed his lips across her cheeks and down her neck, drinking in her fragrance and basking in her velvety skin.

She moaned with pleasure. He opened her robe and found that she was bare breasted. Her delicate bosom were creamy and full, and her nipples the color of a light pink rose. He slid his hands to her breasts, grasping one in each hand, luxuriating in the tenderness of her skin. When he danced his fingertips across her nipples, she sighed and rolled her head back. And the more he massaged, the more erect her nipples became. Newland was overwhelmed with desire. He wanted to ravage Ellen, join with her, be inside of her.

He squeezed the tips of her nipples and she suddenly released an impassioned moan, breathing his name through a rushed whisper. Then he lowered his mouth to one of her breasts, and took the whole of it into his mouth. He slowly pulled forward, circling his tongue around her flesh to taste her sweetness, and then stopped at the nipple to suck, softly at first. But the more her passions intensified, the harder he sucked, rolling the tip of her nipple across his tongue. He had dreamed about this from the moment he had imagined making love to her. But this celestial encounter far exceeded anything that he had imagined. Her scent, her elegant and subtle movements, the touch of her skin against his mouth and tongue, aroused him so completely that he felt as if he were tasting a piece of heaven itself.

With his hand, he continued to massage the other breast, until he moved through her cleavage, where he lingered with his tongue and explored her every curve. Then he moved to the other side, where he again took the full breast into his mouth and pulled forward. He stopped at the nipple to suck lightly and then pulled back so that only his tongue touched the tip. He teased it, driving her wild, but did not take it into his mouth this time. Instead, he swirled his tongue in sensuous circles around the bud, feeling the nipple grow ever more erect. He circled his tongue around the nub tenderly, a rhythmic dance, all the while squeezing her other breast with his hand.

He basked in utter pleasure as he moved his mouth from one of her breasts to the other. As her arousal intensified to white heat, her hips undulated with desire. He opened her robe completely; she was fully naked, exposed to him. Her feminine form was framed by delicate curls of light brown. Craving more, Newland gently opened one of her legs, and slowly lowered his face down her torso. He stopped to circle his tongue at her navel, her body trembling at his touch. And then, he moved farther below and traced the lines of her hip with his mouth and tongue, inhaling her amatory feminine scent. He slipped a hand lower and between her legs, gently squeezing her loins before sliding his fingers through her cream.

"Wonderful," she said the moment he touched her feminine folds. When he began caressing her pearl, she began to moan. The more he played, the more intensely her hips undulated.

"Deeper," she said, and with the other hand he slipped deeper inside her creamy vessel and began strumming his finger in sweet rhythm with her movements.

"Ah-h, Newland," she said, her hips thrusting almost violently.

When he slipped another finger inside, continuing to stroke while also massaging her pearl, her body suddenly quivered, and then trembled. A few moments later, with a tumultuous quaver, she thrust her body forward, and he knew that she had crested. He gently danced his fingertips across her sensitive pearl as she continued to shudder, longer and more intensely than any woman he had ever known. And finally, her body melted under the pull of her climax.

The logs in the fireplace suddenly tumbled, and one rolled from the fireplace.

The Countess opened her eyes. "Newland! Do something."

He turned and saw a burning log on the Persian carpet. Jumping to his feet, he found the poker from the fireplace set. He pushed the log back in the direction of the fireplace, but now the rug was aflame.

The Countess gathered her robe and hurried to a vase of flowers. She tossed the roses from it, and returned to the burning rug to throw the water on it. Instantly, the fire on the carpet was extinguished. But the log kept burning, threatening to set fire to the lace curtain. Newland struggled to move the log back into the fireplace without igniting another fire. The Countess grabbed a shovel from the fireplace set and handed it to him. With both instruments, he managed to scoop up the log and returned it to the fireplace.

The Countess kneeled next to the carpet and expelled a frustrated breath. "I suppose it's not so awfully bad."

He kneeled beside her. "It was my fault. I should have secured the logs."

She kissed his cheek as if dismissing him. "No, not at all. I'm only glad you were here."

"Can I see you to—?"

"It's late, Newland. Perhaps we've had enough excitement for the day. Though you were lovely to stay and keep me company."

"I assure you it was all my pleasure."

She smiled sweetly at him and stood. Then she drew them away from the fireplace and toward the door.

"You are the loveliest," he said, turning back to her at the door. She kissed his cheek again, and then he turned to the door leading into the hall, where he found his coat and hat under the faint gas-light of the hall, and without further ado, plunged outside into the winter night bursting with the belated eloquence of the inarticulate.

# Chapter 13

It was a crowded night at Wallack's theatre.

The play was "The Shaughraun," with Dion Boucicault in the title role and Harry Montague and Ada Dyas as the lovers. The popularity of the admirable English company was at its height, and the Shaughraun always packed the house. In the galleries the enthusiasm was unreserved; in the stalls and boxes, people smiled a little at the hackneyed sentiments and clap- trap situations, and enjoyed the play as much as the galleries did.

There was one episode, in particular, that held the house from floor to ceiling. It was that in which Harry Montague, after a sad, almost monosyllabic scene of parting with Miss Dyas, bade her good-bye, and turned to go. The actress, who was standing near the mantelpiece and looking down into the fire, wore a gray cashmere dress without fashionable loopings or trimmings, moulded to her tall figure and flowing in long lines about her feet. Around her neck was a narrow black velvet ribbon with the ends falling down her back.

When her wooer turned from her she rested her arms against the mantel-shelf and bowed her face in her hands. On the threshold he paused to look at her; then he stole back, lifted one of the ends of velvet ribbon, kissed it, and left the room without her hearing him or changing her attitude. And on this silent parting the curtain fell.

It was always for the sake of that particular scene that Newland Archer went to see "The Shaughraun." He thought the adieux of Montague and Ada Dyas as fine as anything he had ever seen Croisette and Bressant do in Paris, or Madge Robertson and Kendal in London; in its reticence, its dumb sorrow, it moved him more than the most famous histrionic outpourings.

On the evening in question the little scene acquired an added poignancy by reminding him—he could not have said why—of his leave-taking from Madame Olenska after their confidential talk and lovemaking a week or ten days earlier.

It would have been as difficult to discover any resemblance between the two situations as between the appearance of the persons concerned. Newland Archer could not pretend to anything approaching the young English actor's romantic good looks, and Miss Dyas was a tall red-haired woman of monumental build whose pale and pleasantly ugly face was utterly unlike Ellen Olenska's vivid countenance. Nor were Archer and Madame Olenska two lovers parting in heart-broken silence; they parted as two who chose love, and of course, they were client and lawyer separating after a talk which had given the lawyer the worst possible impression of the client's case. Wherein, then, lay the resemblance that made the young man's heart beat with a kind of retrospective excitement? It seemed to be in Madame Olenska's mysterious faculty of suggesting tragic and moving possibilities outside the daily run of experience. She had hardly ever said a word to him to produce this impression, but it was a part of her, either a projection of her mysterious and outlandish background or of something inherently dramatic, passionate and unusual in herself. Archer had always been inclined to think that chance and circumstance played a small part in shaping people's lots compared with their innate tendency to have things happen to them. This tendency he had felt from the first in Madame Olenska. The quiet, almost passive young woman struck him as exactly the kind of person to whom things were bound to happen, no matter how much she shrank from them and went out of her way to avoid them, although she had not shrunk from his affection, but rather welcomed it. The exciting fact was her having lived in an atmosphere so thick with drama that her own tendency to provoke it had apparently passed unperceived. It was precisely the odd absence of surprise in her that gave him the sense of her having been plucked out of a very maelstrom: the things she took for granted gave the measure of those she had rebelled against.

Archer had left her with the conviction that Count Olenska's accusation was not unfounded. The mysterious person who figured in his wife's past as "the secretary" had probably not been unrewarded for his share in her escape. The conditions from which she had fled were intolerable, past speaking of, past believing: she was young, she was frightened, she was desperate—what more natural than that she should be grateful to her rescuer? The pity was that her gratitude put her, in the law's eyes and the world's, on a par with her abominable husband. Archer had made her understand this, as he was bound to do; he had also made her understand that simplehearted kindly New York, on whose larger charity she had apparently counted, was precisely the place where she could least hope for indulgence.

To have to make this fact plain to her—and to witness her resigned acceptance of it—had been intolerably painful to him. He felt himself drawn to her by obscure feelings of jealousy and pity, as if her dumbly- confessed error had put her at his mercy, humbling yet endearing her. He was glad it was to him she had revealed her secret, rather than to the cold scrutiny of Mr. Letterblair, or the embarrassed gaze of her family. He immediately took it upon himself to assure them both that she had given up her idea of seeking a divorce, basing her decision on the fact that she had understood the uselessness of the proceeding; and with infinite relief they had all turned their eyes from the "unpleasantness" she had spared them.

"I was sure Newland would manage it," Mrs. Welland had said proudly of her future son-in-law; and old Mrs. Mingott, who had summoned him for a confidential interview, had congratulated him on his cleverness, and added impatiently: "Silly goose! I told her myself what nonsense it was. Wanting to pass herself off as

Ellen Mingott and an old maid, when she has the luck to be a married woman and a Countess!"

These incidents had made the memory of his last talk with Madame Olenska so vivid to the young man that as the curtain fell on the parting of the two actors his eyes filled with tears, and he stood up to leave the theatre.

In doing so, he turned to the side of the house behind him, and saw the lady of whom he was thinking seated in a box with the Beauforts, Lawrence Lefferts, and one or two other men. He had not spoken with her alone since their evening together, trying to forget, thinking of his obligation to May, and he had tried to avoid being with her in company; but now their eyes met, and as Mrs. Beaufort recognised him at the same time, and made her languid little gesture of invitation, it was impossible not to go into the box.

Beaufort and Lefferts made way for him, and after a few words with Mrs. Beaufort, who always preferred to look beautiful and not have to talk, Archer seated himself behind Madame Olenska. There was no one else in the box but Mr. Sillerton Jackson, who was telling Mrs. Beaufort in a confidential undertone about Mrs. Lemuel Struthers's last Sunday reception (where some people reported that there had been dancing). Under cover of this circumstantial narrative, to which Mrs. Beaufort listened with her perfect smile, and her head at just the right angle to be seen in profile from the stalls, Madame Olenska turned and spoke in a low voice.

"Do you think," she asked, glancing toward the stage, "he will send her a bunch of yellow roses tomorrow morning?"

Archer reddened, and his heart gave a leap of surprise. He had called only twice on Madame Olenska, and each time he had sent her a box of yellow roses, and each time without a card. She had never before made any allusion to the flowers, and he supposed she had never thought of him as the sender. Now her sudden recognition of the gift, and her associating it with the tender leave-taking on the stage, filled him with an agitated pleasure.

"I was thinking of that too—I was going to leave the theatre in order to take the picture away with me," he said.

To his surprise her colour rose, reluctantly and duskily. She rose from her chair and excused herself. "I must speak with a friend. I won't be a minute," she said quietly to Newland and the other gentlemen.

Some moments passed and Newland's curiosity was naturally heightened. With a nod, he excused himself from the box and went in search of the Countess, wondering if she had meant for him to follow. He traveled the length of the corridor, and down the stairs, but with the Countess nowhere in sight, he decided to return to the box to avoid any suspicion.

As he brushed passed an open door, leading to a discrete hallway, he noticed a handkerchief lying on the floor. It wasn't just any piece of cloth, but one embroidered with the Countess's initials like the one he had seen in her lap the first evening he had met her. He entered the hallway and collected the item. But as he stood, he noticed an open door.

He gingerly trod down the hallway and found the Countess standing inside a small sitting room. When he cleared his throat, she turned to him.

"Newland? You followed me?"

"It seems you've lost your handkerchief," he said, his voice lowering.

"So it has."

"May I?" He entered the room and returned the item to her. "Are you quite all right?"

"Yes, I was to meet a friend for a private conversation. A woman I knew from Europe, although it appears that she has lost her way."

"To my fortune," he said. He took a glance at his surroundings. "And this room is very private indeed. Very intimate."

"No Newland, we shouldn't, not again."

He clasped her hand and brought it to his lips. "Yes," he whispered. Then he took a step back and closed the door behind them. "I must have you. I've been desolate without you," he said, returning to her side.

"But you stayed away, avoided me. I thought the matter was settled."

He shook his head and lowered her to the sofa. He dropped to his knees and clasped her feet, bringing them to his face.

"Please, Newland. Don't. We shouldn't." But despite her words, she offered no physical resistance, but perhaps involuntarily parted her legs slightly.

Then he raised the skirt of her dress to her lap and began kissing the length of her legs. He paused to spread her legs when he reached her thighs, and then crossed over to her inner thighs. She sighed helplessly at his touch, her body going limber, and so he continued upwardly, running a slow tongue up to her loins. He slipped a few fingers inside her gold silk undergarment to find that despite her words of denial, her body was impassioned with her seductive cream, which overflowed. Pulling the garment to the side, her orchid was fully revealed, her crimson pearl bursting through its folds. He drew near to inhale her scent, and then slipped his tongue through her passion to taste the richness, which he savored as though it were the most heavenly of desserts.

She moaned and began moving her hips desirously toward him, needing more of his loving touch. He slid his tongue upward to her pearl and with quick tender licks, ran his tongue in a circular motion over it, heightening her arousal.

"Make love to me, Newland," she finally whispered.

He drew back and removed her undergarment. Then he turned her around so that she faced the sofa, with her hands resting upon its back. He raised her dress and positioned himself behind her. She raised her hips to him, undulating impatiently. He unfastened his trousers and prepared to enter her sheath. He wrapped a strong arm around her, and with the other hand, returned to caress her pearl.

She sighed endlessly. But as soon as his manhood touched the opening to her sheath, she said, "Yes. I need you moving inside me now."

He massaged her pearl, circling it several times more, before slowly pushing his manhood inside her. When she was fully filled, they paused to savor the moment, sighing and basking in lust. It wasn't long before they were both overcome with excitement and began moving with more urgency.

"This was the Count's favorite way to take me," she said, unexpectedly.

Newland's thrusts slowed. "Ellen, I don't want to . . ."

"No, Newland, you're different." She thrust her hips back at him, encouraging him to resume the intensity of their lovemaking.

The pleasure of her intimate chamber was too much for him, and he resumed.

"The Count . . ." Her voice was breathless, hoarse with passion. "He was more animal than man. He treated me roughly, while you move like a lover." She looked back at him.

Newland did not want to hear the words, and yet her body and voice inflamed him.

"I learned to love it, Newland, crave his ill-treatment of me, until I woke up and could stand it no more and escaped. I vowed never to allow a man to take me like this again … until you."

Newland stopped his movements and was about to withdraw from her sheath when she reached back with a hand and grabbed his hips.

"Do not stop, I beg you," she said. "With you, it's different. With you, I am your lover. It's wonderful. Please … let me feel your movements." She thrust her hips back hard, twisted, and undulated them, caressing his manhood with the velvety walls of her chamber.

He could not resist and began thrusting, as she preferred. "Harder, harder, Newland," she said, panting and breathless. She suddenly thrust forward, raising her hips higher to allow him easier, deeper access to her intimate chamber. He continued to massage her pearl, round and round, until her body became taut, and then heaved and jerked uncontrollably.

"Yes, yes, I swoon," she cried as she announced her release. And in his next stroke inside her, he groaned and released his seed. His legs convulsed and buckled, and his body collapsed against the weight of hers. Together, they sighed as they felt the electrical impulse race through their limbs.

"Ellen," he whispered as he enveloped her tightly in his arms. "How I need you my darling."

"And I you," she said.

They lay in each other's arms, comforted by their physical union.

"I could stay here forever," he said.

"But we must return to the box before we are suspected."

"Let us forget the others."

"And disparage your good name?"

He exhaled heavily. "Whoever cares?"

She moved so that he had to let her rise. She straightened her hair and smoothed her skirts. "It was lovely, my darling. Lovely. I shall dream of you tonight when you are away from me." She gently kissed his lips.

"Don't go," he said.

But she turned and left the privacy of the room. When Newland returned to the box, their conversation continued exactly where they had left off before their leaving.

She looked down at the mother-of-pearl opera-glass in her smoothly gloved hands, and said, after a pause: "What do you do while May is away?"

"I stick to my work," he answered, faintly annoyed by the question.

In obedience to a long-established habit, the Wellands had left the previous week for St. Augustine, where, out of regard for the supposed susceptibility of Mr. Welland's bronchial tubes, they always spent the latter part of the winter. Mr. Welland was a mild and silent man, with no opinions but with many habits. With these habits none might interfere; and one of them demanded that his wife and daughter should always go with him on his annual journey to the south. To preserve an unbroken domesticity was essential to his peace of mind; he would not have known where his hair-brushes were, or how to provide stamps for his letters, if Mrs. Welland had not been there to tell him.

As all the members of the family adored each other, and as Mr. Welland was the central object of their idolatry, it never occurred to his wife and May to let him go to St. Augustine alone; and his sons, who were both in the law, and could not leave New York during the winter, always joined him for Easter and travelled back with him.

It was impossible for Archer to discuss the necessity of May's accompanying her father. The reputation of the Mingotts' family physician was largely based on the attack of pneumonia which Mr. Welland had never had; and his insistence on St. Augustine was therefore inflexible. Originally, it had been intended that May's engagement should not be announced till her return from Florida, and the fact that it had been made known sooner could not be expected to alter Mr. Welland's plans. Archer would have liked to join the travellers and have a few weeks of sunshine and boating with his betrothed; but he too was bound by custom and conventions. Little arduous as his professional duties were, he would have been convicted of frivolity by the whole Mingott clan if he had suggested asking for a holiday in mid-winter; and he accepted May's departure with the resignation which he perceived would have to be one of the principal constituents of married life.

He was conscious that Madame Olenska was looking at him under lowered lids. "I have done what you wished—what you advised," she said abruptly.

"Ah—I'm glad," he returned, embarrassed by her broaching the subject at such a moment.

"I understand—that you were right," she went on a little breathlessly; "but sometimes life is difficult ... perplexing... "

"I know."

"And I wanted to tell you that I DO feel you were right; and that I'm grateful to you," she ended, lifting her opera-glass quickly to her eyes as the door of the box opened and Beaufort's resonant voice broke in on them.

Archer stood up, and left the box and the theatre.

Only the day before he had received a letter from May Welland in which, with characteristic candour, she had asked him to "be kind to Ellen" in their absence. "She likes you and admires you so much—and you know, though she doesn't show it, she's still very lonely and unhappy. I don't think Granny understands her, or uncle Lovell Mingott either; they really think she's much worldlier and fonder of society than she is. And I can quite see that New York must seem dull to her, though the family won't admit it. I think she's been used to lots of things we haven't got; wonderful music, and picture shows, and celebrities—artists and authors and all the clever people you admire. Granny can't understand her wanting anything but lots of dinners and clothes—but I can see that you're almost the only person in New York who can talk to her about what she really cares for."

His wise May—how he had loved her for that letter! But he had not meant to act on it; he was too busy, to begin with, and he did not care, as an engaged man, to play too conspicuously the part of Madame Olenska's champion. He had an idea that she knew how to take care of herself a good deal better than the ingenuous May imagined. She had Beaufort at her feet, Mr. van der Luyden hovering above her like a protecting deity, and any number of candidates (Lawrence Lefferts among them) waiting their opportunity in the middle distance. Yet he never saw her, or exchanged a word with her, without feeling that, after all, May's ingenuousness almost amounted to a gift of divination. Ellen Olenska was lonely and she was unhappy.

# Chapter 14

As he came out into the lobby Archer ran across his friend Ned Winsett, the only one among what Janey called his "clever people" with whom he cared to probe into things a little deeper than the average level of club and chop-house banter.

He had caught sight, across the house, of Winsett's shabby round-shouldered back, and had once noticed his eyes turned toward the Beaufort box. The two men shook hands, and Winsett proposed a bock at a little German restaurant around the corner. Archer, who was not in the mood for the kind of talk they were likely to get there, declined on the plea that he had work to do at home; and Winsett said: "Oh, well so have I for that matter, and I'll be the Industrious Apprentice too."

They strolled along together, and presently Winsett said: "Look here, what I'm really after is the name of the dark lady in that swell box of yours—with the Beauforts, wasn't she? The one your friend Lefferts seems so smitten by."

Archer, he could not have said why, although he would like to have, but he was more than slightly annoyed with this man. What the devil did Ned Winsett want with Ellen Olenska's name? And above all, why did he couple it with Lefferts's? It was unlike Winsett to manifest such curiosity; but after all, Archer remembered, he was a journalist.

"It's not for an interview, I hope?" he laughed.

"Well—not for the press; just for myself," Winsett rejoined. "The fact is she's a neighbour of mine—queer quarter for such a beauty to settle in—and she's been awfully kind to my little boy, who fell down her area chasing his kitten, and gave himself a nasty cut. She rushed in bareheaded, carrying him in her arms, with his knee all beautifully bandaged, and was so sympathetic and beautiful that my wife was too dazzled to ask her name."

A pleasant glow dilated Archer's heart. There was nothing extraordinary in the tale: any woman would have done as much for a neighbour's child. But it was just like Ellen, he felt, to have rushed in bareheaded, carrying the boy in her arms, and to have dazzled poor Mrs. Winsett into forgetting to ask who she was.

"That is the Countess Olenska—a granddaughter of old Mrs. Mingott's."

"Whew—a Countess!" whistled Ned Winsett. "Well, I didn't know Countesses were so neighbourly. Mingotts ain't."

"They would be, if you'd let them."

"Ah, well—" It was their old interminable argument as to the obstinate unwillingness of the "clever people" to frequent the fashionable, and both men knew that there was no use in prolonging it.

"I wonder," Winsett broke off, "how a Countess happens to live in our slum?"

"Because she doesn't care a hang about where she lives—or about any of our little social sign-posts," said Archer, with a secret pride in his own picture of her.

"H'm—been in bigger places, I suppose," the other commented. "Well, here's my corner."

He slouched off across Broadway, and Archer stood looking after him and musing on his last words.

Ned Winsett had those flashes of penetration; they were the most interesting thing about him, and always made Archer wonder why they had allowed him to accept failure so stolidly at an age when most men are still struggling.

Archer had known that Winsett had a wife and child, but he had never seen them. The two men always met at the Century, or at some haunt of journalists and theatrical people, such as the restaurant where Winsett had proposed to go for a bock. He had given Archer to understand that his wife was an invalid; which might be true of the poor lady, or might merely mean that she was lacking in social gifts or in evening clothes, or in both. Winsett himself had a savage abhorrence of social observances: Archer, who dressed in the evening because he thought it cleaner and more comfortable to do so, and who had never stopped to consider that cleanliness and comfort are two of the costliest items in a modest budget, regarded Winsett's attitude as part of the boring "Bohemian" pose that always made fashionable people, who changed their clothes without talking about it, and were not forever harping on the number of servants one kept, seem so much simpler and less self-conscious than the others. Nevertheless, he was always stimulated by Winsett, and whenever he caught sight of the journalist's lean bearded face and melancholy eyes he would rout him out of his corner and carry him off for a long talk.

Winsett was not a journalist by choice. He was a pure man of letters, untimely born in a world that had no need of letters; but after publishing one volume of brief and exquisite literary appreciations, of which one hundred and twenty copies were sold, thirty given away, and the balance eventually destroyed by the publishers (as per contract) to make room for more marketable material, he had abandoned his real calling, and taken a sub-editorial job on a women's weekly, where fashion- plates and paper patterns alternated with New England love-stories and advertisements of temperance drinks.

On the subject of "Hearth-fires" (as the paper was called) he was inexhaustibly entertaining; but beneath his fun lurked the sterile bitterness of the still young man who has tried and given up. His conversation always made Archer take the measure of his own life, and feel how little it contained; but Winsett's, after all, contained still less, and though their common fund of intellectual interests and curiosities made their talks exhilarating, their exchange of views usually remained within the limits of a pensive dilettantism.

"The fact is, life isn't much a fit for either of us," Winsett had once said. "I'm down and out; nothing to be done about it. I've got only one ware to produce, and there's no market for it here, and won't be in my time. But you're free and you're well-off. Why don't you get into touch? There's only one way to do it: to go into politics."

Archer threw his head back and laughed. There one saw at a flash the unbridgeable difference between men like Winsett and the others—Archer's kind. Every one in polite circles knew that, in America, "a gentleman couldn't go into politics." But, since he could hardly put it in that way to Winsett, he answered evasively: "Look at the career of the honest man in American politics! They don't want us."

"Who's 'they'? Why don't you all get together and be 'they' yourselves?"

Archer's laugh lingered on his lips in a slightly condescending smile. It was useless to prolong the discussion: everybody knew the melancholy fate of the few gentlemen who had risked their clean linen in municipal or state politics in New York. The day was past when that sort of thing was possible: the country was in possession of the bosses and the emigrant, and decent people had to fall back on sport or culture.

"Culture! Yes—if we had it! But there are just a few little local patches, dying out here and there for lack of—well, hoeing and cross-fertilising: the last remnants of the old European tradition that your forebears brought with them. But you're in a pitiful little minority: you've got no centre, no competition, no audience. You're like the pictures on the walls of a deserted house: 'The Portrait of a Gentleman.' You'll never amount to anything, any of you, till you roll up your sleeves and get right down into the muck. That, or emigrate … God! If I could emigrate … "

Archer mentally shrugged his shoulders and turned the conversation back to books, where Winsett, if uncertain, was always interesting. Emigrate! As if a gentleman could abandon his own country! One could no more do that than one could roll up one's sleeves and go down into the muck. A gentleman simply stayed at home and abstained. But you couldn't make a man like Winsett see that; and that was why the New York of literary clubs and exotic restaurants, though a first shake made it seem more of a kaleidoscope, turned out, in the end, to be a smaller box, with a more monotonous pattern, than the assembled atoms of Fifth Avenue.

The next morning Archer scoured the town in vain for more yellow roses. In consequence of this search he arrived late at the office, perceived that his doing so made no difference whatever to any one, and was filled with sudden exasperation at the elaborate futility of his life. Why should he not be, at that moment, on the sands of St. Augustine with May Welland? No one was deceived by his pretense of professional activity. In old-fashioned legal firms like that of which Mr. Letterblair was the head, and which were mainly engaged in the management of large estates and "conservative" investments, there were always two or three young men, fairly well-off, and without professional ambition, who, for a certain number of hours of each day, sat at their desks accomplishing trivial tasks, or simply reading the newspapers. Though it was supposed to be proper for them to have an occupation, the crude fact of money-making was still regarded as derogatory, and the law, being a profession, was accounted a more gentlemanly pursuit than business. But none of these young men had much hope of really advancing in his profession, or any earnest desire to do so; and over many of them the green mould of the perfunctory was already perceptibly spreading.

It made Archer shiver to think that it might be spreading over him too. He had, to be sure, other tastes and interests; he spent his vacations in European travel, cultivated the "clever people" May spoke of, and generally tried to "keep up," as he had somewhat wistfully put it to Madame Olenska. But once he was married, what would become of this narrow margin of life in which his real experiences were lived? He had seen enough of other young men who had dreamed his dream, though perhaps less ardently, and who had gradually sunk into the placid and luxurious routine of their elders.

From the office he sent a note by messenger to Madame Olenska, asking if he might call that afternoon, and begging her to let him find a reply at his club; but at the club he found nothing, nor did he receive any letter the following day. This unexpected silence mortified him beyond reason, and though the next morning he saw a glorious cluster of yellow roses behind a florist's window-pane, he left it there. It was only on the third morning that he received a line by post from the Countess Olenska. To his surprise it was dated from Skuytercliff, whither the van der Luydens had promptly retreated after putting the Duke on board his steamer.

"I ran away," the writer began abruptly (without the usual preliminaries), "the day after I saw you at the play, and these kind friends have taken me in. I wanted to be quiet, and think things over. You were right in telling me how kind they were; I feel myself so safe here. I wish that you were with us." She ended with a conventional "Yours sincerely," and without any allusion to the date of her return.

The tone of the note surprised the young man. What was Madame Olenska running away from, and why did she feel the need to be safe? His first thought was of some dark menace from abroad; then he reflected that he did not know her epistolary style, and that it might run to picturesque exaggeration. Women always exaggerated; and moreover she was not wholly at her ease in English, which she often spoke as if she were translating from the French. "Je me suis evadee—" put in that way, the opening sentence immediately suggested that she might merely have wanted to escape from a boring round of engagements; which was very likely true, for he judged her to be capricious, and easily wearied of the pleasure of the moment.

It amused him to think of the van der Luydens having carried her off to Skuytercliff on a second visit, and this time for an indefinite period. The doors of Skuytercliff were rarely and grudgingly opened to visitors, and a chilly week-end was the most ever offered to the few thus privileged. But Archer had seen, on his last visit to Paris, the delicious play of Labiche, "Le Voyage de M. Perrichon," and he remembered M. Perrichon's dogged and undiscouraged attachment to the young man whom he had pulled out of the glacier. The van der Luydens had rescued Madame Olenska from a doom almost as icy; and though there were many other reasons for being attracted to her, Archer knew that beneath them all lay the gentle and obstinate determination to go on rescuing her.

He felt a distinct disappointment on learning that she was away; and almost immediately remembered that, only the day before, he had refused an invitation to spend the following Sunday with the Reggie Chiverses at their house on the Hudson, a few miles below Skuytercliff.

He had had his fill long ago of the noisy friendly parties at Highbank, with coasting, ice-boating, sleighing, long tramps in the snow, and a general flavour of mild flirting and milder practical jokes. He had just received a box of new books from his London book- seller, and had preferred the prospect of a quiet Sunday at home with his spoils. But he now went into the club writing-room, wrote a hurried telegram, and told the servant to send it immediately. He knew that Mrs. Reggie didn't object to her visitors' suddenly changing their minds, and that there was always a room to spare in her elastic house.

That evening when Newland arrived home, he called for Miranda to ready his portmanteaus. As he smoked his cigar in his private chambers, he held one of his new books in his lap without bothering to read it. All he could think of was that blissful moment when he would knock upon the Countess's door to surprise her. This time he intended to bed her properly and fill his days with her pleasant and amusing company. They would have such delightful conversation in sharing thoughts from books they had read and exhibits they had seen.

"Sir," Miranda said, interrupting his thoughts.

Newland looked up.

"You're all packed."

"Very well, Miranda." He lifted the book on the pretense of reading it.

"Will there be anything further?"

Newland looked up at her, perplexed.

Her voice lowered. "You've always been so kind to me, sir. Never striking a hand of disapproval."

Newland was aghast at the very thought. "I wouldn't dare think of such action."

"No, I don't mean that you're unpleased."

"Oh . . .?"

She twisted her body, seductively.

"Oh. Right. I'm afraid I'm a bit done in for the day," he said.

She neared him. "I could rub your shoulders, ease the tension of the day."

He hesitated, but said, "Yes. That might be nice."

She stepped around to the back of his chair, lowered his smoking jacket from his shoulders and chest, and then began rubbing his shoulders and chest with her strong hands. She hummed lightly, and before long, he was lost in a meditative doze. When his book tumbled from his lap to the rug, she scooted around and retrieved it from the floor. Turning back to him, she noticed the fine build of his chest, and after setting the book to the side, she carefully eased away the belt of his robe, letting the garment slide open to reveal his manhood surrounded in a thick casing of curls. His legs were parted, and she took delight in seeing her master's jewels resting pleasingly upon the seat cushion of the chair.

His naked body taunted her, reminded her of the many moments of intimate pleasure he had given to her. Nevertheless, she left well enough alone because with all her heart, she loved this man. She knew that as a simple servant, the most she would ever have of this man was the privilege of serving his needs, and that was by far good enough for her. Had he not hired her, she would most certainly have ended up in the service of the typical uncaring and brutal master; or worse, she would have become a woman of the streets—such was her desperation so many years ago. Loving him at a distance, serving his manly desires, and tending to his needs had given her comfort and self-respect. These were the only things she could ever ask of life.

She lowered herself to the floor, removed one of his slippers, and began rubbing the sole of his foot. When he groaned quietly from deep within his chest, she knew that he was lost in pleasure.

When he changed position, she glanced up and saw that his member was becoming engorged. She removed the other slipper and began to rub the sole of this foot. And before long, his member stood fully erect, even though he still appeared to be lost in slumber. Unable to resist, she slowly moved her hands up his legs, massaging gently as she worked her way up to his loins. She rubbed his muscular thighs, and still unable to refrain, she continued inching her way further up.

His member began to throb. A moment later, he groaned a little louder, and pressed his hips forward as though needing to be touched.

Taking that as a command, Miranda clasped his jewels in her hands and began gently massaging them, round and round. And when his member throbbed more insistently, she wrapped a hand around the staff and began slowly stroking it up and down.

His groans grew more vocal, his staff more erect. Then she moved up, rolling the palm of her hand around his crown.

His jaw slackened and he began breathing more heavily.

Rising to her knees, she continued stroking his staff, and placed her tongue on his crown, where she began licking around it. He began to move to the rhythm of her tongue, and before long, she enveloped his crown fully inside her mouth. She sucked lightly, swirling her tongue, and soon began suckling him more vigorously as she pumped her hand up and down the length of his staff.

"Ah," he said, his eyes still closed.

Miranda worked her delicate magic, until he gave way and began beating his hips more vigorously. She knew her master's needs well, and how to please him. She suckled more intensely, and at last, he exploded, expelling his seed into her mouth and letting out a loud manly groan. She savored the taste of the man she loved, the man she could never have.

She gently pulled her mouth from his crown and swallowed his seed, savoring her treat, while also letting her lips linger over the top of his crown. She licked the opening and between the folds, until she heard him speak.

"Oh, dear girl. You've spoiled me again," he said, his voice hoarse.

She rose up and smiled.

He bent down and kissed the top of her head. "You're a good girl. I bid you good night, Miranda."

# Chapter 15

Newland Archer arrived at the Chiverses's on Friday evening, and on Saturday went conscientiously through all the rites appertaining to a week-end at Highbank.

In the morning he had a spin in the ice-boat with his hostess and a few of the hardier guests; in the afternoon he "went over the farm" with Reggie, and listened, in the elaborately appointed stables, to long and impressive disquisitions on the horse; after tea he talked in a corner of the firelit hall with a young lady who had professed herself broken-hearted when his engagement was announced, but was now eager to tell him of her own matrimonial hopes; and finally, about midnight, he assisted in putting a goldfish in one visitor's bed, dressed up a burglar in the bath-room of a nervous aunt, and saw in the small hours by joining in a pillow-fight that ranged from the nurseries to the basement. But on Sunday after luncheon he borrowed a cutter, and drove over to Skuytercliff.

People had always been told that the house at Skuytercliff was an Italian villa. Those who had never been to Italy believed it; so did some who had. The house had been built by Mr. van der Luyden in his youth, on his return from the "grand tour," and in anticipation of his approaching marriage with Miss Louisa Dagonet. It was a large square wooden structure, with tongued and grooved walls painted pale green and white, a Corinthian portico, and fluted pilasters between the windows. From the high ground on which it stood a series of terraces bordered by balustrades and urns descended in the steel-engraving style to a small irregular lake with an asphalt edge overhung by rare weeping conifers. To the right and left, the famous weedless lawns studded with "specimen" trees (each of a different variety) rolled away to long ranges of grass crested with elaborate cast-iron ornaments; and below, in a hollow, lay the four-roomed stone house which the first Patroon had built on the land granted him in 1612.

Against the uniform sheet of snow and the greyish winter sky the Italian villa loomed up rather grimly; even in summer it kept its distance, and the boldest coleus bed had never ventured nearer than thirty feet from its awful front. Now, as Archer rang the bell, the long tinkle seemed to echo through a mausoleum; and the surprise of the butler who at length responded to the call was as great as though he had been summoned from his final sleep.

Happily Archer was of the family, and therefore, irregular though his arrival was, entitled to be informed that the Countess Olenska was out, having driven to afternoon service with Mrs. van der Luyden exactly three quarters of an hour earlier.

"Mr. van der Luyden," the butler continued, "is in, sir; but my impression is that he is either finishing his nap or else reading yesterday's Evening Post. I heard him say, sir, on his return from church this morning, that he intended to look through the Evening Post after luncheon; if you like, sir, I might go to the library door and listen—"

But Archer, thanking him, said that he would go and meet the ladies; and the butler, obviously relieved, closed the door on him majestically.

A groom took the cutter to the stables, and Archer struck through the park to the high-road. The village of Skuytercliff was only a mile and a half away, but he knew that Mrs. van der Luyden never walked, and that he must keep to the road to meet the carriage. Presently, however, coming down a foot-path that crossed the highway, he caught sight of a slight figure in a red cloak, with a big dog running ahead. He hurried forward, and Madame Olenska stopped short with a smile of welcome.

"Ah, you've come!" she said, and drew her hand from her muff.

The red cloak made her look gay and vivid, like the Ellen Mingott of old days; and he laughed as he took her hand, and answered: "I came to see what you were running away from."

Her face clouded over, but she answered: "Ah, well—you will see, presently."

The answer puzzled him. "Why—do you mean that you've been overtaken?"

She shrugged her shoulders, with a little movement like Nastasia's, and rejoined in a lighter tone: "Shall we walk on? I'm so cold after the sermon. And what does it matter, now you're here to protect me?"

The blood rose to his temples and he caught a fold of her cloak. "Ellen—what is it? You must tell me."

"Oh, presently—let's run a race first: my feet are freezing to the ground," she cried; and gathering up the cloak she fled away across the snow, the dog leaping about her with challenging barks. For a moment Archer stood watching, his gaze delighted by the flash of the red meteor against the snow; then he started after her, and they met, panting and laughing, at a wicket that led into the park.

She looked up at him and smiled. "I knew you'd come!"

"That shows you wanted me to," he returned, with a disproportionate joy in their nonsense. The white glitter of the trees filled the air with its own mysterious brightness, and as they walked on over the snow the ground seemed to sing under their feet.

"Where did you come from?" Madame Olenska asked.

He told her, and added: "It was because I got your note."

After a pause she said, with a just perceptible chill in her voice: "May asked you to take care of me."

"I didn't need any asking."

"You mean—I'm so evidently helpless and defenceless? What a poor thing you must all think me! But women here seem not—seem never to feel the need: any more than the blessed in heaven."

He lowered his voice to ask: "What sort of a need?"

"Ah, don't ask me! I don't speak your language," she retorted petulantly.

The answer smote him like a blow, and he stood still in the path, looking down at her.

"What did I come for, if I don't speak yours?"

"Oh, my friend—!" She laid her hand lightly on his arm, and he pleaded earnestly: "Ellen—why won't you tell me what's happened?"

She shrugged again. "Does anything ever happen in heaven?"

He was silent, and they walked on a few yards without exchanging a word. Finally she said: "I will tell you—but where, where, where? One can't be alone for a minute in that great seminary of a house, with all the doors wide open, and always a servant bringing tea, or a log for the fire, or the newspaper! Is there nowhere in an American house where one may be by one's self? You're so shy, and yet you're so public. I always feel as if I were in the convent again—or on the stage, before a dreadfully polite audience that never applauds."

"Ah, you don't like us!" Archer exclaimed.

They were walking past the house of the old Patroon, with its squat walls and small square windows compactly grouped about a central chimney. The shutters stood wide, and through one of the newly-washed windows Archer caught the light of a fire.

"Why—the house is open!" he said.

She stood still. "No; only for today, at least. I wanted to see it, and Mr. van der Luyden had the fire lit and the windows opened, so that we might stop there on the way back from church this morning." She ran up the steps and tried the door. "It's still unlocked—what luck! Come in and we can have a quiet talk. Mrs.

van der Luyden has driven over to see her old aunts at Rhinebeck and we shan't be missed at the house for another hour."

He followed her into the narrow passage. His spirits, which had dropped at her last words, rose with an irrational leap. The homely little house stood there, its panels and brasses shining in the firelight, as if magically created to receive them. A big bed of embers still gleamed in the kitchen chimney, under an iron pot hung from an ancient crane. Rush-bottomed arm-chairs faced each other across the tiled hearth, and rows of Delft plates stood on shelves against the walls. Archer stooped over and threw a log upon the embers.

Madame Olenska, dropping her cloak, sat down in one of the chairs. Archer leaned against the chimney and looked at her.

"You're laughing now; but when you wrote me you were unhappy," he said.

"Yes." She paused. "But I can't feel unhappy when you're here."

"I sha'n't be here long," he rejoined, his lips stiffening with the effort to say just so much and no more.

"No; I know. But I'm improvident: I live in the moment when I'm happy."

The words stole through him like a temptation, and to close his senses to it he moved away from the hearth and stood gazing out at the black tree-boles against the snow. But it was as if she too had shifted her place, and he still saw her, between himself and the trees, drooping over the fire with her indolent smile. Archer's heart was beating insubordinately. What if it were from him that she had been running away, and if she had waited to tell him so till they were here alone together in this secret room?

"Ellen, if I'm really a help to you—if you really wanted me to come—tell me what's wrong, tell me what it is you're running away from," he insisted.

He spoke without shifting his position, without even turning to look at her: if the thing was to happen, it was to happen in this way, with the whole width of the room between them, and his eyes still fixed on the outer snow.

For a long moment she was silent; and in that moment Archer imagined her, almost heard her, stealing up behind him to throw her light arms about his neck. He imagined a sublime sweetness from her touch, beautiful and loving words from her lips. She might first whisper in his ear the most precious term of endearment, "My love." He would not turn to her, but would savor her words, replaying them over and again in his mind. He would not turn to her, but would feel the touch of her delicate arms and hands resting gently against him as though she had been standing behind him all of his life. He would not turn to her, but would breathe in her fragrance, letting all of his senses be filled with only her. And when she would say, "Kiss me and tell me what you must feel inside," he would lose all sense of obligation, except to her.

Clasping her hand, he would bring it to his mouth and gently pressed his lips to her palm. Lingering, he would feel the distinctive lines that defined her. He would turn her hand over and kiss the back of it before turning around to face her. Gazing deeply into her eyes, he would feel the air catch in his lungs. Her beauty and magnificent expression would touch his innermost soul.

She would tilt her head upward with half-closed eyes. He knew she would expect a kiss, one so passionate that it would seem as if the fate of the world rested upon it. But somehow, almost incomprehensibly, he would be so captivated by her gaze that all he would be able to do was stand there helplessly, stock-still, staring at her. He would be unable to draw his eyes from hers. All rationality would be gone. And he would be able to see and understand and absorb only the foundation of her being.

Two souls had touched, merged, and united as one—a heavenly encounter.

While he waited, soul and body throbbing with the miracle to come, his eyes mechanically received the image of a heavily-coated man with his fur collar turned up who was advancing along the path to the house. The man was Julius Beaufort.

"Ah—!" Archer cried, bursting into a laugh.

Madame Olenska had sprung up and moved to his side, slipping her hand into his; but after a glance through the window her face paled and she shrank back.

"So that was it?" Archer said derisively.

"I didn't know he was here," Madame Olenska murmured. Her hand still clung to Archer's; but he drew away from her, and walking out into the passage threw open the door of the house.

"Hallo, Beaufort—this way! Madame Olenska was expecting you," he said.

During his journey back to New York the next morning, Archer relived with a fatiguing vividness his last moments at Skuytercliff.

Beaufort, though clearly annoyed at finding him with Madame Olenska, had, as usual, carried off the situation high-handedly. His way of ignoring people whose presence inconvenienced him actually gave them, if they were sensitive to it, a feeling of invisibility, of nonexistence. Archer, as the three strolled back through the park, was aware of this odd sense of disembodiment; and humbling as it was to his vanity it gave him the ghostly advantage of observing unobserved.

Beaufort had entered the little house with his usual easy assurance; but he could not smile away the vertical line between his eyes. It was fairly clear that Madame Olenska had not known that he was coming, though her words to Archer had hinted at the possibility; at any rate, she had evidently not told him where she was going when she left New York, and her unexplained departure had exasperated him. The ostensible reason of his appearance was the discovery, the very night before, of a "perfect little house," not in the market, which was really just the thing for her, but would be snapped up instantly if she didn't take it; and he was loud in mock-reproaches for the dance she had led him in running away just as he had found it.

"If only this new dodge for talking along a wire had been a little bit nearer perfection I might have told you all this from town, and been toasting my toes before the club fire at this minute, instead of tramping after you through the snow," he grumbled, disguising a real irritation under the pretence of it; and at this opening Madame Olenska twisted the talk away to the fantastic possibility that they might one day actually converse with each other from street to street, or even—incredible dream!—from one town to another. This struck from all three allusions to Edgar Poe and Jules Verne, and such platitudes as naturally rise to the lips of the most intelligent when they are talking against time, and dealing with a new invention in which it would seem ingenuous to believe too soon; and the question of the telephone carried them safely back to the big house.

Mrs. van der Luyden had not yet returned; and Archer took his leave and walked off to fetch the cutter, while Beaufort followed the Countess Olenska indoors. It was probable that, little as the van der Luydens encouraged unannounced visits, he could count on being asked to dine, and sent back to the station to catch the nine o'clock train; but more than that he would certainly not get, for it would be inconceivable to his hosts that a gentleman travelling without luggage should wish to spend the night, and distasteful to them to propose it to a person with whom they were on terms of such limited cordiality as Beaufort.

Beaufort knew all this, and must have foreseen it; and his taking the long journey for so small a reward gave the measure of his impatience. He was undeniably in pursuit of the Countess Olenska; and Beaufort had only one object in view in his pursuit of pretty women. His dull and childless home had long since palled on him; and in addition to more permanent consolations he was always in quest of amorous adventures in his own set. This was the man from whom Madame Olenska was avowedly flying: the question was whether she had fled because his importunities displeased her, or because she did not wholly trust herself to resist them; unless, indeed, all her talk of flight had been a blind, and her departure no more than a manoeuvre.

Archer did not really believe this. Little as he had actually seen of Madame Olenska, he was beginning to think that he could read her face, and if not her face, her voice; and both had betrayed annoyance, and even dismay, at Beaufort's sudden appearance. But, after all, if this were the case, was it not worse than if she had left New York for the express purpose of meeting him? If she had done that, she ceased to be an object of interest, she threw in her lot with the vulgarest of dissemblers: a woman engaged in a love affair with Beaufort "classed" herself irretrievably.

No, it was worse a thousand times if, judging Beaufort, and probably despising him, she was yet drawn to him by all that gave him an advantage over the other men about her: his habit of two continents and two societies, his familiar association with artists and actors and people generally in the world's eye, and his careless contempt for local prejudices. Beaufort was vulgar, he was uneducated, he was purse-proud; but the circumstances of his life, and a certain native shrewdness, made him better worth talking to than many men, morally and socially his betters, whose horizon was bounded by the Battery and the Central Park. How should any one coming from a wider world not feel the difference and be attracted by it?

Madame Olenska, in a burst of irritation, had said to Archer that he and she did not talk the same language; and the young man knew that in some respects this was true. But Beaufort understood every turn of her dialect, and spoke it fluently: his view of life, his tone, his attitude, were merely a coarser reflection of those revealed in Count Olenska's letter. This might seem to be to his disadvantage with Count Olenska's wife; but Archer was too intelligent to think that a young woman like Ellen Olenska would necessarily recoil from everything that reminded her of her past. She might believe herself wholly in revolt against it; but what had charmed her in it would still charm her, even though it were against her will.

Thus, with a painful impartiality, did the young man make out the case for Beaufort, and for Beaufort's victim. A longing to enlighten her was strong in him; and there were moments when he imagined that all she asked was to be enlightened.

That evening he unpacked his books from London. The box was full of things he had been waiting for impatiently; a new volume of Herbert Spencer, another collection of the prolific Alphonse Daudet's brilliant tales, and a novel called "Middlemarch," as to which there had lately been interesting things said in the reviews. He had declined three dinner invitations in favour of this feast; but though he turned the pages with the sensuous joy of the book-lover, he did not know what he was reading, and one book after another dropped from his hand. Suddenly, among them, he lit on a small volume of verse which he had ordered because the name had attracted him: "The House of Life." He took it up, and found himself plunged in an atmosphere unlike any he had ever breathed in books; so warm, so rich, and yet so ineffably tender, that it gave a new and haunting beauty to the most elementary of human passions. All through the night he pursued through those enchanted pages the vision of a woman who had the face of Ellen Olenska; but when he woke the next morning, and looked out at the brownstone houses across the street, and thought of his desk in Mr. Letterblair's office, and the family pew in Grace Church, his hour in the park of Skuytercliff became as far outside the pale of probability as the visions of the night.

"Mercy, how pale you look, Newland!" Janey commented over the coffee-cups at breakfast; and his mother added: "Newland, dear, I've noticed lately that you've been coughing; I do hope you're not letting yourself be overworked?" For it was the conviction of both ladies that, under the iron despotism of his senior partners, the young man's life was spent in the most exhausting professional labours—and he had never thought it necessary to undeceive them.

The next two or three days dragged by heavily. The taste of the usual was like cinders in his mouth, and there were moments when he felt as if he were being buried alive under his future. He heard nothing of the Countess Olenska, or of the perfect little house, and though he met Beaufort at the club they merely nodded at each other across the whist-tables. It was not till the fourth evening that he found a note awaiting him on his return home. "Come late tomorrow: I must explain to you. Ellen." These were the only words it contained.

The young man, who was dining out, thrust the note into his pocket, smiling a little at the Frenchness of the "to you." After dinner he went to a play; and it was not until his return home, after midnight, that he drew Madame Olenska's missive out again and re-read it slowly a number of times. There were several ways of answering it, and he gave considerable thought to each one during the watches of an agitated night. That on which, when morning came, he finally decided was to pitch some clothes into a portmanteau and jump on board a boat that was leaving that very afternoon for St. Augustine.

# Chapter 16

When Archer walked down the sandy main street of St. Augustine to the house which had been pointed out to him as Mr. Welland's, and saw May Welland standing under a magnolia with the sun in her hair, he wondered why he had waited so long to come.

Here was the truth, here was reality, here was the life that belonged to him; and he, who fancied himself so scornful of arbitrary restraints, had been afraid to break away from his desk because of what people might think of his stealing a holiday! He told himself to believe these thoughts because the truth was, he was running away this time. He was running away from his need for passion with the Countess and into the safe, loving arms of May. Perhaps in time, simple, frivolous, innocent May would become the passionate woman he so needed. She was young after all, so time would be her friend, while he would be her educationalist.

May's eyes widened when she saw him. Her first exclamation was: "Newland—has anything happened?" and it occurred to him that it would have been more "feminine" if she had instantly read in his eyes why he had come. But when he answered: "Yes—I found I had to see you," her happy blushes took the chill from her surprise, and he saw how easily he would be forgiven, and how soon even Mr. Letterblair's mild disapproval would be smiled away by a tolerant family.

Early as it was, the main street was no place for any but formal greetings, and Archer longed to be alone with May, and to pour out all his tenderness and his impatience. It still lacked an hour to the late Welland breakfast-time, and instead of asking him to come in she proposed that they should walk out to an old orange-garden beyond the town. She had just been for a row on the river, and the sun that netted the little waves with gold seemed to have caught her in its meshes. Across the warm brown of her cheek her blown hair glittered like silver wire; and her eyes too looked lighter, almost pale in their youthful limpidity. As she walked beside Archer with her long swinging gait her face wore the vacant serenity of a young marble athlete.

To Archer's strained nerves the vision was as soothing as the sight of the blue sky and the lazy river. They sat down on a bench under the orange-trees and he put his arm about her and kissed her. It was like drinking at a cold spring with the sun on it; but his pressure may have been more vehement than he had intended, for the blood rose to her face and she drew back as if he had startled her.

"What is it?" he asked, smiling; and she looked at him with surprise, and answered: "Nothing."

A slight embarrassment fell on them, and her hand slipped out of his. It was one of the only times that he had kissed her on the lips except for their fugitive embrace in the Beaufort conservatory, and he saw that she was disturbed, and shaken out of her cool boyish composure.

"Tell me what you do all day," he said, crossing his arms under his tilted-back head, and pushing his hat forward to screen the sun-dazzle. To let her talk about familiar and simple things was the easiest way of carrying on his own independent train of thought; and he sat listening to her simple chronicle of swimming, sailing and riding, varied by an occasional dance at the primitive inn when a man-of-war came in. A few pleasant people from Philadelphia and Baltimore were picknicking at the inn, and the Selfridge Merrys had come down for three weeks because Kate Merry had had bronchitis. They were planning to lay out a lawn tennis court on the sands; but no one but Kate and May had racquets, and most of the people had not even heard of the game.

All this kept her very busy, and she had not had time to do more than look at the little vellum book that Archer had sent her the week before (the "Sonnets from the Portuguese"); but she was learning by heart "How they brought the Good News from Ghent to Aix," because it was one of the first things he had ever read to her; and it amused her to be able to tell him that Kate Merry had never even heard of a poet called Robert Browning.

Presently she started up, exclaiming that they would be late for breakfast; and they hurried back to the tumble-down house with its pointless porch and unpruned hedge of plumbago and pink geraniums where the Wellands were installed for the winter. Mr. Welland's sensitive domesticity shrank from the discomforts of the slovenly southern hotel, and at immense expense, and in face of almost insuperable difficulties, Mrs. Welland was obliged, year after year, to improvise an establishment partly made up of discontented New York servants and partly drawn from the local African supply.

"The doctors want my husband to feel that he is in his own home; otherwise he would be so wretched that the climate would not do him any good," she explained, winter after winter, to the sympathising Philadelphians and Baltimoreans; and Mr. Welland, beaming across a breakfast table miraculously supplied with the most varied delicacies, was presently saying to Archer: "You see, my dear fellow, we camp—we literally camp. I tell my wife and May that I want to teach them how to rough it."

Mr. and Mrs. Welland had been as much surprised as their daughter by the young man's sudden arrival; but it had occurred to him to explain that he had felt himself on the verge of a nasty cold, and this seemed to Mr. Welland an all-sufficient reason for abandoning any duty.

"You can't be too careful, especially toward spring," he said, heaping his plate with straw-coloured griddle- cakes and drowning them in golden syrup. "If I'd only been as prudent at your age May would have been dancing at the Assemblies now, instead of spending her winters in a wilderness with an old invalid."

"Oh, but I love it here, Papa; you know I do. If only Newland could stay I should like it a thousand times better than New York."

"Newland must stay till he has quite thrown off his cold," said Mrs. Welland indulgently; and the young man laughed, and said he supposed there was such a thing as one's profession.

He managed, however, after an exchange of telegrams with the firm, to make his cold last a week; and it shed an ironic light on the situation to know that Mr. Letterblair's indulgence was partly due to the satisfactory way in which his brilliant young junior partner had settled the troublesome matter of the Olenska divorce. Mr. Letterblair had let Mrs. Welland know that Mr. Archer had "rendered an invaluable service" to the whole family, and that old Mrs. Manson Mingott had been particularly pleased; and one day when May had gone for a drive with her father in the only vehicle the place produced Mrs. Welland took occasion to touch on a topic which she always avoided in her daughter's presence.

"I'm afraid Ellen's ideas are not at all like ours. She was barely eighteen when Medora Manson took her back to Europe—you remember the excitement when she appeared in black at her coming-out ball? Another of Medora's fads—really this time it was almost prophetic! That must have been at least twelve years ago; and since then Ellen has never been to America. No wonder she is completely Europeanised."

"But European society is not given to divorce: Countess Olenska thought she would be conforming to American ideas in asking for her freedom." It was the first time that the young man had pronounced her name since he had left Skuytercliff, and he felt the colour rise to his cheek.

Mrs. Welland smiled compassionately. "That is just like the extraordinary things that foreigners invent about us. They think we dine at two o'clock and countenance divorce! That is why it seems to me so foolish to entertain them when they come to New

York. They accept our hospitality, and then they go home and repeat the same stupid stories."

Archer made no comment on this, and Mrs. Welland continued: "But we do most thoroughly appreciate your persuading Ellen to give up the idea. Her grandmother and her uncle Lovell could do nothing with her; both of them have written that her changing her mind was entirely due to your influence—in fact she said so to her grandmother. She has an unbounded admiration for you. Poor Ellen—she was always a wayward child. I wonder what her fate will be?"

"What we've all contrived to make it," he felt like answering. "If you'd all of you rather she should be Beaufort's mistress than some decent fellow's wife you've certainly gone the right way about it." Upon recalling Beaufort's intrusion upon his privacy with the Countess, Newland felt a deep-rooted anger. But if the man was truly Ellen's paramour, then it was fortuitous that he had appeared before Newland professed his feelings to her.

He wondered what Mrs. Welland would have said if he had uttered the words instead of merely thinking them. He could picture the sudden decomposure of her firm placid features, to which a lifelong mastery over trifles had given an air of factitious authority. Traces still lingered on them of a fresh beauty like her daughter's; and he asked himself if May's face was doomed to thicken into the same middle-aged image of invincible innocence.

Ah, no, he did not want May to have that kind of innocence, the innocence that seals the mind against imagination and the heart against experience!

"I verily believe," Mrs. Welland continued, "that if the horrible business had come out in the newspapers it would have been my husband's death-blow. I don't know any of the details; I only ask not to, as I told poor Ellen when she tried to talk to me about it. Having an invalid to care for, I have to keep my mind bright and happy. But Mr. Welland was terribly upset; he had a slight temperature every morning while we were waiting to hear what had been decided. It was the horror of his girl's learning that such things were possible—but of course, dear Newland, you felt that too. We all knew that you were thinking of May."

"I'm always thinking of May," the young man rejoined, rising to cut short the conversation.

He had meant to seize the opportunity of his private talk with Mrs. Welland to urge her to advance the date of his marriage. But he could think of no arguments that would move her, and with a sense of relief he saw Mr. Welland and May driving up to the door.

His only hope was to plead again with May, and on the day before his departure he walked with her to the ruinous garden of the Spanish Mission. The background lent itself to allusions to European scenes; and May, who was looking her loveliest under a wide-brimmed hat that cast a shadow of mystery over her too-clear eyes, kindled into eagerness as he spoke of Granada and the Alhambra.

"We might be seeing it all this spring—even the Easter ceremonies at Seville," he urged, exaggerating his demands in the hope of a larger concession.

"Easter in Seville? And it will be Lent next week!" she laughed.

"Why shouldn't we be married in Lent?" he rejoined; but she looked so shocked that he saw his mistake.

"Of course I didn't mean that, dearest; but soon after Easter—so that we could sail at the end of April. I know I could arrange it at the office."

She smiled dreamily upon the possibility; but he perceived that to dream of it sufficed her. It was like hearing him read aloud out of his poetry books the beautiful things that could not possibly happen in real life.

"Oh, do go on, Newland; I do love your descriptions."

"But why should they be only descriptions? Why shouldn't we make them real?"

"We shall, dearest, of course; next year." Her voice lingered over it.

"Don't you want them to be real sooner? Can't I persuade you to break away now?"

She bowed her head, vanishing from him under her conniving hat-brim.

"Why should we dream away another year? Look at me, dear! Don't you understand how I want you for my wife?"

For a moment she remained motionless; then she raised on him eyes of such despairing dearness that he half-released her waist from his hold. But suddenly her look changed and deepened inscrutably. "I'm not sure if I DO understand," she said. "Is it—is it because you're not certain of continuing to care for me?"

Archer sprang up from his seat. "My God—perhaps—I don't know," he broke out angrily.

May Welland rose also; as they faced each other she seemed to grow in womanly stature and dignity. Both were silent for a moment, as if dismayed by the unforeseen trend of their words: then she said in a low voice: "If that is it—is there some one else?"

"Some one else—between you and me?" He echoed her words slowly, as though they were only half- intelligible and he wanted time to repeat the question to himself. She seemed to catch the uncertainty of his voice, for she went on in a deepening tone: "Let us talk frankly, Newland. Sometimes I've felt a difference in you; especially since our engagement has been announced."

"Dear—what madness!" he recovered himself to exclaim.

She met his protest with a faint smile. "If it is, it won't hurt us to talk about it." She paused, and added, lifting her head with one of her noble movements: "Or even if it's true: why shouldn't we speak of it? You might so easily have made a mistake."

He lowered his head, staring at the black leaf-pattern on the sunny path at their feet. "Mistakes are always easy to make; but if I had made one of the kind you suggest, is it likely that I should be imploring you to hasten our marriage?"

She looked downward too, disturbing the pattern with the point of her sunshade while she struggled for expression. "Yes," she said at length. "You might want—once for all—to settle the question: it's one way."

Her quiet lucidity startled him, but did not mislead him into thinking her insensible. Under her hat-brim he saw the pallor of her profile, and a slight tremor of the nostril above her resolutely steadied lips.

"Well—?" he questioned, sitting down on the bench, and looking up at her with a frown that he tried to make playful.

She dropped back into her seat and went on: "You mustn't think that a girl knows as little as her parents imagine. One hears and one notices—one has one's feelings and ideas. And of course, long before you told me that you cared for me, I'd known that there was some one else you were interested in; every one was talking about it two years ago at Newport. And once I saw you sitting together on the verandah at a dance—and when she came back into the house her face was sad, and I felt sorry for her; I remembered it afterward, when we were engaged."

Her voice had sunk almost to a whisper, and she sat clasping and unclasping her hands about the handle of her sunshade. The young man laid his upon them with a gentle pressure; his heart dilated with an inexpressible relief.

"My dear child—was THAT it? If you only knew the truth!"

She raised her head quickly. "Then there is a truth I don't know?"

He kept his hand over hers. "I meant, the truth about the old story you speak of."

"But that's what I want to know, Newland—what I ought to know. I couldn't have my happiness made out of a wrong—an unfairness—to somebody else. And I want to believe that it would be the same with you. What sort of a life could we build on such foundations?"

Her face had taken on a look of such tragic courage that he felt like bowing himself down at her feet. "I've wanted to say this for a long time," she went on. "I've wanted to tell you that, when two people really love each other, I understand that there may be situations which make it right that they should—should go against public opinion. And if you feel yourself in any way pledged ... pledged to the person we've spoken of ... and if there is any way ... any way in which you can fulfill your pledge ... even by her getting a divorce ... Newland, don't give her up because of me!"

His surprise at discovering that her fears had fastened upon an episode so remote and so completely of the past as his love-affair with Mrs. Thorley Rushworth gave way to wonder at the generosity of her view. There was something superhuman in an attitude so recklessly unorthodox, and if other problems had not pressed on him he would have been lost in wonder at the prodigy of the Wellands' daughter urging him to marry his former mistress. But he was still dizzy with the glimpse of the precipice they had skirted, and full of a new awe at the mystery of young-girlhood.

For a moment he could not speak; then he said: "There is no pledge—no obligation whatever—of the kind you think. Such cases don't always—present themselves quite as simply as ... But that's no matter ... I love your generosity, because I feel as you do about those things ... I feel that each case must be judged individually, on its own merits ... irrespective of stupid conventionalities ... I mean, each woman's right to her liberty—" He pulled himself up, startled by the turn his thoughts had taken, and went on, looking at her with a smile: "Since you understand so many things, dearest, can't you go a little farther, and understand the uselessness of our submitting to another form of the same foolish conventionalities? If there's no one and nothing between us, isn't that an argument for marrying quickly, rather than for more delay?"

She flushed with joy and lifted her face to his; as he bent to it he saw that her eyes were full of happy tears.

"I want to marry you, May," he said. "Is that so unreasonable?"

"No, dearest. We shall."

"I want to be with you, as man and wife."

"Newland, if that is all, then I think I might have the solution that can satisfy both our needs."

He looked at the strange expression on her face—a sly grin, eyelids narrowed sultrily. Her eyes were no longer filled with girlish tears, but with a womanly look of lust.

"May? What ever are you thinking?"

"Newland, the night we announced our engagement, you brought me great joy and satisfaction in the conservatory. You remember, when you kissed me. And not just on the lips, but . . ." She did not have to remind him of the places on her body that he had kissed; his recollection of that night was vivid.

Newland was surprised by her apparent change of heart and now did not want to pressure her. "But what about your desire to remain a virgin, my dear?" he said.

She smiled wickedly. "There are other ways a man and a woman can gain satisfaction."

"You intrigue me."

She glanced around, her eyes resting on a potting shed. "I mean to intrigue you, Newland." She rose and held her hand to his. "Shall we?"

Newland allowed her to lead him to the shed. She closed the door and locked it, and then opened a small leather pouch she wore around her wrist. "I was in the pharmacy the other day with Mother," she said. "When she was busy shopping for tonics, I stole away to the opposite end of the shop and found this rather interesting gel. I think it allows certain male appendages to glide freely in other places rather easily. Shall we try it?" She held the tube to him.

He studied the ointment and glanced back at her. "You don't mean?"

"Yes, Newland. If you enter the forbidden door, my virginity will remain intact. I will still be pure on our wedding night." She smiled at him as though she were a mature woman.

"Do you desire this?"

"I must admit, though I am ashamed somewhat to do so, that I have found one or two of the local servants' French magazines. They're quite a bit different from anything one could purchase at the shops I frequent. And much more ... shall we say, instructive?"

He nodded, beginning to fully understand her intentions. What a delightful surprise this was to him. All along, he had believed she was only an innocent and naïve young woman, but all the while, she was much worldlier than he could ever have imagined.

"You see," she said. "There's so much to learn about life, Newland. I didn't think it would matter so much if I made a study of ... well, relations between men and women."

"No, of course not. Women should have their independence, their liberties." And at hearing himself repeat the words aloud, he began to feel quite excited over May's newest proposition. It was one matter for him to please her by touching and kissing her intimate femininity, but to make love to her and satisfy his needs without destroying her chastity was quite another matter— an exhilarating matter. This was the last thing he expected her to propose.

"I may not be so experienced as others..." She looked at him coyly. "As my cousin, Ellen, for instance. For she is . . ."

Newland was unseated at hearing May mention Ellen's name. In his mind, he might have made the comparison, but never would have expected May to desire to emulate Ellen's worldliness, not yet. "My dear, your cousin is—"

"I know—a married woman."

"It may be more than just the idea of being married. What you are proposing is quite intimate." He did not want to miss this splendid opportunity, but he also did not want to hurt or disillusion May either. "Perhaps this is much more difficult than you might imagine, with your being so inexperienced, my dear."

"Newland," she said, with a faux frown that appeared to be nothing more than a playful pout. "I am quite prepared, as I do have my nursemaid, who I've … well, if I must admit, I've consulted with." She placed her arm on his shoulder, leaned in confidentially, and whispered in his ear. "I have practiced with her, Newland. And I am now ready for you."

He slowly nodded his head. "Ah, I see."

"Enough talk," May said. She began to undress. The sight of her youthful and seductive body overwhelmed Newland's senses. Any more thoughts of the Countess soon vanished.

"You mustn't keep me waiting," May said once she was fully unclothed, standing before him as his very own Aphrodite.

Newland quickly ripped the clothes from his body, careful to place them upon a shelf to avoid the dirt on the floors. "There," he said, pointing toward an outdoor recliner. Then he led her to it. He took her into his arms, feeling the naked flesh of her body against his, and then kissed her lips tenderly. He felt his erection growing and beginning to throb against her pelvis. He feared the worst. He feared that after this exploration, she might turn him away. He drew in a long breath, trying to decide what he should do, but she would not allow him any further thought.

"Enter me now," she said, her voice hoarse and intense.

Knowing that this was her idea, he ventured forward without any further discussion. He turned her around so that she faced the recliner. She placed her hands and upper body against the chair for support and wiggled her sweet derrière at him.

"We can't be terribly long, dear. Breakfast will be soon." She glanced over her shoulder, narrowed her eyes, and slowly slid her tongue across her lower lip.

With that, he pulled her hips toward him. He began to massage her breasts with one of his hands, and with the other, he quickly found his way to her intimate folds, where he found that she was indeed deluged with passion. He slid his hands through her wet, hot passion, and circled her pearl relentlessly until she danced with irresistible desire.

"Oh, Newland," she whispered between moans. "I'm, I'm . . ."

He kissed her neck, slowly licking his tongue along the length of its delicate lines. "Are you sure, sweetness?" he whispered.

"Oh, yes, Newland, yes. Please make haste.

He withdrew and applied the viscous ointment to himself, and then slid a loving hand along her back anatomy doing the same to her. With his other hand, he began massaging her pearl again, and then he tentatively pressed his member between the tight crease of her bottom cheeks. She was exceedingly aroused by his touch, as her body trembled and rippled the further he advanced. And the moment his member touched her back entrance, she shrieked with lubricious pleasure. Encouraged by her cries of desire, he gently, but with some force probed his rampant, pulsing member more intently between her inner fold.

"Oh, Newland, it feels so . . ."

"Shall I stop?"

"Don't you dare! If you do, I shall forever be disappointed in you, Newland. This is gorgeous, so delicious."

He bumped his pulsating cock to her door, feeling the ointment slide easily over her anatomy. Then with his hand, he immersed the orchid's cream into the mix, lathering her with a healthy and fragrant wetness.

"Oh," she moaned, desperately, desirously. "Now, Newland. Now."

Slowly, he pushed, breaking through the barrier.

She gasped.

He couldn't stop, not now. He encircled an arm around her hips and pulled her closer as he slowly pushed inside her forbidden and exotic door of astounding passion, so soft, so tight.

"Oh," she said. "Oh, my, I . . ."

"Are you all right, my dear?" he said, his words only sounding above a breath.

"Yes," she hissed. "Glorious."

And upon hearing her words, feeling her desire, he began to thrust in and out of her tight cavern, feeling the ultimate squeeze of a man's desire. He was transported—no longer in control of his mind or senses. His carnal cravings were in complete control. There was no stopping, no beginning, no end. It just was—my God—blissful unwed carnal knowledge. His darling, May, had taken him into another universe and time. Minutes ago, she was only a girl of whom he was unsure; now she was the woman he very much desired.

Then to his heightened surprise, she grasped a hand between her legs and clasped his baubles in her hands. She began to massage, rolling his prize between her fingers.

"May, my dear, May," he said, gasping. This was more heavenly than any man could ever expect to have.

He felt his jewels tighten. His member became more erect. He was at the point where he could not return. But he wanted her to finish with him, the ultimate desire of lovers. He circled a finger around her pearl, stroking her, heightening her arousal, until her body finally tightened. He knew that she was cresting, and so he let loose. He let his body take over as nature had so intended. Her heart, his soul, was untamed. He beat harder, faster, more intensely, until at last, in a hard thrust, he once and for all exploded, breaking the bars that imprison a man's soul. He spilled his seed, while she overflowed, her body thrusting in perfect time as though they were parts of a celestial clock moving in perfect synchronization. As one, they smoldered in a vastness beyond measure.

"My heavens, May. How you enthrall me." He withdrew from her cavity, which was still teasing and nipping at his member. He turned her and kissed her. How she excited him. And it was right then that he saw glimpses of his future, a wonderful future.

"May, my darling," he said, and then he grasped her hand so that they could sit together a moment before they departed. "If there is nothing between us, isn't that an argument for marrying quickly, rather than for more delay? You must know how I feel. How I need you so desperately."

"I have pleased you, Newland?"

"Of course, my dearest."

"And you have pleased me," she said. "My body seems to have been built for such activities."

But in another moment, perhaps in her next breath, she seemed to have descended from her womanly eminence to helpless and timorous girlhood; and he understood that her courage and initiative were all for others, and that she had none for herself. That she had allowed their present pleasure for him more so than herself. It was evident that the effort of speaking and lovemaking had been much greater than her studied composure betrayed, and that at his first word of reassurance she had dropped back into the usual, as a too-adventurous child takes refuge in its mother's arms.

Archer had no heart to go on pleading with her; he was too much disappointed at the vanishing of the new being who had cast that one deep look at him from her transparent eyes. That she had ascended to a woman only to drop back to a child. May seemed to be aware of his disappointment, but without knowing how to alleviate it; and they stood up and walked silently home.

# Chapter 17

"Your cousin the Countess called on mother while you were away," Janey Archer announced to her brother on the evening of his return.

The young man, who was dining alone with his mother and sister, glanced up in surprise and saw Mrs. Archer's gaze demurely bent on her plate. Mrs. Archer did not regard her seclusion from the world as a reason for being forgotten by it; and Newland guessed that she was slightly annoyed that he should be surprised by Madame Olenska's visit.

"She had on a black velvet polonaise with jet buttons, and a tiny green monkey muff; I never saw her so stylishly dressed," Janey continued. "She came alone, early on Sunday afternoon; luckily the fire was lit in the drawing-room. She had one of those new card- cases. She said she wanted to know us because you'd been so good to her."

Newland laughed. "Madame Olenska always takes that tone about her friends. She's very happy at being among her own people again."

"Yes, so she told us," said Mrs. Archer. "I must say she seems thankful to be here."

"I hope you liked her, mother."

Mrs. Archer drew her lips together. "She certainly lays herself out to please, even when she is calling on an old lady."

"Mother doesn't think her simple," Janey interjected, her eyes screwed upon her brother's face.

"It's just my old-fashioned feeling; dear May is my ideal," said Mrs. Archer.

"Ah," said her son, "they're not alike."

Archer had left St. Augustine charged with many messages for old Mrs. Mingott; and a day or two after his return to town he called on her.

The old lady received him with unusual warmth; she was grateful to him for persuading the Countess Olenska to give up the idea of a divorce; and when he told her that he had deserted the office without leave, and rushed down to St. Augustine simply because he wanted to see May, she gave an adipose chuckle and patted his knee with her puff-ball hand.

"Ah, ah—so you kicked over the traces, did you? And I suppose Augusta and Welland pulled long faces, and behaved as if the end of the world had come? But little May—she knew better, I'll be bound?"

"I hoped she did; but after all she wouldn't agree to what I'd gone down to ask for."

"Wouldn't she indeed? And what was that?"

"I wanted to get her to promise that we should be married in April. What's the use of our wasting another year?"

Mrs. Manson Mingott screwed up her little mouth into a grimace of mimic prudery and twinkled at him through malicious lids. "'Ask Mamma,' I suppose—the usual story. Ah, these Mingotts—all alike! Born in a rut, and you can't root 'em out of it. When I built this house you'd have thought I was moving to California! Nobody ever HAD built above Fortieth Street—no, says I, nor above the Battery either, before Christopher Columbus discovered America. No, no; not one of them wants to be different; they're as scared of it as the small-pox. Ah, my dear Mr. Archer, I thank my stars I'm nothing but a vulgar Spicer; but there's not one of my own children that takes after me but my little Ellen." She broke off, still twinkling at him, and asked, with the casual irrelevance of old age: "Now, why in the world didn't you marry my little Ellen?"

Archer laughed. "For one thing, she wasn't there to be married."

"No—to be sure; more's the pity. And now it's too late; her life is finished." She spoke with the cold- blooded complacency of the aged throwing earth into the grave of young hopes. The young man's heart grew chill, and he said hurriedly: "Can't I persuade you to use your influence with the Wellands, Mrs. Mingott? I wasn't made for long engagements."

Old Catherine beamed on him approvingly. "No; I can see that. You've got a quick eye. When you were a little boy I've no doubt you liked to be helped first." She threw back her head with a laugh that made her chins ripple like little waves. "Ah, here's my Ellen now!" she exclaimed, as the portieres parted behind her.

Madame Olenska came forward with a smile. Her face looked vivid and happy, and she held out her hand gaily to Archer while she stooped to her grandmother's kiss.

"I was just saying to him, my dear: `Now, why didn't you marry my little Ellen?'"

Madame Olenska looked at Archer, still smiling. "And what did he answer?"

"Oh, my darling, I leave you to find that out! He's been down to Florida to see his sweetheart."

"Yes, I know." She still looked at him. "I went to see your mother, to ask where you'd gone. I sent a note that you never answered, and I was afraid you were ill."

He muttered something about leaving unexpectedly, in a great hurry, and having intended to write to her from St. Augustine.

"And of course once you were there you never thought of me again!" She continued to beam on him with a gaiety that might have been a studied assumption of indifference.

"If she still needs me, she's determined not to let me see it," he thought, stung by her manner. He wanted to thank her for having been to see his mother, but under the ancestress's malicious eye he felt himself tongue- tied and constrained.

"Look at him—in such hot haste to get married that he took French leave and rushed down to implore the silly girl on his knees! That's something like a lover—that's the way handsome Bob Spicer carried off my poor mother; and then got tired of her before I was weaned—though they only had to wait eight months for me! But there—you're not a Spicer, young man; luckily for you and for May. It's only my poor Ellen that has kept any of their wicked blood; the rest of them are all model Mingotts," cried the old lady scornfully.

Archer was aware that Madame Olenska, who had seated herself at her grandmother's side, was still thoughtfully scrutinising him. The gaiety had faded from her eyes, and she said with great gentleness: "Surely, Granny, we can persuade them between us to do as he wishes."

Archer rose to go, and as his hand met Madame Olenska's he felt that she was waiting for him to make some allusion to her unanswered letter.

"When can I see you?" he asked, as she walked with him to the door of the room.

"Whenever you like; but it must be soon if you want to see the little house again. I am moving next week."

A pang shot through him at the memory of his lamplit hours in the low-studded drawing-room. Few as they had been, they were thick with memories.

"Tomorrow evening?"

She nodded. "Tomorrow; yes; but early. I'm going out."

The next day was a Sunday, and if she were "going out" on a Sunday evening it could, of course, be only to Mrs. Lemuel Struthers's. He felt a slight movement of annoyance, not so much at her going there (for he rather liked her going where she pleased in spite of the van der Luydens), but because it was the kind of house at which she was sure to meet Beaufort, where she must have known beforehand that she would meet him—and where she was probably going for that purpose.

"Very well; tomorrow evening," he repeated, inwardly resolved that he would not go early, and that by reaching her door late he would either prevent her from going to Mrs. Struthers's, or else arrive after she had started—which, all things considered, would no doubt be the simplest solution.

It was only half-past eight, after all, when he rang the bell under the wisteria; not as late as he had intended by half an hour—but a singular restlessness had driven him to her door. He reflected, however, that Mrs. Struthers's Sunday evenings were not like a ball, and that her guests, as if to minimise their delinquency, usually went early.

The one thing he had not counted on, in entering Madame Olenska's hall, was to find hats and overcoats there. Why had she bidden him to come early if she was having people to dine? On a closer inspection of the garments besides which Nastasia was laying his own, his resentment gave way to curiosity. The overcoats were in fact the very strangest he had ever seen under a polite roof; and it took but a glance to assure himself that neither of them belonged to Julius Beaufort. One was a shaggy yellow ulster of "reach-me- down" cut, the other a very old and rusty cloak with a cape—something like what the French called a "Macfarlane." This garment, which appeared to be made for a person of prodigious size, had evidently seen long and hard wear, and its greenish-black folds gave out a moist sawdusty smell suggestive of prolonged sessions against bar-room walls. On it lay a ragged grey scarf and an odd felt hat of semiclerical shape.

Archer raised his eyebrows enquiringly at Nastasia, who raised hers in return, and then pressed a finger to her lips to quiet him. She tiptoed to the drawing room doors and peered through the crack between them. Then she turned back to Newland and beckoned him to follow.

Newland inched forward and looked through the crack, and what he saw astounded him.

"Bacchanalia," she said.

Newland glanced over his shoulder at her. "You mean an orgy!"

Nastasia started for the door handle, but Newland pushed her hand away. "No," he whispered, and then dismissed her with a wave. When she disappeared down the hallway and passed through a door, he looked again inside the room. He had not seen the Countess in there, but that didn't mean she wasn't present, writhing on the floors or furniture, stark naked like the rest of them.

A woman laughed loudly. Newland found it disquieting. Then the woman rose from the carpet and stood in front of the blazing fire, her back toward him. All he could see was her naked derrière and her long, faded silver hair running down the length of her back. He had not been able to see her face, and he could not be certain, but had the impression that the woman must be of some considerable age, although her physique was quite extraordinary.

Two men rose up, the first of prodigious size, and the second leaner. The larger man moved in front of the woman, grasped her waist with his hands, and pulled her near. She didn't resist, but pressed up against him willingly. Then he raised one of her legs and placed it on top of a chair so that her legs were spread wide open.

The leaner man approached the woman from behind and began sliding his hands along her back and down to her derrière. The larger man lowered his face to the woman's full breasts and took one into his mouth. With his other hand, he slid it to her loins and slowly began raising his hand until he was touching her intimate form.

The woman moaned hoarsely as she rolled her head back, clearly lost in the heat.

The thinner man slid a hand between her legs and began touching her intimate form. The larger man moved his hand forward and continued massaging, undoubtedly caressing and teasing her pearl. From Newland's perspective, he was able to see the thin man slide one, two, and then three fingers inside of the woman's vessel as she thrust her hips up and back to allow him more open access.

The larger man rose from her breast and began stroking his large, erect cock. Then he encouraged the woman to lower her head and touch his member with her mouth. She licked the crown of his staff as he continued to stroke, and some moments later, he stopped stroking, and she took the crown inside her mouth. He grasped her shoulders and slowly began grinding his hips so that he stroked his member inside her mouth, some strokes dipping deeper, others just teasing her lips.

The thin man took his enormous cock in his hand and stroked the length of it a few times, clearly preparing himself. He neared the woman from behind and slowly slid his cock through the length of her feminine form. He pulled back, and on his next stroke, he plunged his cock inside her sheath.

The woman withdrew the cock in her mouth and cried with pleasure, "Ah-h. My God! You're good."

The thin man grasped her hips and began moving inside her with mounting vigor, while also beginning to groan lustfully.

The woman moaned louder and with more enthusiasm, and then took the larger man's cock back inside her mouth. Together, the three moved as one, each vocally expressing their inflamed passion, all moving with a sublime primal thirst.

Newland was glad the Countess was nowhere in sight; his jealousy over her would undoubtedly have prevented him from sharing her with the others. However, watching this passionate scene unfold, he found himself becoming more aroused by the idea of joining in their carnal games Then it occurred to him that perhaps he should go in search of the Countess. He glanced away from the crack in the door and down the hallway. Ellen was likely in her private chambers, he thought.

Then a loud roar echoed from inside the parlor. Newland quickly turned back and peered through the crack just in time to witness the multiple orgasmic climaxes of all three participants, their train thrusting violently in the final moments of their release. The woman's entire body undulated and convulsed and the men thrust deep as they spilled their seed.

From down the hallway, a door opened and closed. Newland glanced back. It was Nastasia again. Only this time, she was chattering away unintelligibly, while waving her arms.

Newland stepped back as she muscled her way toward the door. She opened it and spoke to the three inside the room, and then she closed the door and stood in front of it. Baffled, Newland waited. And some minutes later, with a fatalistic "Gia!" as she threw open the drawing-room door, Nastasia stepped out of the way and permitted Newland to enter. The three individuals were fully clothed. The young man saw at once that his hostess was as he had previously determined not in the room, and that she had not entered the parlor from an adjoining door; and then, with little surprise, he discovered not another lady standing by the fire, but the lady he had witnessed having wild sex with the two men. This lady, who was long, lean and loosely put together, was clad in raiment intricately looped and fringed, with plaids and stripes and bands of plain colour disposed in a design to which the clue seemed missing. Her hair, which had tried to turn white and only succeeded in fading, was surmounted by a Spanish comb and black lace scarf, and silk mittens, visibly darned, covered her rheumatic hands.

Beside her, in a cloud of cigar-smoke, stood the owners of the two overcoats, both in morning clothes that they had evidently not taken off since morning, except for this saturnalia that Newland had voyeuristically witnessed. In one of the two, the thinner man, Archer, to his surprise, recognised Ned Winsett; the other and older, who was unknown to him, and whose gigantic frame declared him to be the wearer of the "Macfarlane," had a feebly leonine head with crumpled grey hair, and moved his arms with large pawing gestures, as though he were distributing lay blessings to a kneeling multitude.

These three persons stood together on the hearth- rug, with their eyes now fixed on an extraordinarily large bouquet of crimson roses, with a knot of purple pansies at their base, that lay on the sofa where Madame Olenska usually sat. It was as if they had not noticed the flowers until now, or perhaps they were only acting coy, as Nastasia had interrupted their play, putting an end to their fun. Little did they realize that Newland had seen the highlights of the affair, although it was not a matter he would speak openly of to them.

"What they must have cost at this season—though of course it's the sentiment one cares about!" the lady was saying in a sighing staccato as Archer came in.

When Newland cleared his throat, the three turned with surprise at his appearance, and the lady, advancing, held out her hand.

"Dear Mr. Archer—almost my cousin Newland!" she said. "I am the Marchioness Manson."

Archer bowed, and she continued: "My Ellen has taken me in for a few days. I came from Cuba, where I have been spending the winter with Spanish friends—such delightful distinguished people: the highest nobility of old Castile—how I wish you could know them! But I was called away by our dear great friend here, Dr. Carver. You don't know Dr. Agathon Carver, founder of the Valley of Love Community?"

Dr. Carver inclined his leonine head, and the Marchioness continued: "Ah, New York—New York—how little the life of the spirit has reached it! But I see you do know Mr. Winsett."

"Oh, yes—I reached him some time ago; but not by that route," Winsett said with his dry smile.

The Marchioness shook her head reprovingly. "How do you know, Mr. Winsett? The spirit bloweth where it listeth."

"List—oh, list!" interjected Dr. Carver in a stentorian murmur.

"But do sit down, Mr. Archer. We four have been having a delightful little dinner together, and my child has gone up to dress. She expects you; she will be down in a moment. We were just admiring these marvellous flowers, which will surprise her when she reappears."

Winsett remained on his feet. "I'm afraid I must be off. Please tell Madame Olenska that we shall all feel lost when she abandons our street. This house has been an oasis."

"Ah, but she won't abandon YOU. Poetry and art are the breath of life to her. It IS poetry you write, Mr. Winsett?"

"Well, no; but I sometimes read it," said Winsett, including the group in a general nod and slipping out of the room.

"A caustic spirit—un peu sauvage. But so witty; Dr. Carver, you DO think him witty?"

"I never think of wit," said Dr. Carver severely.

"Ah—ah—you never think of wit! How merciless he is to us weak mortals, Mr. Archer! But he lives only in the life of the spirit; and tonight he is mentally preparing the lecture he is to deliver presently at Mrs. Blenker's. Dr. Carver, would there be time, before you start for the Blenkers' to explain to Mr. Archer your illuminating discovery of the Direct Contact? But no; I see it is nearly nine o'clock, and we have no right to detain you while so many are waiting for your message."

Dr. Carver looked slightly disappointed at this conclusion, but, having compared his ponderous gold time-piece with Madame Olenska's little travelling-clock, he reluctantly gathered up his mighty limbs for departure.

"I shall see you later, dear friend?" he suggested to the Marchioness, who replied with a smile: "As soon as Ellen's carriage comes I will join you; I do hope the lecture won't have begun."

Dr. Carver looked thoughtfully at Archer. "Perhaps, if this young gentleman is interested in my experiences, Mrs. Blenker might allow you to bring him with you?"

"Oh, dear friend, if it were possible—I am sure she would be too happy. But I fear my Ellen counts on Mr. Archer herself."

"That," said Dr. Carver, "is unfortunate—but here is my card." He handed it to Archer, who read on it, in Gothic characters:

**Agathon Carver**

**The Valley of Love**

**Kittasquattamy, N. Y.**

Dr. Carver bowed himself out, and Mrs. Manson, with a sigh that might have been either of regret or relief, again waved Archer to a seat.

"Ellen will be down in a moment; and before she comes, I am so glad of this quiet moment with you."

Archer murmured his pleasure at their meeting, and the Marchioness continued, in her low sighing accents: "I know everything, dear Mr. Archer—my child has told me all you have done for her. Your wise advice: your courageous firmness—thank heaven it was not too late!"

The young man listened with considerable embarrassment. Was there any one, he wondered, to whom Madame Olenska had not proclaimed his intervention in her private affairs?

"Madame Olenska exaggerates; I simply gave her a legal opinion, as she asked me to."

"Ah, but in doing it—in doing it you were the unconscious instrument of—of—what word have we moderns for Providence, Mr. Archer?" cried the lady, tilting her head on one side and drooping her lids mysteriously. "Little did you know that at that very moment I was being appealed to: being approached, in fact—from the other side of the Atlantic!"

She glanced over her shoulder, as though fearful of being overheard, and then, drawing her chair nearer, and raising a tiny ivory fan to her lips, breathed behind it: "By the Count himself—my poor, mad, foolish Olenska; who asks only to take her back on her own terms."

"Good God!" Archer exclaimed, springing up.

"You are horrified? Yes, of course; I understand. I don't defend poor Stanislas, though he has always called me his best friend. He does not defend himself—he casts himself at her feet: in my person." She tapped her emaciated bosom. "I have his letter here."

"A letter?—Has Madame Olenska seen it?" Archer stammered, his brain whirling with the shock of the announcement.

The Marchioness Manson shook her head softly. "Time—time; I must have time. I know my Ellen—haughty, intractable; shall I say, just a shade unforgiving?"

"But, good heavens, to forgive is one thing; to go back into that hell—"

"Ah, yes," the Marchioness acquiesced. "So she describes it—my sensitive child! But on the material side, Mr. Archer, if one may stoop to consider such things; do you know what she is giving up? Those roses there on the sofa—acres like them, under glass and in the open, in his matchless terraced gardens at Nice! Jewels—historic pearls: the Sobieski emeralds—sables,—but she cares nothing for all these! Art and beauty, those she does care for, she lives for, as I always have; and those also surrounded her. Pictures, priceless furniture, music, brilliant conversation—ah, that, my dear young man, if you'll excuse me, is what you've no conception of here! And she had it all; and the homage of the greatest. She tells me she is not thought handsome in New York—good heavens! Her portrait has been painted nine times;

the greatest artists in Europe have begged for the privilege. Are these things nothing? And the remorse of an adoring husband?"

As the Marchioness Manson rose to her climax her face assumed an expression of ecstatic retrospection which would have moved Archer's mirth had he not been numb with amazement.

He would have laughed if any one had foretold to him that his first sight of poor Medora Manson would have been in the guise of a messenger of Satan; but he was in no mood for laughing now, and she seemed to him to come straight out of the hell from which Ellen Olenska had just escaped.

"She knows nothing yet—of all this?" he asked abruptly.

Mrs. Manson laid a purple finger on her lips. "Nothing directly—but does she suspect? Who can tell? The truth is, Mr. Archer, I have been waiting to see you. From the moment I heard of the firm stand you had taken, and of your influence over her, I hoped it might be possible to count on your support—to convince you ... "

"That she ought to go back? I would rather see her dead!" cried the young man violently.

"Ah," the Marchioness murmured, without visible resentment. For a while she sat in her arm-chair, opening and shutting the absurd ivory fan between her mittened fingers; but suddenly she lifted her head and listened.

"Here she comes," she said in a rapid whisper; and then, pointing to the bouquet on the sofa: "Am I to understand that you prefer THAT, Mr. Archer? After all, marriage is marriage ... and my niece is still a wife... "

# Chapter 18

"What are you two plotting together, aunt Medora?" Madame Olenska cried as she came into the room.

She was dressed as if for a ball. Everything about her shimmered and glimmered softly, as if her dress had been woven out of candle-beams; and she carried her head high, like a pretty woman challenging a roomful of rivals.

"We were saying, my dear, that here was something beautiful to surprise you with," Mrs. Manson rejoined, rising to her feet and pointing archly to the flowers.

Madame Olenska stopped short and looked at the bouquet. Her colour did not change, but a sort of white radiance of anger ran over her like summer lightning. "Ah," she exclaimed, in a shrill voice that the young man had never heard, "who is ridiculous enough to send me a bouquet? Why a bouquet? And why tonight of all nights? I am not going to a ball; I am not a girl engaged to be married. But some people are always ridiculous."

She turned back to the door, opened it, and called out: "Nastasia!"

The ubiquitous handmaiden promptly appeared, and Archer heard Madame Olenska say, in an Italian that she seemed to pronounce with intentional deliberateness in order that he might follow it: "Here—throw this into the dustbin!" and then, as Nastasia stared protestingly: "But no—it's not the fault of the poor flowers. Tell the boy to carry them to the house three doors away, the house of Mr. Winsett, the dark gentleman who dined here. His wife is ill—they may give her pleasure ... The boy is out, you say? Then, my dear one, run yourself; here, put my cloak over you and fly. I want the thing out of the house immediately! And, as you live, don't say they come from me!"

She flung her velvet opera cloak over the maid's shoulders and turned back into the drawing-room, shutting the door sharply. Her bosom was rising high under its lace, and for a moment Archer thought she was about to cry; but she burst into a laugh instead, and looking from the Marchioness to Archer, asked abruptly: "And you two—have you made friends!"

"It's for Mr. Archer to say, darling; he has waited patiently while you were dressing." She did not mention the carnal fun she had shared with the two men.

"Yes—I gave you time enough: my hair wouldn't go," Madame Olenska said, raising her hand to the heaped-up curls of her chignon. "But that reminds me: I see Dr. Carver is gone, and you'll be late at the Blenkers'. Mr. Archer, will you put my aunt in the carriage?"

She followed the Marchioness into the hall, saw her fitted into a miscellaneous heap of overshoes, shawls and tippets, and called from the doorstep: "Mind, the carriage is to be back for me at ten!" Then she returned to the drawing-room, where Archer, on re-entering it, found her standing by the mantelpiece, examining herself in the mirror. It was not usual, in New York society, for a lady to address her parlour-maid as "my dear one," and send her out on an errand wrapped in her own opera-cloak; and Archer, through all his deeper feelings, tasted the pleasurable excitement of being in a world where action followed on emotion with such Olympian speed.

Madame Olenska did not move when he came up behind her, and for a second their eyes met in the mirror; then she turned, threw herself into her sofa- corner, and sighed out: "There's time for a cigarette."

He handed her the box and lit a spill for her; and as the flame flashed up into her face she glanced at him with laughing eyes and said: "What do you think of me in a temper?"

Archer paused a moment; then he answered with sudden resolution: "It makes me understand what your aunt has been saying about you."

"I knew she'd been talking about me. Well?"

"She said you were used to all kinds of things—splendours and amusements and excitements—that we could never hope to give you here."

Madame Olenska smiled faintly into the circle of smoke about her lips.

"Medora is incorrigibly romantic. It has made up to her for so many things!"

Archer hesitated again, thinking just how passionate the woman he saw through the crack in the door really was, and then he again took his risk. "Is your aunt's romanticism always consistent with accuracy?"

"You mean: does she speak the truth?" Her niece considered. "Well, I'll tell you: in almost everything she says, there's something true and something untrue. But why do you ask? What has she been telling you?"

He looked away into the fire, and then back at her shining presence. His heart tightened with the thought that this was their last evening by that fireside, and that in a moment the carriage would come to carry her away.

"She says—she pretends that Count Olenska has asked her to persuade you to go back to him."

Madame Olenska made no answer. She sat motionless, holding her cigarette in her half-lifted hand. The expression of her face had not changed; and Archer remembered that he had before noticed her apparent incapacity for surprise.

"You knew, then?" he broke out.

She was silent for so long that the ash dropped from her cigarette. She brushed it to the floor. "She has hinted about a letter: poor darling! Medora's hints—"

"Is it at your husband's request that she has arrived here suddenly?"

Madame Olenska seemed to consider this question also. "There again: one can't tell. She told me she had had a 'spiritual summons,' whatever that is, from Dr. Carver. I'm afraid she's going to marry Dr. Carver ... poor Medora, there's always some one she wants to marry. But perhaps the people in Cuba just got tired of her! I think she was with them as a sort of paid companion. Really, I don't know why she came."

"But you do believe she has a letter from your husband?"

Again Madame Olenska brooded silently; then she said: "After all, it was to be expected."

The young man rose and went to lean against the fireplace. A sudden restlessness possessed him, and he was tongue-tied by the sense that their minutes were numbered, and that at any moment he might hear the wheels of the returning carriage.

"You know that your aunt believes you will go back?"

Madame Olenska raised her head quickly. A deep blush rose to her face and spread over her neck and shoulders. She blushed seldom and painfully, as if it hurt her like a burn.

"Many cruel things have been believed of me," she said.

"Oh, Ellen—forgive me; I'm a fool and a brute!"

She smiled a little. "You are horribly nervous; you have your own troubles. I know you think the Wellands are unreasonable about your marriage, and of course I agree with you. In Europe people don't understand our long American engagements; I suppose they are not as calm as we are." She pronounced the "we" with a faint emphasis that gave it an ironic sound.

Archer felt the irony but did not dare to take it up. After all, she had perhaps purposely deflected the conversation from her own affairs, and after the pain his last words had evidently caused her he felt that all he could do was to follow her lead. But the sense of the waning hour made him desperate: he could not bear the thought that a barrier of words should drop between them again.

"Yes," he said abruptly; "I went south to ask May to marry me after Easter. There's no reason why we shouldn't be married then."

"And May adores you—and yet you couldn't convince her? I thought her too intelligent to be the slave of such absurd superstitions."

"She IS too intelligent—she's not their slave."

Madame Olenska looked at him. "Well, then—I don't understand."

Archer reddened, and hurried on with a rush. "We had a frank talk—almost the first. She thinks my impatience a bad sign."

"Merciful heavens—a bad sign?"

"She thinks it means that I can't trust myself to go on caring for her. She thinks, in short, I want to marry her at once to get away from some one that I—care for more."

Madame Olenska examined this curiously. "But if she thinks that—why isn't she in a hurry too?"

"Because she's not like that: she's so much nobler. She insists all the more on the long engagement, to give me time—"

"Time to give her up for the other woman?"

"If I want to."

Madame Olenska leaned toward the fire and gazed into it with fixed eyes. Down the quiet street Archer heard the approaching trot of her horses.

"That IS noble," she said, with a slight break in her voice.

"Yes. But it's ridiculous."

"Ridiculous? Because you don't care for any one else?"

"Because I don't mean to marry any one else."

"Ah." There was another long interval. At length she looked up at him and asked: "This other woman—does she love you?"

"Oh, there's no other woman; I mean, the person that May was thinking of is—was never—"

"Then, why, after all, are you in such haste?"

"There's your carriage," said Archer.

She half-rose and looked about her with absent eyes. Her fan and gloves lay on the sofa beside her and she picked them up mechanically.

"Yes; I suppose I must be going."

"You're going to Mrs. Struthers's?"

"Yes." She smiled and added: "I must go where I am invited, or I should be too lonely. Why not come with me?"

Archer felt that at any cost he must keep her beside him, must make her give him the rest of her evening. Ignoring her question, he continued to lean against the chimney-piece, his eyes fixed on the hand in which she held her gloves and fan, as if watching to see if he had the power to make her drop them.

"May guessed the truth," he said. "There is another woman—but not the one she thinks."

Ellen Olenska made no answer, and did not move. After a moment he sat down beside her, and, taking her hand, softly unclasped it, so that the gloves and fan fell on the sofa between them.

She started up, and freeing herself from him moved away to the other side of the hearth. "Ah, don't make love to me! Too many people have done that," she said, frowning.

Archer, changing colour, stood up also: it was the bitterest rebuke she could have given him. "I have never made anything other than love to you," he said, "and I never shall. But you are the woman I would have married if it had been possible for either of us."

"Possible for either of us?" She looked at him with unfeigned astonishment. "And you say that—when it's you who've made it impossible?"

He stared at her, groping in a blackness through which a single arrow of light tore its blinding way.

"I'VE made it impossible—?"

"You, you, YOU!" she cried, her lip trembling like a child's on the verge of tears. "Isn't it you who made me give up divorcing—give it up because you showed me how selfish and wicked it was, how one must sacrifice one's self to preserve the dignity of marriage … and to spare one's family the publicity, the scandal? And because my family was going to be your family—for May's sake and for yours—I did what you told me, what you proved to me that I ought to do. Ah," she broke out with a sudden laugh, "I've made no secret of having done it for you!"

She sank down on the sofa again, crouching among the festive ripples of her dress like a stricken masquerader; and the young man stood by the fireplace and continued to gaze at her without moving.

"Good God," he groaned. "When I thought—"

"You thought?"

"Ah, don't ask me what I thought!"

Still looking at her, he saw the same burning flush creep up her neck to her face. She sat upright, facing him with a rigid dignity.

"I do ask you."

"Well, then: there were things in that letter you asked me to read—"

"My husband's letter?"

"Yes."

"I had nothing to fear from that letter: absolutely nothing! All I feared was to bring notoriety, scandal, on the family—on you and May."

"Good God," he groaned again, bowing his face in his hands.

The silence that followed lay on them with the weight of things final and irrevocable. It seemed to Archer to be crushing him down like his own grave-stone; in all the wide future he saw nothing that would ever lift that load from his heart. He did not move from his place, or raise his head from his hands; his hidden eyeballs went on staring into utter darkness.

"At least I loved you—" he brought out.

On the other side of the hearth, from the sofa-corner where he supposed that she still crouched, he heard a faint stifled crying like a child's. He started up and came to her side.

"Ellen! What madness! Why are you crying? Nothing's done that can't be undone. I'm still free, and you're going to be." He had her in his arms, her face like a wet flower at his lips, and all their vain terrors shrivelling up like ghosts at sunrise. The one thing that astonished him now was that he should have stood for five minutes arguing with her across the width of the room, when just touching her made everything so simple.

She gave him back all his kiss, but after a moment he felt her stiffening in his arms, and she put him aside and stood up.

"Ah, my poor Newland—I suppose this had to be. But it doesn't in the least alter things," she said, looking down at him in her turn from the hearth.

"It alters the whole of life for me."

"No, no—it mustn't, it can't. You're engaged to May Welland; and I'm married."

He stood up too, flushed and resolute. "Nonsense! It's too late for that sort of thing. We've no right to lie to other people or to ourselves. We won't talk of your marriage; but do you see me marrying May after this?"

She stood silent, resting her thin elbows on the mantelpiece, her profile reflected in the glass behind her. One of the locks of her chignon had become loosened and hung on her neck; she looked haggard and almost old.

"I don't see you," she said at length, "putting that question to May. Do you?"

He gave a reckless shrug. "It's too late to do anything else."

"You say that because it's the easiest thing to say at this moment—not because it's true. In reality it's too late to do anything but what we'd both decided on."

"Ah, I don't understand you!"

She forced a pitiful smile that pinched her face instead of smoothing it. "You don't understand because you haven't yet guessed how you've changed things for me: oh, from the first—long before I knew all you'd done."

"All I'd done?"

"Yes. I was perfectly unconscious at first that people here were shy of me—that they thought I was a dreadful sort of person. It seems they had even refused to meet me at dinner. I found that out afterward; and how you'd made your mother go with you to the van der Luydens'; and how you'd insisted on announcing your engagement at the Beaufort ball, so that I might have two families to stand by me instead of one—"

At that he broke into a laugh.

"Just imagine," she said, "how stupid and unobservant I was! I knew nothing of all this till Granny blurted it out one day. New York simply meant peace and freedom to me: it was coming home. And I was so happy at being among my own people that every one I met seemed kind and good, and glad to see me. But from the very beginning," she continued, "I felt there was no one as kind as you; no one who gave me reasons that I understood for doing what at first seemed so hard and—unnecessary. The very good people didn't convince me; I felt they'd never been tempted. But you knew; you understood; you had felt the world outside tugging at one with all its golden hands—and yet you hated the things it asks of one; you hated happiness bought by disloyalty and cruelty and indifference. That was what I'd never known before—and it's better than anything I've known."

She spoke in a low even voice, without tears or visible agitation; and each word, as it dropped from her, fell into his breast like burning lead. He sat bowed over, his head between his hands, staring at the hearthrug, and at the tip of the satin shoe that showed under her dress. Suddenly he knelt down and kissed the shoe.

She bent over him, laying her hands on his shoulders, and looking at him with eyes so deep that he remained motionless under her gaze.

"Ah, don't let us undo what you've done!" she cried. "I can't go back now to that other way of thinking. I can't love you unless I give you up."

His arms were yearning up to her; but she drew away, and they remained facing each other, divided by the distance that her words had created. Then, abruptly, his anger overflowed.

"And Beaufort? Is he to replace me?"

As the words sprang out he was prepared for an answering flare of anger; and he would have welcomed it as fuel for his own. But Madame Olenska only grew a shade paler, and stood with her arms hanging down before her, and her head slightly bent, as her way was when she pondered a question.

"He's waiting for you now at Mrs. Struthers's; why don't you go to him?" Archer sneered.

She turned to ring the bell. "I shall not go out this evening; tell the carriage to go and fetch the Signora Marchesa," she said when the maid came.

After the door had closed again Archer continued to look at her with bitter eyes. "Why this sacrifice? Since you tell me that you're lonely I've no right to keep you from your friends."

She smiled a little under her wet lashes. "I shan't be lonely now. I WAS lonely; I WAS afraid. But the emptiness and the darkness are gone; when I turn back into myself now I'm like a child going at night into a room where there's always a light."

Her tone and her look still enveloped her in a soft inaccessibility, and Archer groaned out again: "I don't understand you!"

"Yet you understand May!"

He reddened under the retort, but kept his eyes on her. "May is ready to give me up."

"What! Three days after you've entreated her on your knees to hasten your marriage?"

"She's refused; that gives me the right—"

"Ah, you've taught me what an ugly word that is," she said.

He turned away with a sense of utter weariness. He felt as though he had been struggling for hours up the face of a steep precipice, and now, just as he had fought his way to the top, his hold had given way and he was pitching down headlong into darkness.

If he could have got her in his arms again he might have swept away her arguments; but she still held him at a distance by something inscrutably aloof in her look and attitude, and by his own awed sense of her sincerity. At length he began to plead again.

"If we do this now it will be worse afterward—worse for every one—"

"No—no—no!" she almost screamed, as if he frightened her.

At that moment the bell sent a long tinkle through the house. They had heard no carriage stopping at the door, and they stood motionless, looking at each other with startled eyes.

Outside, Nastasia's step crossed the hall, the outer door opened, and a moment later she came in carrying a telegram which she handed to the Countess Olenska.

"The lady was very happy at the flowers," Nastasia said, smoothing her apron. "She thought it was her signor marito who had sent them, and she cried a little and said it was a folly."

Her mistress smiled and took the yellow envelope. She tore it open and carried it to the lamp; then, when the door had closed again, she handed the telegram to Archer.

It was dated from St. Augustine, and addressed to the Countess Olenska. In it he read: "Granny's telegram successful. Papa and

Mamma agree marriage after Easter. Am telegraphing Newland. Am too happy for words and love you dearly. Your grateful May."

The envelope fell from Newland's hand to the floor. He stepped toward Ellen and drew her into his arms. This time the tears spilled from his eyes. His chest heaved. Ellen did not push him away, but embraced him, rubbing his back to console him as though he were a wounded child. Yet at the same time, he was a devastated man who could only be healed by her touch.

"Dear Newland," she said. "I could not love you if you were a different man. You must do what is right so that we both can live."

Newland sobbed disconsolately.

"Come now," she said, drawing back from his clinging grasp. She clasped his arms and gently shook him. When he raised his head, she looked deeply into his eyes. "You know what I am saying is true." She raised a hand to his cheek and brushed away the tears.

To taste heaven and then to be thrown into the fiery pit of hell was unjust. Had he never known the paradise of Ellen—her body and soul—he would have been able to live more simply. He would never have realized the depths to which unbridled love can sink inside the soul.

"Let me take you to my bed, one last time," she said.

It was all that Newland longed for, that he dreamt of—to make love to Ellen, to embrace her, to feel her near him, but to do so now would only deepen the wound, further expand the incomparable loss. Yet, to deny himself this heavenly pleasure would destroy him more. Every passing day, he would be plagued by having lost the opportunity to touch her one last time. There was no reason to perplex his mind any further. He offered her his hand, and she grasped it.

She led him to her private chamber and secured the latch on the door. When she turned, he stood before her, no longer a helpless child, but rather a man who accepted his destiny. Before she spoke, he drew her into his arms and held her tightly, and then he lowered his lips to hers, and with all of his being, kissed her.

She returned his affection and held him so tightly that their bodies seemed to merge as one flesh. They kissed deeply. Like the French, their tongues touched sublimely, caressing with a reckless hunger, and they began undressing one another. When they stood naked, their bodies again united, they slowed the kiss to a more sensuous rhythm, both sighing with extreme delight.

Newland did not allow himself to think, nor to question any of the inequities of life. He had completely lost himself to the desires of the physical flesh. It was the only way he could live. It was the only way that he could be free to make love to Ellen without thinking the world a wicked place.

He grasped her waist and slowly lowered his head so that he could lick her bare breasts. He inhaled deeply. Her marvelous fragrance, a mixture of sweet perfume and her natural scent, intoxicated him. He brushed his lips slowly across her breasts, letting his tongue linger when he reached her nipples. Then he grasped one of her supple breasts in his hand and began circling the tip of it with his tongue, while slowly caressing the other with the fingertips of free hand. She sighed quietly, and her body began to writhe to his gentle touch. She moved her hands from his shoulders to his head, where she began running her slender fingers through his thick dark hair. Then she moved her fingers to the side and delicately began circling the outer rims of his ears, stopping to massage his earlobes, before moving to outline his jaw. Newland groaned quietly, pleased by her touch, but found his desires mounting, his manhood throbbing impatiently.

"Come," she said and led him to her bed.

He hastily threw back the covers and swept her off her feet, cradled her in his arms and kissed her softly before laying her on her back. He stood over her, admiring the beauty of her creamy skin, as she let down her chignon. Her loose hair tumbled beside her neck and shoulders. With a hand, he traced the long lines of her toned body, from her shoulders to the ends of her toes, and then returned upward toward her hips, where he stopped to circle the sensuous curve of her torso.

She let out a sigh of encouragement as she opened her legs, and he quickly moved his hand to touch her. She was impassioned, moist with desire, and the more he explored, the more fully she opened her legs, until he could wait no longer. He grasped one of her thighs and urged her legs open more fully, until nothing remained hidden. Her orchid was enflamed, a deep crimson. Her pearl, bursting through its stigma, awaited his touch. And the moment he touched her jewel, she gasped.

"Newland," she whispered, as she reached for his manhood. Once she held the crown in her hand, she began caressing him as he gently circled her pearl. Then he slid his fingers lower to mix her passion and dip a finger inside her velvety sheath. She was tight, supple, and needy.

"Make love to me," she said.

He lowered his head and ran his tongue along her delicate flower before he positioned himself over her. He circled her in his arms and pulled her close so that her breasts were next to his chest. Then he touched the crown of his staff to her sheath. They stared deeply into each other's eyes, anticipating the moment that they would finally be complete. And when she moved her hips desirously toward him, he waited no longer and pushed inside her wet, velvety purse, sliding slowly to the end.

"You're so beautiful," he whispered as he closed his eyes and began to thrust.

They moved slowly with their bodies sliding easily over one another. But as their passion flourished, their pace hastened until they were racing through the final measures. Like a symphonic masterpiece, the crescendo intensified with each thrust, and then finally, they climaxed in a perfect beat. With her locked in his embrace, Newland rolled to his side, and they continued to kiss.

When their lips parted, they held each other near, and continued to swirl the tips of their tongues. And when their tongues withdrew, they continued to share gentle kisses.

He kissed her forehead, and then he said softly, "How shall I ever live without you?"

She offered no reply.

He wished he had never asked the question. Her silence was more painful than if she had sent him away with words. The ache in his heart was debilitating. He dreaded to think about tomorrow or the future, or how he would he ever leave her tonight. He glanced down at her face. Her eyes were closed, and she wore a pleasant, satisfied expression, almost as if she had not heard a word he had said.

Pushing the thoughts from his mind, he embraced her tightly and began stroking her head. As long as he held her close, she belonged to him, and he to her. If he lived not a second more in this life, he could rightfully say that it had been a life worth living. He closed his eyes because it was all he could do to hold onto the moment. They lay arm in arm, dozing and sharing one and the same breath, until sometime late in the night, he was compelled to take his leave.

Half an hour later, when Archer unlocked his own front-door, he found a similar envelope to the one Ellen had received, it was lying on the hall-table on top of his pile of notes and letters. The message inside the envelope was also from May Welland, and ran as follows: "Parents consent wedding Tuesday after Easter at twelve Grace Church eight bridesmaids please see Rector so happy love May."

Archer crumpled up the yellow sheet as if the gesture could annihilate the news it contained. Then he pulled out a small pocket-diary and turned over the pages with trembling fingers;

but he did not find what he wanted, and cramming the telegram into his pocket he mounted the stairs.

A light was shining through the door of the little hall-room which served Janey as a dressing-room and boudoir, and her brother rapped impatiently on the panel. The door opened, and his sister stood before him in her immemorial purple flannel dressing-gown, with her hair "on pins." Her face looked pale and apprehensive.

"Newland! I hope there's no bad news in that telegram? I waited on purpose, in case—" (No item of his correspondence was safe from Janey.)

He took no notice of her question. "Look here—what day is Easter this year?"

She looked shocked at such unchristian ignorance. "Easter? Newland! Why, of course, the first week in April. Why?"

"The first week?" He turned again to the pages of his diary, calculating rapidly under his breath. "The first week, did you say?" He threw back his head with a long laugh.

"For mercy's sake what's the matter?"

"Nothing's the matter, except that I'm going to be married in a month."

Janey fell upon his neck and pressed him to her purple flannel breast. "Oh Newland, how wonderful! I'm so glad! But, dearest, why do you keep on laughing? Do hush, or you'll wake Mamma."

# About the Authors

Coco Rousseau
After successfully adapting E. M. Forster's *A Room with a View* to explore that novel's erotic potential, Coco decided she would continue her passion for retelling classic love stories on a more intimate level by adapting an American classic.

Edith Wharton
In 1921, Edith Wharton became the first woman to win the Pulitzer Prize for Fiction for her twelfth book, The Age of Innocence. A remarkable chronicle of an important period in American history, the story portrays the public and private lives of the upper class in nineteenth-century New York. Wharton creates a tragic, poignant love story among Newland Archer, an idealistic young lawyer, May, his society-conscious wife, and the Countess Olenska, a beautiful, mysterious woman with a scandalous past. In Coco's adaption of the timeless classic, the plot takes on a new twist, while also more explicitly exploring human passion and sexuality in ways that Wharton could not.

# More from This Author

## (From *A Room with a View: The Wild and Wanton Edition* by Coco Rousseau and E.M. Forster)

"The Signora had no business to do it," said Miss Bartlett, "no business at all. She promised us south rooms with a view close together, instead of which here are north rooms, looking into a courtyard, and a long way apart. Oh, Lucy!"

"And a Cockney, besides!" said Lucy to her cousin, Miss Bartlett, who had been further saddened by the Signora's unexpected accent. "It might be London," Lucy continued. Then she looked at the two rows of English people who were sitting at the table; at the row of white bottles of water and red bottles of wine that ran between the English people; at the portraits of the late Queen and the late Poet Laureate that hung behind the English people, heavily framed; at the notice of the English church (Rev. Cuthbert Eager, M. A. Oxon.), that was the only other decoration of the wall; and she might have remained saddened had her eyes not swept past an older gentleman and came to rest upon the dashingly handsome face of a young man. She studied the lines of his face, absorbing all of his features at once. There was a softness to his fair complexion and cerulean eyes, yet the man in him was strong and exuded all that was masculine, all that she so longed to know.

Lucy's bosom swelled, her heart began to flutter, and her breath hastened. She was utterly mesmerized, unable to break her gaze, though she lingered a measure too long when the young man suddenly met her stare.

Bursting from within, Lucy's heart pulsed against its cage: a cage that she had never once been allowed to escape.

The couple stared longingly into each other's eyes as though they shared a secret: one of intimacy, one that might have revealed they had been lovers from the birth of time. Despite her attempt to stay calm, she felt her cheeks flush with heat and her pulse quicken. When a fork clinked loudly against the older man's plate, Lucy quickly cast her eyes down and toward her own plate. Searching for her breath, she could hardly believe her boldness, a brazenness that had sprung from hidden depths inside her that she had not even known existed. How could she have permitted herself to be partner to this surreptitious exchange with a stranger?

Was she to blame for these strange new feelings that were beginning to stir deep within her—feelings that glided like lightning from the tips of her bosoms through her loins and down to the very ends of her toes.

How could she feel such yearning desire to be in the arms of a man she had never once laid eyes upon before this day in her life? She felt as though she was possessed by some inexplicable and captivating allure. Lucy questioned whether she would be able to eat another bite much less converse with the others while they took their evening meal.

She could not stop herself. Her imagination sprang forth and began to roam through the wilds of her mind. The handsome young man lying next to her; her body cradled in his. Their breath as one. Their hands freely exploring. Her legs slowly unfolding to allow his caressing hand to know her intimate flesh.

"Ah." The very thought of his touch befell Lucy with such an intense sensation that a surge of lust shot through her loins. Try as she might, she could not calm her nerves. She felt the urge to run.

All aflutter, she placed a hand on her Cousin Charlotte's lap. "I must fetch my handkerchief from the room, I will return shortly," Lucy whispered.

"My dear Lucia, can it not wait?" Miss Bartlett said in an attempt to suppress her young cousin.

"No, I am quite sorry. Pardon me. I won't be long."

Lucy quickly slipped away from her chaperon and hurried from the dining room hall. As she rounded the corner, she hurried to stairs, which led to the sleeping quarters upstairs. The clock in the hallway struck; the surprise of it almost shattered her nerves. Her head spinning, Lucy hastened to an unexpected stop and braced herself against the wall. Closing her eyes, she took a moment to catch her breath as she listened to the clock wend its way through its chords.

"Is it possible to be love-struck?" she thought. "Hit by a bolt of lightning clapping the earth?"

Lucy felt an overwhelming urge to be taken, to be ravaged, to be made love to in the most intimate and devouring of manners. Although what did she know of these matters? She knew nothing of such delicacies; these affairs were not to be spoken of till the bedroom door closed on one's wedding night; though, the primal urge could not be denied.

"What's come over me?" she thought. "Perhaps it's just fatigue." Lucy brought her hands to her raised bosom. "That must be it, only tiredness from travel." She drew in a long savoring breath. "To be sure, that must be it, nothing more."

The clock reached its final stanza and the only sound that remained was the faint echoes of the bells. Breathing more steadily, Lucy opened her eyes and leaned over to straighten her skirts. She would forego the handkerchief and return to the dining room instead.

Only as she turned to go, the very gentleman who had stolen her breath completely away was standing right there, in front of her, unnaturally close, in this lone hallway. It was just the two of them. Man and woman. He was so close.

Could it be a dream? Did her eyes deceive her?

It could not be. No, it could not. She felt the heat radiating from his body and pouring into her soul.

The air in the hallway instantly drained.

Frightened and filled with insatiable desire, Lucy gasped, trying desperately to draw in a breath, trying to scream, although the presence of this man had shaken her to down to her innermost core, stealing not only her breath but also her words.

Surely, his intentions were not …

Without uttering a word, without asking for permission, he grasped her arms and held her firm. He stared deeply into her eyes. Still, he spoke not a word, although his labored breath was hot against hers.

Braced against the wall, she could not escape. There was nowhere to go. Her heart beat uncontrollably. Inside she ached, her legs weakened. And then he took his liberty. He leaned closer and before she could form a word, her face was in his hands. His strong, warm hands, holding her ever so gently. He paused for a moment to study her face, then softly pressed his lips against hers.

Lucy was unable to resist. Never before kissed, she relinquished every bit of control to this man. With his tongue, he parted her lips to slip inside and find her tongue. Soft and delicate, he began sliding his tongue against hers in a rhythm that played like a sonata.

As if tasting honey for the first time in his life, he kissed her ever so gently till the beast in him emerged unfettered. All at once, he closed the distance between them till he pressed himself against her skirts. There was no mistaking his intention. He kissed her harder. More wildly. Passionately. She could not have stopped him had she wanted to—and she did not want him to stop.

His hands released from her face and slid over the fabric of her dress toward her bosom, where he grasped the fullness of each breast in his hands. He found the aroused tips of her bosom pressing against the cloth and began to circle them with his fingertips.

Through their kisses, Lucy surrendered a light sigh. His touch was so pleasureful, she began to purr until the purr became a moan. A moan filled with such indulgence that it begged for him to lift her skirts. If only his hands would find her intimate flesh. Oh, the pleasure she had longed for—the desire to be caressed, the need to be released. Oh my love, don't stop.

He lifted his lips from hers and began kissing the line of her jaw, moving ever so slowly toward her neck. Unable to speak, she could only gasp with that unspeakable desire. Not asking, he slipped his fingers through her blouse, but just as he was about to clasp the buds of her bosoms, footsteps pattered across the wooden floors downstairs and toward the staircase.

Charlotte!

The young man straightened, then whispered into Lucy's ear, "Please do not think ill of me. Your beauty drew me to you, my darling."

The stranger drew back, parted himself from her, and rushed toward the stairs.

Bewildered, Lucy raced to her room, and before she closed her door, she heard the voice of Charlotte speaking to the Signora.

Safe inside the sleeping quarters, Lucy hurried to settle herself. She raced to her looking glass mirror and saw that her face was flushed a crimson red. Reaching quickly for her powder brush, she began painting her face.

There was a rap on the door.

Lucy straightened her hair, but before she could open the door, it burst open.

"Are you quite all right, my dear, Lucia?" Miss Bartlett inquired of her young cousin.

"Of course. Shall we go back down?" Without waiting for a reply, Lucy hurried past Miss Bartlett, and before long, the two were once again situated at the dining room table with all of its members assembled exactly as they had left them, including the handsome young man who had so intimately descended upon Lucy in that upper hallway only moments ago. Had the two of them been left there alone for a moment longer, pray tell what would have become of her chaste virtue?

Lucy was a shambles, confused, and filled with unspeakable thoughts. How would he dare? Should she feel shame? Lucy glimpsed at him, but what she saw astonished her; he appeared exactly as she had left him when he was seated at the table—untouched.

"Lucia," said Miss Bartlett. "Do eat."

Sweeping her eyes past the young man, Lucy forced herself to speak pleasantly to her cousin. "Charlotte," Lucy said, "don't you feel, too, that we might be in London? I can hardly believe that all kinds of other things are just outside. I suppose it is one's being so tired."

"This meat has surely been used for soup," said Miss Bartlett, laying down her fork.

"I want so to see the Arno. The rooms the Signora promised us in her letter would have looked over the Arno. The Signora had no business to do it at all. Oh, it is a shame!"

"Any nook does for me," Miss Bartlett continued; "but it does seem hard that you shouldn't have a view."

Lucy felt that she had been selfish. "Charlotte, you mustn't spoil me: of course, you must look over the Arno, too. I meant that. The first vacant room in the front—"

"You must have it," said Miss Bartlett, part of whose travelling expenses were paid by Lucy's mother—a piece of generosity to which she made many a tactful allusion.

"No, no. You must have it."

"I insist on it. Your mother would never forgive me, Lucy."

"She would never forgive me."

The ladies' voices grew animated, and—if the sad truth be owned—a little peevish. They were tired, and under the guise of unselfishness they wrangled. Some of their neighbours interchanged glances, and one of them—one of the ill-bred people whom one does meet abroad—leant forward over the table and actually intruded into their argument. He said:

"I have a view, I have a view."

Miss Bartlett was startled. Generally at a pension people looked them over for a day or two before speaking, and often did not find out that they would "do" till they had gone. She knew that the intruder was ill-bred, even before she glanced at him. He was an old man, of heavy build, with a fair, shaven face and large eyes. There was something childish in those eyes, though it was not the childishness of senility. What exactly it was Miss Bartlett did not stop to consider, for her glance passed on to his clothes. These did not attract her. He was probably trying to become acquainted with them before they got into the swim. So she assumed a dazed expression when he spoke to her, and then said: "A view? Oh, a view! How delightful a view is!"

"This is my son," said the old man; "his name's George. He has a view too."

"Ah," said Miss Bartlett, repressing Lucy, who was about to speak.

"Ah, the name. He has a name," Lucy thought. "One wouldn't simply be a handsome young man who took liberties to kiss a complete stranger; he must of course have a name: George. Her Dear George."

For a better definition, Lucy considered George at length. He was not only a handsome young man who sat contentedly, appearing quite untouched as though it were perfectly natural to go about seducing another's affections without speaking a word. He was genuinely the most desirable man she had ever set eyes upon in her life.

The kiss—the very kiss—they shared just moments ago thrilled Lucy so that her toes still tingled. She knew she had to restrain her desire, but it was only heightened.

"What I mean," the older man continued, "is that you can have our rooms, and we'll have yours. We'll change."

The better class of tourist was shocked at this, and sympathized with the new-comers. Miss Bartlett, in reply, opened her mouth as little as possible, and said "Thank you very much indeed; that is out of the question."

Lucy wriggled her toes at the very thought of lying in the same bed in which George had slept.

"Why?" said the old man, with both fists on the table.

"Because it is quite out of the question, thank you," replied Miss Bartlett.

"You see, we don't like to take—" began Lucy. Her cousin again repressed her.

"But why?" he persisted. "Women like looking at a view; men don't." And he thumped with his fists like a naughty child, and turned to his son, saying, "George, persuade them!"

"It's so obvious they should have the rooms," said the son. "There's nothing else to say … "

Though calm on the outside, George did not look at Lucy for fear that his desires would be laid upon the table for all to inspect. His hands moistened at the thought of touching her bare breasts, separated only by the thin cloth of her dress. He had been so close to claiming his prize, so close to making her his own. His fingers hungered at the thought of finding the tips of her bare breasts, the very act which had been denied.

George's heart began to pound within the confines of his chest. The young woman had bedazzled him like no other. Her beauty had allured him, compelled him to act upon impulse. He wanted her. The touch of her soft lips against his, to feel her, to know her quiet sighs, to see her blissful expression.

He turned toward the window, stealing a lingering glance at Lucy's voluptuous bosom. He would have her, but if he did not regain his inner composure this instant, their secret was sure to be discovered. "Yes," George said, "we insist." He still did not look at the ladies as he spoke, but his voice was perplexed and sorrowful. He forced himself to slow his breathing and continued to gaze out the window. The view was lush and flawless as Italy, herself, would have it; the canvas lacked only the merged flesh of a man and a woman. If only he could take Lucy now, and together the two might escape the mundane and meld into an eternal perfection …

Lucy, too, was perplexed; but she saw that they were in for what is known as "quite a scene," and she had an odd feeling that whenever these ill-bred tourists spoke the contest widened and deepened till it dealt, not with rooms and views, but with— well, with something quite different, whose existence she had not realized before. Now the old man attacked Miss Bartlett almost violently: Why should she not change? What possible objection had she? They would clear out in half an hour.

Miss Bartlett, though skilled in the delicacies of conversation, was powerless in the presence of brutality. It was impossible to snub any one so gross. Her face reddened with displeasure. She looked around as much as to say, "Are you all like this?" And two little old ladies, who were sitting further up the table, with shawls hanging over the backs of the chairs, looked back, clearly indicating "We are not; we are genteel."

"Eat your dinner, dear," she said to Lucy, and began to toy again with the meat that she had once censured.

Lucy mumbled that those seemed very odd people opposite, excepting George, of course. She would most certainly have to give the thought of him more consideration.

"Eat your dinner, dear. This pension is a failure. To-morrow we will make a change," said Miss Bartlett.

Lucy felt her heart twist. To be forced to leave George whom she had only just met was simply unthinkable. How could Charlotte take her away from him? She would not stand for it.

Hardly had Miss Bartlett announced this fell decision when she reversed it. She felt her breath catch in her throat as soon as the curtains at the end of the room parted, and revealed a clergyman, stout but pleasingly attractive, who hurried forward to take his place at the table, cheerfully apologizing for his lateness. Lucy, who had not yet acquired decency, at once rose to her feet, exclaiming: "Oh, oh! Why, it's Mr. Beebe! Oh, how perfectly lovely! Oh, Charlotte, we must stop now, however bad the rooms are. Oh!"

Miss Bartlett whose head was now beginning to spin with thoughts she had never known said, forcing herself to profess with more restraint:

"How do you do, Mr. Beebe? I expect that you have forgotten us: Miss Bartlett and Miss Honeychurch, who were at Tunbridge Wells when you helped the Vicar of St. Peter's that very cold Easter."

The clergyman, who had the air of one on a holiday, did not remember the ladies quite as clearly as they remembered him. But he came forward pleasantly enough and accepted the chair into which he was beckoned by Lucy.

"I AM so glad to see you," said the girl, who was in a state of spiritual starvation, and would have been glad to see the waiter, if her cousin had permitted it had George not been present. "Just fancy how small the world is. Summer Street, too, makes it so specially funny." Lucy knew Miss Bartlett would never take her away from the Bertolini, not now, not with the presentation of their new vicar so close at hand.

"Miss Honeychurch lives in the parish of Summer Street," said Miss Bartlett, filling up the gap for fear that she might give way to swooning like some silly young girl. "And," Miss Bartlett continued, "she happened to tell me in the course of conversation that you have just accepted the living—"

"Yes, I heard from mother so last week. She didn't know that I knew you at Tunbridge Wells; but I wrote back at once, and I said: 'Mr. Beebe is—'"

"Quite right," said the clergyman. "I move into the Rectory at Summer Street next June. I am lucky to be appointed to such a charming neighbourhood."

"Oh, how glad I am! The name of our house is Windy Corner." Mr. Beebe bowed.

"There is mother and me generally, and my brother, though it's not often we get him to ch—The church is rather far off, I mean."

"Lucy, dearest, let Mr. Beebe eat his dinner." At hearing Lucy prattle on with the vicar, Miss Bartlett had now regained her countenance as her young cousin's chaperon.

"I am eating it, thank you, and enjoying it." Mr. Beebe stole a glance Miss Barlett's way. A careful observer might have gleaned an added twinkle in his eye, though the vicar was sure to mask any gesture that might appear untoward in polite society.

To be safe at present, he preferred to talk to Lucy, whose playing he remembered, rather than to Miss Bartlett, who probably remembered his sermons. He asked the girl whether she knew Florence well, and was informed at some length that she had never been there before. It is delightful to advise a newcomer, and he was first in the field. "Don't neglect the country round," his advice concluded. "The first fine afternoon drive up to Fiesole, and round by Settignano, or something of that sort."

"No!" cried a voice from the top of the table. "Mr. Beebe, you are wrong. The first fine afternoon your ladies must go to Prato."

"That lady looks so clever," whispered Miss Bartlett to her cousin. "We are in luck."

And, indeed, a perfect torrent of information burst on them. People told them what to see, when to see it, how to stop the electric trams, how to get rid of the beggars, how much to give for a vellum blotter, how much the place would grow upon them. The Pension Bertolini had decided, almost enthusiastically, that they would do. Whichever way they looked, kind ladies smiled and shouted at them. And above all rose the voice of the clever lady, crying: "Prato! They must go to Prato. That place is too sweetly squalid for words. I love it; I revel in shaking off the trammels of respectability, as you know."

The young man named George glanced at the clever lady, and then returned moodily to his plate. Obviously he and his father did not do. Lucy, in the midst of her success, found time to wish they did. It gave her no extra pleasure that any one should be left in the cold: especially George, whom she so longed to be near. When she rose to go, she turned back and gave the two outsiders a nervous little bow.

The father did not see it; the son acknowledged it, not by another bow, but by raising his eyebrows and smiling; he seemed to be smiling across something, and Lucy knew exactly why— their kiss.

She hastened after her cousin, who had already disappeared through the curtains—curtains which smote one in the face, and seemed heavy with more than cloth. Beyond them stood the unreliable Signora, bowing good-evening to her guests, and supported by 'Enery, her little boy, and Victorier, her daughter. It made a curious little scene, this attempt of the Cockney to convey the grace and geniality of the South. And even more curious was the drawing-room, which attempted to rival the solid comfort of a Bloomsbury boarding-house. Was this really Italy?

Miss Bartlett was already seated on a tightly stuffed arm-chair, which had the colour and the contours of a tomato. She was talking to Mr. Beebe, and as she spoke, her long narrow head drove backwards and forwards, slowly, regularly, as though she were demolishing some invisible obstacle. "We are most grateful to you," she was saying. "The first evening means so much. When you arrived we were in for a peculiarly mauvais quart d'heure."

He expressed his regret.

"I must say it is so delightful to see a friendly face." Miss Bartlett's eyes met Mr. Beebe's and before she thought to check herself, she released a delicate smile.

Nodding, Mr. Beebe returned the smile.

Charlotte felt her bosom swell. Again, she was struck with fanciful thoughts usually reserved exclusively for young girls.

"Do you, by any chance, know the name of an old man who sat opposite us at dinner?" she asked, forcing herself back into her role of restraint.

"Emerson."

"Is he a friend of yours?"

"We are friendly—as one is in pensions."

"Then I will say no more."

He pressed her very slightly, and she said more.

"I am, as it were," she concluded, "the chaperon of my young cousin, Lucy, and it would be a serious thing if I put her under an obligation to people of whom we know nothing. His manner was somewhat unfortunate. I hope I acted for the best."

"You acted very naturally," said he. He seemed thoughtful, and after a few moments added: "All the same, I don't think much harm would have come of accepting."

"No harm, of course. But we could not be under an obligation." His rather casual response to their becoming obliged to the wrong sort of person beckoned Charlotte to steal dangerous, impure glances at Mr. Beebe. She wondered what knowledge of the world he might harbor. But then she looked away when shame overtook her.

She scolded herself for allowing her thoughts of the clergyman to roam beyond the boundaries of decent society. Then she forced herself to glance at the severest of paintings mounted on the wall off to the side of Mr. Beebe. Straightening her posture, she smoothed the arm of the chair and reclaimed her matronly position by folding her hands to her lap.

The vicar continued. "He is rather a peculiar man." Again he hesitated, and then said gently: "I think he would not take advantage of your acceptance," he gave Charlotte a peculiar smile, which she did her best to ignore before he continued to say, "nor would he expect you to show gratitude. He has the merit—if it is one—of saying exactly what he means. He has rooms he does not value, and he thinks you would value them. He no more thought of putting you under an obligation than he thought of being polite. It is so difficult—at least, I find it difficult—to understand people who speak the truth."

Charlotte stiffened, but spoke not.

Lucy was pleased, and said: "I was hoping that he was nice; I do so always hope that people will be nice." Moreover, if Lucy were to sleep in the bed where George slept, she would have heavenly dreams. Lucy felt herself becoming aroused again by the thought of sharing his bed. Was it wrong to think like this when the thoughts came so naturally to her?

The vicar continued. "I think he is; nice and tiresome. I differ from him on almost every point of any importance, and so, I expect—I may say I hope—you will differ. But his is a type one disagrees with rather than deplores. When he first came here he not unnaturally put people's backs up. He has no tact and no manners—I don't mean by that that he has bad manners—and he will not keep his opinions to himself. We nearly complained about him to our depressing Signora, but I am glad to say we thought better of it."

"Am I to conclude," said Miss Bartlett, "that he is a Socialist?"

Mr. Beebe accepted the convenient word, not without a slight twitching of the lips.

"And presumably he has brought up his son to be a Socialist, too?"

"I hardly know George, for he hasn't learnt to talk yet." Lucy listened in silence, but she smiled inwardly when she thought, "he may not know how to talk but he has learned how to kiss. "He seems a nice creature, and I think he has brains. Of course, he has all his father's mannerisms, and it is quite possible that he, too, may be a Socialist."

"Oh, you relieve me," said Miss Bartlett. "So you think I ought to have accepted their offer? You feel I have been narrow-minded and suspicious?"

"Not at all," he answered; "I never suggested that."

"But ought I not to apologize, at all events, for my apparent rudeness?"

He replied, with some irritation, that it would be quite unnecessary, and got up from his seat to go to the smoking-room.

"Was I a bore?" said Miss Bartlett, as soon as he had disappeared, surprising herself at this sudden, unfamiliar desire for a man's attention. "Why didn't you talk, Lucy? He prefers young people, I'm sure. I do hope I haven't monopolized him. I hoped you would have him all the evening, as well as all dinner-time."

"He is nice," exclaimed Lucy. "Just what I remember. He seems to see good in every one. No one would take him for a clergyman." Lucy thought how delightful it was that the vicar had seemed so playful, that he would not be one to stand in the way of her having fun with George; but, oh dear, least he should discover her secret. It would be most uncivil, scandalous, to discuss the matter. But this was all assuming Dear George would return to her. Lucy fretted. Oh surely —

"My dear Lucia—"

"Well," Lucy quickly recovered herself and promptly addressed her cousin's concerns, "you know what I mean. And you know how clergymen generally laugh; Mr. Beebe laughs just like an ordinary man."

"Funny girl! How you do remind me of your mother. I wonder if she will approve of Mr. Beebe." She secretly hoped so, although she must remember in future to keep such thoughts in check.

"I'm sure she will; and so will Freddy."

"I think every one at Windy Corner will approve; it is the fashionable world. I am used to Tunbridge Wells, where we are all hopelessly behind the times."

"Yes," said Lucy despondently.

There was a haze of disapproval in the air, but whether the disapproval was of herself, or of Mr. Beebe, or of the fashionable world at Windy Corner, or of the narrow world at Tunbridge Wells, she could not determine. She tried to locate it, but as usual she blundered. Miss Bartlett sedulously denied disapproving of any one, and added, "I am afraid you are finding me a very depressing companion."

And the girl again thought: "I must have been selfish or unkind; I must be more careful. It is so dreadful for Charlotte, being poor, and I am certain she has never once in her entire solitary life had a kiss; certainly not like the one I received from my Dear George."

Fortunately one of the little old ladies, who for some time had been smiling very benignly, now approached and asked if she might be allowed to sit where Mr. Beebe had sat. Permission granted, she began to chatter gently about Italy, the plunge it had been to come there, the gratifying success of the plunge, the improvement in her sister's health, the necessity of closing the bed-room windows at night, and of thoroughly emptying the water-bottles in the morning. She handled her subjects agreeably, and they were, perhaps, more worthy of attention than the high discourse upon Guelfs and Ghibellines which was proceeding tempestuously at the other end of the room. It was a real catastrophe, not a mere episode, that evening of hers at Venice, when she had found in her bedroom something that is one worse than a flea, though one better than something else.

"But here you are as safe as in England. Signora Bertolini is so English."

"Yet our rooms smell," said poor Lucy. "We dread going to bed," although to bed was exactly where Lucy wanted to go—to George's bed.

"Ah, then you look into the court." She sighed. "If only Mr. Emerson was more tactful! We were so sorry for you at dinner."

"I think he was meaning to be kind."

"Undoubtedly he was," said Miss Bartlett.

"Mr. Beebe has just been scolding me for my suspicious nature. Of course, I was holding back on my cousin's account."

"Of course," said the little old lady; and they murmured that one could not be too careful with a young girl.

Lucy tried to look demure, but could not help feeling a great fool. No one was careful with her at home; or, at all events, she had not noticed it. And now, Charlotte would spoil her opportunity by trying to do what she thought right.

"About old Mr. Emerson—I hardly know. No, he is not tactful; yet, have you ever noticed that there are people who do things which are most indelicate, and yet at the same time—beautiful?"

"Beautiful?" said Miss Bartlett, puzzled at the word. "Are not beauty and delicacy the same?"

"So one would have thought," said the other helplessly. "But things are so difficult, I sometimes think." Or do we make them difficult by not following our feelings, thought Lucy.

She proceeded no further into things, for Mr. Beebe reappeared, looking extremely pleasant.

"Miss Bartlett," he cried, "it's all right about the rooms. I'm so glad. Mr. Emerson was talking about it in the smoking-room, and knowing what I did, I encouraged him to make the offer again. He has let me come and ask you. He would be so pleased."

"Oh, Charlotte," cried Lucy to her cousin, "we must have the rooms now. The old man is just as nice and kind as he can be."

Miss Bartlett was silent.

"I fear," said Mr. Beebe, after a pause, "that I have been officious. I must apologize for my interference."

Gravely displeased, he turned to go. Not till then did Miss Bartlett reply: "My own wishes, dearest Lucy, are unimportant in comparison with yours. It would be hard indeed if I stopped you doing as you liked at Florence, when I am only here through your kindness. If you wish me to turn these gentlemen out of their rooms, I will do it. Would you then, Mr. Beebe, kindly tell Mr. Emerson that I accept his kind offer, and then conduct him to me, in order that I may thank him personally?"

She raised her voice as she spoke; it was heard all over the drawing room, and silenced the Guelfs and the Ghibellines. The clergyman, inwardly cursing the female sex, but only for his lack of knowing what pleasures the intimate company of the right woman might bring, bowed, glanced at Charlotte, and then departed the room with her message.

"Remember, Lucy, I alone am implicated in this. I do not wish the acceptance to come from you. Grant me that, at all events."

Mr. Beebe was back, saying rather nervously:

"Mr. Emerson is engaged, but here is his son instead."

The young man gazed down on the three ladies, who felt seated on the floor at the intensity of his eyes, so low were their chairs.

Lucy held her breath as she sat motionless, waiting for George to speak. His presence caused her heart to flutter and she wondered if he noticed when her cheeks flushed a pale shade of pink.

"My father," he said, "is in his bath, so you cannot thank him personally. But any message given by you to me will be given by me to him as soon as he comes out." George glimpsed at Lucy, a glint of light shone from his fiery eyes, and then he quickly looked away.

Indeed, George would return to her. She clearly saw his intentions in that fleeting expression of his; he was so apparent to her, but thank goodness to her alone. Lucy's heart raced, her bosom rose higher with each and every breath, and she felt the buds of her bosom beginning to flower.

To feel his touch, those fingers of his reaching for her …

Miss Bartlett was unequal to the bath. All her barbed civilities came forth wrong end first. Young Mr. Emerson scored a notable triumph to the delight of Mr. Beebe and to the secret delight of Lucy.

"Poor young man!" said Miss Bartlett, as soon as he had gone.

"How angry he is with his father about the rooms! It is all he can do to keep polite."

Or not, as Lucy secretly knew. Not anger. It was that beast in him, anticipating what joy they would share together.

"In half an hour or so your rooms will be ready," said Mr. Beebe. Then looking rather thoughtfully at the two cousins, he retired to his own rooms, to write up his philosophic diary.

"Oh, dear!" breathed the little old lady, and shuddered as if all the winds of heaven had entered the apartment. "Gentlemen sometimes do not realize—" Her voice faded away, but Miss Bartlett seemed to understand and a conversation developed, in which gentlemen who did not thoroughly realize played a principal part. Lucy, not realizing either, was reduced to literature. Taking up Baedeker's Handbook to Northern Italy, she committed to memory the most important dates of Florentine History. For she was determined to enjoy herself on the morrow. Thus the half-hour crept profitably away, and at last Miss Bartlett rose with a sigh, and said:

"I think one might venture now. No, Lucy, do not stir. I will superintend the move."

"How you do everything," said Lucy.

"Naturally, dear. It is my affair."

"But I would like to help you."

"No, dear."

Charlotte's energy! And her unselfishness! She had been thus all her life, but really, on this Italian tour, she was surpassing herself. So Lucy felt, or strove to feel. And yet—there was a rebellious spirit in her brought about by George's kiss, which wondered whether the acceptance might not have been less delicate and more beautiful. At all events, she entered her own room without any feeling of joy.

"I want to explain," said Miss Bartlett, "why it is that I have taken the largest room. Naturally, of course, I should have given it to you; but I happen to know that it belongs to the young man, and I was sure your mother would not like it."

Lucy was bewildered. She felt deprived of not being able to lie in the bed that George had slept.

"If you are to accept a favour it is more suitable you should be under an obligation to his father than to him. I am a woman of the world, in my small way, and I know where things lead to. However, Mr. Beebe is a guarantee of a sort that they will not presume on this."

"Mother wouldn't mind I'm sure," said Lucy, but again had the sense of larger and unsuspected, as yet unlabeled issues.

Miss Bartlett only sighed, and enveloped her in a protecting embrace as she wished her good-night. It gave Lucy the sensation of a fog, and when she reached her own room she opened the window and breathed the clean night air, thinking of the kind old man who had enabled her to see the lights dancing in the Arno and the cypresses of San Miniato, and the foot-hills of the Apennines, black against the rising moon. As Lucy drew in a deep breath, savoring the pristine air, she longed to escape through the window with her Dear George and experience life.

Miss Bartlett, in her room, fastened the window-shutters and locked the door, and then made a tour of the apartment to see where the cupboards led, and whether there were any oubliettes or secret entrances. It was then that she saw, pinned up over the washstand, a sheet of paper on which was scrawled an enormous note of interrogation. Nothing more.

"What does it mean?" she thought, and she examined it carefully by the light of a candle. Meaningless at first, it gradually became menacing, obnoxious, portentous with evil. She was seized with an impulse to destroy it, but fortunately remembered that she had no right to do so, since it must be the property of young Mr. Emerson. So she unpinned it carefully, and put it between two pieces of blotting-paper to keep it clean for him. Then she completed her inspection of the room, sighed heavily according to her habit, and went to bed, knowing within her bosom that her window to life was closing, if not already closed.

In the mood for more Crimson Romance?
Check out *Lorna Doone: The Wild and Wanton Edition*
by M.J. Porteus at *CrimsonRomance.com*.